WHAT TOMORROW BRINGS

WHAT
TOMORROW
BRINGS

S J THOMPSON

Troubador Publishing Ltd
Unit E2 Airfield Business Park,
Harrison Road, Market Harborough,
Leicestershire LE16 7UL
Tel: 0116 279 2299
Email: books@troubador.co.uk
Web: www.troubador.co.uk

ISBN 978 1 80514 180 8

British Library Cataloguing in Publication Data.
A catalogue record for this book is available from the British Library.

Printed and bound in Great Britain by 4edge Limited
Typeset in 10.5pt Garamond Pro by Troubador Publishing Ltd, Leicester, UK

Matador is an imprint of Troubador Publishing Ltd

Dedications
To my family and friends, Dr. Mike Scanlan and
Dr. Deborah Harkness who have supported me
through my dark times.

PROLOGUE

Eleanor Sutherland, a junior doctor in her late twenties, sits at a small square table in the staff canteen of a London Hospital, with a cup of tea and an open pack of sandwiches in front of her. She scrolls down through her incoming emails, deleting each one in turn without reading the content. Taking a bite out of her late lunch, she stops when noting her police officer father has left a voicemail.

Placing the phone to her ear, she listens to his curt, missive 'need you home and don't fart arse about getting here'.

Out the corner of her eye, she sees her mentor Sir George Khan standing in the doorway of the now emptying room.

Witnessing the confused look on her face, he gently asks, "Is there a problem, Eleanor?"

Being a man that can spot a lie at twenty paces, she replies honestly before her courage wanes. "My father requires me to return home. I do not know why, but it did sound serious."

Much to her surprise, he holds up a hand, signalling the topic is not open for discussion, before softly murmuring, "Then you must go." He moves back into the corridor, leaving her in a confused state.

If she had taken time to read the obituaries section in the national newspapers, which reported the death of retired

MP Nigel Trevisa. Was an observer at the Trevisa's London home in Mayfair last night at 10pm, what awaits her in Northamptonshire may not come as a complete surprise. . But she doesn't have time to read anything other than medical journals and patient records, and last night she was observing Sir George in surgery before taking on an extra shift.

All she wants to do now is finish her shift, get home, find out what her father wants and get back to her beloved career; little does she know it is not going to be that easy – an innocuous task given to her father decades ago has morphed into something more dangerous and is about to reach its deadly climax. Without her knowledge, she has been cast as the leading lady, a role that will require her to become brave and fearless if she wishes to see another day.

CHAPTER 1

SUNDAY

Walking, leisurely, through the deserted streets of Mayfair, one of the most desirable districts of London, if not the world, on a cold evening that heralds an early start to autumn, the 'Man' ponders why anyone would want to live here. It is a vastly different environment to his South London stomping ground, where he was born and raised. He is at odds with himself, as he knows why the posh, affluent and privileged do, as he is told why by all those fashion magazines his wife buys. This is a place to be seen with its elegant, stylish homes, boutiques and coffee houses. Also, it's close to Town – to you and me the City of London, but it is known here as Town – theatre land, ballet, opera, and the playhouses. But the 'Man' prides himself, being a person of the 'real' world, he can look at this most expensive area of England and dub it pretentious, in his very basic terms, 'up itself'. Although he doesn't have a great amount of dealings with its inmates, he paints a lucid picture in his mind of those in residency.

Thin, leggy blondes married to rich, old guys, who they hope will pop their clogs and leave them a fortune. There are lords and ladies who live here for the status and have second, or even third, homes somewhere, just as aristocratic. When asked where they reside, all haughtily they would say, 'my address? Oh! We winter on the Continent, darling, either at our little place in - *some ski resort*-, or when we want to escape the crowd, we toddle off to our beach house, but while in London it's Mayfair, don't you know?'.

Next to get his undivided attention are the Members of Parliaments (MPs), who have invariably been voted into Government by constituencies living in a deprived area of the country. These hardworking folk were fed the standard line, that their views matter and they could look forward to a rosier future, for them and their family. But our Mayfair-loving MPs will not be seen dead in those areas again, if they can help it. When asked why they live here and not there, the answer is always the same: 'easier to get to the House (the Houses of Parliament) so I can have my finger on the pulse of the nation and ensure my constituents have a voice'. Rather, I want my finger in every pie going and my snout in the trough.

Then there are those with non-domicile status, so they will definitely pay zero to the taxman, while ensuring their employees do.

Lastly, the football player and his wife or girlfriend, the WAG. She saw the property while having various beauty treatments and, on reaching home, cried in a whiney tone, "Babe, look at this house; we must have it – your teammates will be so jealous of you, please, please, please." Since moving in, he has rung his agent every day to see if one of the big northern clubs want him: Liverpool, either of the Manchester clubs, United or City, he's not fussed just to get away from his snobby neighbours. And with these thoughts firmly taking root, the 'Man' shudders and not from the cold, even though he is not wearing a topcoat.

Moving slowly past gated properties, in dimly lit streets, he ticks off numbers and names before arriving at his destination. A quick glance at his expensive watch tells him it is time. Stealing himself for what is about to take place, he opens the well-oiled front gate. Other than two impressive olive bushes, in very classy pots on either side of the three stone steps, the front garden, if you can call it that, is covered in handmade and finished slabs, not a blade of grass in sight. He only needs to stand on the first step in order to reach the immaculately cleaned brass knocker. *Bang*, one wallop is all he is going to give it, but it is enough to wake the dead, let alone the residents of the property. He steps down in order not to give an intimidating display of himself, to whoever opens the door. Since being an adult, he has become mindful of what impression his height, bulk and accent may say about him.

On hearing the distinct sound of the metal doorknocker hitting its metal plate, a petite young woman opens the pillar-box red, oak front door. Looking at her watch in order to check that it is 10pm, the visitor is given a cursory once-over. While he is expected, the look on her face makes it abundantly clear that he is going to be admitted, and his presence tolerated, reluctantly. It's not her property, but her deportment speaks volumes. Under no circumstances is he to be allowed to disturb the equilibrium of the household. And with that she lets him in, but only as far as to be able to close the door behind him. Once this is done, she moves in front of him in order to inspect his appearance in the full light of the illuminated porch area.

The 'Man' stands erect, deliberately not making eye contact. His whole persona cries out bodyguard: his build, his look, his dress and his stance. Standing well over six foot two and built like the preverbal brick wall. He wears the regulation uniform and has the air of a 'Man' whom you would not mess with: black suit, black tie, black shoes, white shirt and no hair.

Tattooed free hands rest in front of him in a passive position but ready, if called upon, to strike out. The downturned palms of these hands are crossed lightly over each other, as though protecting his 'privates' from attack. His eyes are sharp, taking in his surroundings in a well-practised manner, which is very quickly. Summing up the woman and her role as dogsbody dressed up in the title of personal assistant, he has a great amount of sympathy for her – he knows what it is like to be downtrodden; he wasn't born this tall and with these muscles.

Satisfied with what she sees, she allows him to move further into the house, once again only as far as to allow her to close the two stained-glass inner porch doors behind him. She moves economically, clip-clopping to the hall table, on which an antique Louis Comfort Tiffany lamp rests majestically.

The 'Man' is forever vigilant to his own security, making a mental note of the number of doors on the ground floor, and what might be behind each. Continuing his observation of the area, he registers the wide staircase and the rooms that are visible to him on the upper floors of the property. Through experience, he had deliberately undertaken a reconnaissance of the outside of the building before knocking. He knew there were cellars and a large attic. Any chance of hearing voices, to establish how many people are in the house, is hampered by thick walls and solid oak doors.

As to where he is standing, an extremely long hall still retains the obligatory black-and-white marble floor tiles for the period and style of the house. Although fashion ebbs and wanes, the present owner has not carpeted over them or, heaven forbid, taken them up. The white panelled walls have four various-sized gilded mirrors on them. Each one has been strategically placed to reflect the light, emanating from two silver and gold vintage Murano glass chandeliers, hanging down from an ornate plastered ceiling. There are no family pictures, or paintings of any kind; this is unusual as these items are often to be found on such an expanse of wall. However, his eyes register that paintings had once been on the walls, due to a hardly noticeable colour change where each would have hung.

The PA lets out a slight cough; it is then when he half expects Alice to run past him. And on reaching the end she would consume the liquid, from the bottle marked 'drink me', in order to shrink. Once again inwardly smiling, a mechanism to elevate the tedium of his situation, his attention is drawn back to his escort. Opening the left-hand drawer of the hall table, which gives a squeak of wood on wood, she extracts a pair of blue, plastic shoe coverings. She hands them to him, as though they are dangerous objects, and motions, with her head, from the shoe coverings to his shoes. He grabs them with hands the size of large dinner plates and, in a well-practised way, puts them on as though doing a partial yoga tree pose. There is no verbal conversation between them, only a series of pointing and nods. As a 'Man' of few words, this form of communication suits him. He is not here as protector; he is to report on the assignment he has been given by his boss yesterday lunchtime:

The boss came straight to the point. "Discretion, secrecy and professionalism are our watchwords, as you are aware, and the following job is no different. A very important and rich client has instructed us to undertake 'a mission of great magnitude'. Following this briefing, you are to go straight to their family estate in Wales." He was shown an address on a piece of paper and, once he had memorised the details, the sheet of A4 was put through the shredder. Once the machine had stopped its mastication, the boss continued, "Make sure you are not seen; just check on the property. You are not required to go in; the client made this point very clear to me, so check the locks only. Here are the keys; you will need them for the gates. As I said, all you need to do is ensure the locks have not been changed and that the property is secure. There will be no need for you to come back to the office; don't put anything in writing, but go to this house in Mayfair." Another address to commit to memory was shown, then the shredder was utilised again. "Give the client a verbal report only. The client will be waiting to see you tomorrow, Sunday, at 10pm on the dot. Don't be late, or early. Also, hand over the keys while you are there." With that, the meeting was concluded, and we both went our separate ways.

Coming back to the here and now, he notices she is now standing by the first door on the right and is ushering him, with her small pin-like eyes, to join her. Walking, in his unfaltering blue plastic bags, he approaches her, as though on a military parade ground. No matter how hard he tries, he cannot stop the coverings making a rude noise on the tiles. Before he takes his final stride, the door is pushed open by her left, child-sized, hand. Regardless of female liberation, inborn manners dictate he allows the young woman to precede him into the room.

Used to seeing the inside of many homes, occupied by the rich and powerful classes, he was momentarily taken aback by the sheer opulence of this single room. His grandad had been an antiques trader, a bit of a wheeler and dealer type, not always legitimate but definitely knew a genuine item from a fake. This knowledge had been passed on to his grandson, which is now invaluable as he gives the room a fleeting glance. Conclusion, it contains no fakes; if it does, then they are good, very good.

His eyes linger on a particularly fine four-panelled, Japanese landscape silkscreen. The intricate workmanship of the craftsman is wonderful. The depiction of red cranes on a clifftop, with the ocean crashing onto rocks below, is masterful. *Surprised nobody has burgled this place*, he thinks.

Not invited to sit, but motioned where to stand, the PA leaves the room, closing the door silently behind her. He knows this is purely business, not social, and is as welcome as a fart in a lift. Loosening his shoulders, pulling at his jacket front before checking his flies, now taking up the de rigueur 'doorman stance', he gives his surroundings another brief once-over, knowing that the client is behind the silkscreen and is watching him, through a slight gap between two of its panels. Waiting, he moves his feet slightly in order to steady himself before giving his report.

Having been told it was 'a mission of great magnitude', he found it had been quite mundane:

He reached the target inconspicuously. Any attempt to gain access via the gates failed. In order to check the house locks, he scaled a wall at the back of the property. Ever alert, he swiftly checked all doors, including the outbuildings, but no keys in his possession fitted any of the doors or padlocks. For one brief second, he was tempted to break in. However, mindful of his task, he retraced his footsteps and retreated back up the Welsh mountain.

And here he is, his mission nearly completed, but whoever is hiding behind the screen is not going to be happy with his pronouncement. While he waits to be given the order to speak, he contents himself with the knowledge that in ten minutes he will be out the door, gone and hopefully never to return, to this house or this area, again.

It soon becomes apparent there is going to be no preamble. When she speaks, the high-handedness in her voice bares out the utter contempt she has for him. "Well?"

An emotionless and carefully worded report is given by the 'Man': "I was unable to gain access to the property through the main entrance. But I was able to ascertain all locks had been changed, the gates as well as the mansion and outbuildings. A new, highly sophisticated security system has also been installed."

"And?" Spoken as though her patience has just run out.

He continues in a calm manner, "There is nothing more to report."

This is not the answer she wanted. She will now have to break cover, to become conspicuous and, worst of all, deal with certain people herself. Shuddering at the very thought of mixing with common people, she screams, between clenched, white veneered teeth bordered by blood-red lips, "Out."

Not waiting to be told a second time, he exits the room, leaving the now obsolete keys on a small piecrust table in a wall recess. One thing he failed to tell her was that he had observed a gang of men emptying the contents of the mansion into three, logo-free, exceptionally large removal lorries. His boss's remit was to check locks; he is not paid to think, only to do as ordered. So, with that last thought in his head, he deposits his plastic shoe covers on the hall table, shrugs and goes on his way, thrusting his hands into his trouser pockets. Looking around the street, he wonders if it's too late for a drink at a local pub.

Anticipating the front door has been closed behind the 'Man', the client appears from the rear of the screen, moving as elegantly as possible, in her tight-fitting dress, towards the unlit fireplace. Every step is calculated as she attempts to gain her composure. Getting close to the mantel, her eyes focus on a small rectangle of good-quality, cream-coloured card, with black Times New Roman typeface and gold embossing. With long, thin fingers, each adorned with red talons, she reaches out for this small, imprinted business card. She silently reads, 'R

Smyth-Tompkins and Partners Solicitors – Oxford, England'. This is to be her first destination, and with it will be her road to mind-boggling riches.

"Beth," shouting as though her PA is on the other side of the world, "I need to be in Oxford tomorrow morning – arrange things?" Still carrying the business card, while playing with her chunky gold, diamond-encrusted necklace, which harmonise with her earrings, she sashays rather than walks her cold, frigid body to the large white leather sofa. She looks fiercely at the name on the card, as though sending the named individual a telepathic message of intent before sitting, her petite posterior on the equally cold surface. Crossing her feet at the ankle, she ponders her next move and the next move after that. A menacing grimace plays on her face for she knows how far to take 'it', the answer being, all the way. And when needed, if circumstances are not to her liking, she will arrange to have everyone who steps in her path destroyed, whatever the cost to them, but not to her. She tells herself that she is her father's daughter, and he always told her that she could have whatever her heart desires, because Daddy wills it so. Eyeing an elegant antique, nineteenth-century French *escritoire*, she muses, *ah! Daddy's book of famous people*; deep down, she really means infamous.

Unknown to her employer, Beth has heard every word that passed between Madam and the 'Man' and has meticulously entered the date, time and content of the conversation in her personal journal. She prides herself on entering every detail regarding visitors to the house. Who they were, how they looked, dressed, spoke, did they bring anything with them or take anything away? If they smoked, drank, stayed to lunch, dinner, supper or the night. Were they alone? Did they have a guardian with them or were they a regular visitor, turning up at a certain time on a certain day? She locks all this data away somewhere in the house, knowing these records are worth millions in the right hands, in exchange for her own reward.

The secretary has talents, a degree in fine arts and the ability to open safes and pick locks. When alone in the property, she discretely photographs the contents of both house safes, putting everything back as though no one has been there; she has turned this skill into an art form. This information, like the rest of the contents of the house, she proficiently records.

Now hearing her name and what is required of her, she hurriedly moves away from her vantage place. Sitting at the kitchen table, she opens her laptop to organise her employer's, Madam Cassandra Trevisa, travel arrangements.

CHAPTER 2

MONDAY

The five-carriage train, the 12:13pm, pulls into Oxford Railway Station from its starting point of Paddington Station in London, with a loud whoosh as the brakes are applied.

Passengers, who have been alerted to the arrival of this London to Manchester train by the station announcer, are now shuffling while eagerly gathering up their belongings. They then position themselves, behind the yellow line, trying to anticipate where the carriage doors will be. Each undertakes a sideways crab motion, a few metres left then right, hoping they will be the first on and their reward will be a seat, on their own preferably. But first, now the train has stopped, they must let passengers off, some with luggage, pushchairs and bikes. For those who take the trouble to ignore this regular spectacle of people coming and going and look round at their environment, they would be forgiven for thinking there is nothing special about this terminus, and they would be correct. If it wasn't for the numerous signs with the city's name emblazoned across them, you could be forgiven for believing you have arrived anywhere on the 'Rail Network', whose buildings are constructed in a similar style and made up of brick, metal, plastic and concrete. This one does not have the Victorian architectural beauty a few have managed to cling on to; Oxford's edifice is merely functional and an obligatory dirty grey. No doubt Oxford Railway Station suits the seasoned traveller, whose only interests are that the trains run and, hopefully, on time.

The station clock ticks over to now show 12:15pm and Madam – Cassandra Trevisa – descends as elegantly as possible onto the less-than-welcoming platform, from the door nearest to the first-class carriage. If you stop to study her, you will notice she is trying to neither touch nor be touched by fellow passengers, who are now jostling for position in order to exit the station. The reluctant train traveller has already had to suffer the initial indignity of having, begrudgingly, to activate the flashing OPEN button on the panel next to the carriage door, be it with gloved hand. The carriage door had opened seamlessly to welcome her to a damp, dank grey day in Oxfordshire. She had already been told to 'mind the gap when stepping down from the train onto the platform' and to 'take all your belongings' by the electronic messenger on the train. It is doubtful that she is going to take any notice of a mere functionary, especially one without a body. The train doors close like magic, and with a whistle and a wave of a paddle by the station guard, the train continues on its way north, leaving Madam standing statuesque but somewhat perplexed by her surroundings. Her demeanour speaks volumes; her very expensive shoes will now have to share the same uninspiring, concrete floor lesser individuals have walked on.

Her poor PA, Beth, had deliberately booked a late morning train for the demanding Madam. She had done this in order that her employer avoids the commuter crush, both in London and of students, tutors and tourists in Oxford.

Grasping the nettle be it with gloved hands, Madam Trevisa clip-clops her way along the platform to the waiting barrier, after checking which way the exit is. Inserting her outbound ticket in the machine displaying the green tick, the depressing grey, saloon-type barrier doors swing open, while in the process retaining the ticket. She holds herself and her Gucci handbag tight, in order that neither her clothes nor herself touch the unwelcome object. Passing through its open arms with her nose held high, she surveys the area as though arriving on an alien planet. Other passengers are behind her, voicing their displeasure; her only option is to move a few begrudging steps and, under sufferance, into the main terminus building. Quickly finding her bearings, she advances, in a hauteur fashion, towards the exit with its taxi rank and city tour buses. The greyness enveloping the station appears to have gravitated to the area beyond, as the sky is leaden and heavy, as though rain is not far off. She lets out a sigh that conveys displeasure, not only at the weather but also at her predicament.

Although the journey to the heart of the city is just a short transit, on foot, Madam has no intentions of bringing herself down to such a base level. Not for her, walking to her destination like the common person, and in these shoes. Now moving down the station steps, refusing to hold the metal rail, she arrives at the taxi rank.

She peruses the selection on offer, as though picking what to wear. By her body language, there is a noticeable agitation in her manner as she waits for a taxi to pull up. Avoiding the presence of fellow travellers, she taps an expensive shoe on the grey pavement, waiting impatiently for her turn to come. Waiting, even for a moment, is a new concept for her and one she definitely does not like, by the mounting restlessness of her body. Although Oxford is overcast, it is not overly cold, but she raises her coat collar tight around her mouth, wondering if the air here is safe to breath. After ten minutes, it is now her turn. The cabbie draws up, in a new-model, freshly washed and polished black taxi and, in a well-practised manner, reaches behind, from his open window to the rear passenger door handle. Pushing down, the door springs open to allow his fare access to where the black leatherette seat awaits her. Not for her an ungraceful entry, as her tight dress calls for a more dignified approach to the task. One leg in, bending down in the doorway. Once in, swing round so her petite bottom is on the seat. Then in one swift movement bringing her other leg quickly to meet its mate. A seamless wriggle, a patting-down of her coat and then seat belt on. Lastly, a sniff of her surroundings to check for odious smells of peasants.

Without any preamble, while looking in his rear-view mirror, the patter and jolly tone is the same for all his female customers, "Comfortable, love? Where to?" He might as well have been speaking a foreign language by her astonished reaction to being called 'love'.

"The Chambers of Smyth-Tompkins, I take it you know where that is, my man?" She speaks in a self-important fashion, sounding out each word, in pronounced diction.

With her reply, the driver employs the meter to register the fare, which will now tick over with a regular beat. He puts the cab into drive mode, releases the brake and eases off the taxi rank into the throng of lunchtime traffic.

The short ten-minute walk would have been much quicker. Buses, delivery vans, traffic lights, other taxis and cars, as well as bicycles, students and sightseers, oblivious to the dangers, have to be overcome by the driver. While the cabbie knows where to go, the taxi, it would appear, has another idea by approaching the solicitor's office via the scenic route. Although not in his nature, today man and machine are simpatico; if his passenger wants to be taken for a ride, that is what she is going to get, in more ways than one.

He congratulates himself when he only has to brake once, and not too harshly, to avoid killing a student on a bike, and in all this time, not a peep has emanated from his passenger, as she appears to be more interested in her mobile.

Thinking it is now time to get his customer to the Chambers of Smyth-Tompkins before she wises up to what he is doing, he stops the unscheduled journey and proceeds to her destination. Pulling up outside, and with a well-practised cheerfulness, the taxi driver gets straight to the point so he can return to the station, by a much quicker route, to collect another fare. "We're here, love, £25, cash or card?"

As though barking out an order to a subordinate, which she believes he is, she says, "The solicitors will pay you – *wait*."

Despite not being happy with the reaction, he deactivates the locks to allow her to exit the cab in order to get his fare. Now standing on the pavement while smoothing down her coat and passing a hand through her hair, the cabbie makes it clear that he is not finished with her. Putting his arm on the open window and nodding to the large, oversized door, he says, "Tell them, clock's still ticking... *love*."

Oh, you can tell how he enjoys that little bit of 'love' baiting. Then he turns on his radio and gently strums his fingers on the steering wheel in time to the music. Out the corner of his eye he watches her saunter; he knows what she is doing. She walks as though she hopes someone is looking and likes what they see.

Not giving the driver a second glance, she ascends the well-maintained steps, leading to her destination. As she stands at the imposing door, she gives a cursory glance, to her left, at the shining brass plate attached to the brick façade. This is done in order to confirm she has been taken to the correct place. She reads: 'R. Smyth-Tompkins and Partners Solicitors. Oxford, England'. Satisfied, she pushes, with gloved hand, on the equally shiny door handle, attached to the glossy midnight-blue door, to gain access. She steps over the threshold into an immaculate waiting area to be welcomed by an agreeable man, who rises from his leather seat behind a large, solid, mahogany desk.

He is immaculately turned out in a dark suit and tie of an army regiment. His manners are impeccable as demonstrated by the way he addresses the 'client'. "Good afternoon, madam. Welcome to the Chambers of Mr Smyth-Tompkins and Partners – do you have an appointment?" Before giving her one of his best smiles and a slight bow.

Drawing herself up to her full height while taking in most of the available air in the room, she spits out the reply. "No, and pay the cabbie outside? And I need to see Smyth-Tompkins. Now."

The clerk can't help but think he has just been confronted by a petulant teenager, only thing missing is her stomping a foot. Ever a professional, an unflustered clerk ignores her arrogance and bad manners, while coming out from behind his designated position. He indicates in a gracious way and speaks with an equally pleasant countenance. "Yes, madam, if you would like to take a seat?"

The seat in question is a small, light brown, expensive, leather sofa. It harmonises with the space well. To one side of the seat is a walnut coffee table, on which sit an array of *Horse and Hound* magazines, a brass angle poise lamp and an old-style black telephone. A conscientiously attended large palm, in a wicker basket, adorns another corner of the room, to give the area a more inviting ambience. The only other addition is an umbrella stand that holds an array of brollies. Most have elegant dark wooden handles, a couple carrying the logos of various Oxfordshire companies the solicitors do business with, and then there is one solitary golf umbrella belonging to its golf-mad owner, who is not in the office today.

She doesn't sit but looks at him utterly baffled. Appraising the situation, the clerk knows what she's thinking. *Sit and wait, I don't believe so.* Continuing undaunted, "If Madam would allow, please let me pay the cabbie and I will then enquire of Mr Smyth-Tompkins, if he is available to do your bidding?"

Leaving her alone in the main reception area, he goes outside to pay the taxi driver and cool down. Handing over the required amount, with a tip, he raises an eyebrow to the waiting cabbie. The clerk doesn't have to say anything; the driver says it for them both while flicking his head towards the building. "Good luck, mate, you have a right one there. No please, thank you or kiss my arse. If she needs a cab back to the station, get one of the other companies to take Her Highness. Can do without her type, better money and manners from the tourists." With that he touches his forelock to the clerk and pulls out into the line of traffic, cutting up a tourist bus in the process.

The clerk takes in a few more welcome breaths before resuming his position in the solicitors' chambers, but not before acknowledging a well-dressed couple on the opposite side of the road. Entering the reception area, he notes she is still standing and now taking stock of the paintings, by local artists, on the walls.

Hearing the front door close, she turns to the clerk in order to make direct eye contact, and like her tone to the cabbie, she barks at him also, "Well, I'm waiting, chop, chop, my good man, I need to speak to Smyth-Tompkins *now*. I don't have all day."

Attempting not to audibly breathe in, the clerk answers in a calm and practised voice, "Of course, madam, if you would like to give me your name and a brief summary of your business today, I will then make an enquiry on your behalf to *Mr* Smyth-Tompkins?"

Looking utterly aghast she replies with venom, "I don't tell all and sundry my business, especially not subordinates like you. Are you a solicitor? No, of course you are not, you are just what?" Waving a gloved hand in the air while becoming agitated, she continues unabated, "If I need to see a doctor, then I go to my private physician; if I need to fly to Geneva, or Milan, or Roma, then my pilot takes me; if I want to discuss my family's business with my solicitor, I don't want to converse with his clerk."

Letting her remarks wash over him, he tries to unruffle her feathers. "My apologies, madam, I am sorry if I have caused offence in any way, but I will need to retrieve your file from our archives, and unless I have your name, I cannot facilitate your request to see Mr Smyth-Tompkins. I hope that you understand my need for this information?"

Begrudgingly, she gives him her name and the very bare bones of why she is in Oxford.

Once again, the clerk smiles, but this time with tight lips, and then gives her a resentful bow, pointing to the leather sofa with an open hand. You may think he would like to hit her with it but he is a gentleman. Firstly he would never hit a woman regardless, even if she provoked him, and secondly, he loves his job too much to jeopardise it on an impulse. "If Madam would like to take a seat, I will only be a moment. Thank you for your forbearing."

If one looked and listened closely, you would think that the clerk of the chambers has been made to be subservient, browbeaten by this woman, but actually his phrasing and countenance is in strict contrast; he is being sarcastic. He knows she is the type who has no concept of irony. Leaving her, in a state of agitation, he moves to the next room, the Offices Strong Room, situated behind his desk, which he unlocks using a key he has extracted from his inner jacket pocket. As promised, he is only a brief moment. With her family file under his arm, he locks the door securely and pockets the key. He is now ready to rid the area of the creature before him.

CHAPTER 3

MONDAY

Although he has spent the last five minutes being verbally abused by the client, who has just waltzed in, the clerk to the chambers, Henry, does not give that impression when he buzzes the only solicitor in the office today. He has managed to obtain the client's name in order to locate her family file. With much reluctance, she has told Henry she is here to discuss her father's estate. It has been like pulling teeth. However, while his calm, unruffled manner is on show, inside he is angry, very angry. To the outside world, he looks completely composed, but he feels those stolen two minutes outside the office, when he paid the cabbie, were not nearly enough time for him to internally cool down. It's times like this, the very rare occasion when he has to deal with a rude client, he relies on his military background for encouragement. It is not 'solider on' but more akin to 'don't let the buggers grind you down'.

His dark brown eyes do not have to look at the internal telephone to know the number his fingers have to press, number seven. This allows him to keep his eyes fully focused on the client. Over the years, he has found this little trick either intimidates or reassures; right now, he hopes it intimidates, but he very strongly doubts it.

Within two rings, the phone is answered. "Henry here, sir," he says in an upbeat manner, for he knows this information is superfluous; it does, however, put the person on the other end on alert.

"Yes, Henry," a young, mellow voice replies before continuing in a friendly and open way, "problem?"

Ever mindful of his tone, the clerk continues, "No, sir. I have a young lady with me, and she is wondering if you could discuss a family matter with her? I have the family file to hand. Oh! I have taken the liberty of paying her cab fare from the railway station, sir."

The solicitor, knowing the vagaries of clients who turn up at their door without a prior appointment and expect them to pay for the privilege – in this case a taxi fare – has to make it clear it is going to be a quick meeting. "I am not due at my next appointment until 1:30pm," an engagement that does not exist, "so if a ten-minute consultation is agreeable to the young lady, I will be happy to see her?"

Henry gives an audible sigh, followed by, "Thank you, sir," still looking at the young lady while returning the handset to its cradle. Once again, he can tell what she is thinking, *ten minutes, I don't think so.* But all he wants is her away from him as she is starting to make his skin crawl. So, with a fairly thick file in hand, Henry leads the way to the solicitor's office on the first floor, up a very grand staircase, which is only to be expected in such an impressive house in such a prestigious part of Oxford. Reaching the desired room, the clerk gives the door a most audible tap before turning the highly polished brass doorknob.

When the heavy oak door swings open, the first thing the client is greeted with is the unmistakable smell of beeswax and leather. Once inside, it becomes obvious this large, opulent room belongs to a bygone era, when a solicitor's office was deliberately made very foreboding and masculine in its appearance. Regardless of passing fashions, leaps forward in technology, as well as equal opportunities, it does not take much to imagine that these chambers have remained relatively untouched over the decades. Scanning the space, eyes cannot not help but observe the crowning glory of the high, ornate white ceiling, an astonishing and grandiose crystal chandelier, which bathes in the early afternoon sun, now the grey clouds are dissipating. Its multitude of prisms split the sunrays emanating from large windows, sending a full spectrum of coloured lights dancing on the walls. You can tell that the austere portraits of previous occupants of the company, which grace the walls, look down with utter contempt of such luminosity. They cannot speak; they don't have to but are still judging from their lofty position. They judge the staff, the clients, but most of all, they judge the newest incumbent of the room, for none escape their steely glare.

Also adorning the snow-white walls are impressive, magnificent and highly polished mahogany and walnut bookcases. Each filled with leather-bound books in regimental order, like little soldiers in brown, gold and red uniforms. A steady, reassuring *tick, tock, tick*, as though the room has a beating heart, emanates from the proud grandfather clock, which blends into the façade too. Prominent are two, very comfortable-looking, dark brown leather Chesterfield chairs, now showing the wear of much use. To one corner are an additional two sturdy tapestry chairs. These stand like sentinels on either side of a small, round, wood inlaid table on which sits a stunning tantalus containing whisky and sherry, as indicated by the silver tags around the necks of each decanter. There is also a large carafe of water. The display is finished with corresponding glasses for each drink, sitting on an oval silver salver complemented by a small silver container holding coasters. But the pièce de resistance in the room is the solicitor's desk. Words cannot do justice to this single most glorious of items; it oozes class out of every pore. It begs to be touched, to be admired, dare it be said, worshipped for its craftsmanship. Behind this behemoth sits, in a very comfortable-looking leather captain's chair, an extremely well-turned-out young gentleman, born to the position and the responsibility it holds.

Suit Savile Row, of course, pristine white shirt complemented by plain silver bevel-edged cufflinks, tie conservative so as not to offend, expensive Northamptonshire-made shoes, but whoever the maker, they are lovingly polished and cared for by their owner. As is his habit, his watch rests on the desk rather than worn while in the office. His personal appearance harmonises with his dress. Height average, build slight but toned. Hair neat, short and dark, eyes that sparkle behind reading glasses, clean-shaven, hands manicured with a single gold signet ring that depicts the Freemason symbol of square and compass. The ring, which he has a nervous habit of rubbing and moving on his pinkie finger, is a family heirloom that he received from his father at his graduation. He sits bolt upright across his desk from the person entering his domain. Subconsciously, he breathes in deeply before rising to greet the intruder, done out of habit and good manners.

His hand rests lightly on the file in front of him that Henry passed over before departing the room, but not before giving the solicitor a look of abject apology. For his part, the solicitor does not need to consult its content, as he is very well aware of what is inside. His eyes, unwavering, meet the client's. This is a woman he has to play, for he knows that she wants a cat-and-mouse relationship. Little does she know that it is his father whose name appears on the wall plate; he is merely a junior partner, Ptolemy Smyth-Tompkins, known to his closest friends as just plain Smithy and by his family as Tolly. At times, his life can be a little bit dull, so he tells himself that he is going to enjoy the next few minutes.

He makes sure that she is seated before he takes his own chair. Speaking slowly but deliberately, he asks, "How may I be of service to you?"

Ruminating for a few more brief moments waiting for her to answer, he can tell without too much trouble that all of her is false. Her hair, although beautifully coiffured, has been dyed jet black; her eyes have an unnatural piecing blue hue due to the addition of contact lenses. Fillers that enhance her facial features, together with the blood-red colour of her lipstick, give her a macabre look. The red gels adorning her long fingers add to the spectacle. Her clothes make her appear as though she has just alighted from the catwalk, however she is purely the coat hanger on which they sit. As she perches in the leather chair, barely taking up more than half its width, she wraps her fake fur-collared coat tight around her in order to emphasise her small frame. Sheer stockings cover her long, thin, bird-like legs, crossed at her ankles, which reach down into three-inch-high red shoes. Why is it that the only thing that Smithy can think of is a high-class hooker?

When she replies to his enquiry, he has a nagging doubt regarding her accent. As a boy, and then as a man, he wonders if he ever accompanied his father to visit the gentleman – who is now going to be the topic of conversation – the deceased, retired MP Nigel Trevisa. He is aware that he never met a daughter; he would have remembered. For some reason, he is expecting to hear an accent that carries an element of the soft lilt of the West Country, as the Cornish name of Trevisa suggests. But instead, he hears very clipped vowels in pronounced diction.

"On medical advice, my father had taken up residence in an excellent, first-class nursing home I felt was only fitting for a person of his standing in society; money, of course, being no object. I took it upon myself to ensure my dear father had all he needed in his retirement from Government. Alas, his time left with me was short and he has since passed. Such a loss to the world." If by magic, she clutches a small handkerchief to an invisible tear. Looking up, she pauses as though waiting for a standing ovation, and when none is forthcoming, she continues, "Therefore…"

The solicitor thinks, *wait for it; here comes, the* but, *because it is going to be one big story, and let me guess who the princess is…*

"Being his only child, I require all documentation regarding Hailstone Court Mansion, the family home in Wales, passed to me. I know this is what he would have wanted. He was always such a generous papa. Daddy said if I wanted to go to Oxbridge then he could arrange it. I don't know if I would have liked Oxbridge, would have preferred to go to either Oxford or Cambridge."

Smithy feels himself sitting even more upright following that last remark. Resisting the urge to say something sarcastic, it didn't stop him thinking it. *What a dingbat, and did you just say papa and then daddy? My clients are usually a bit more mum and dad types. Me thinks you have been reading too much Jane Austen; I take it you can read, or was it an audiobook? I bet if I turn round, a string quartet is behind me about to start playing a heart-wrenching tune.*

With great candour, while forcing his face to remain in a neutral poise, he decides he has had enough of all this sickly hearts and flowers. And with the need to rid himself of this woman, he delivers the first-round knockout blow, keeping his voice low and non-committal. "According to our records," tapping the file lightly, "and those of the land registry, your father owned no properties, I repeat no properties. This includes Hailstone Court Mansion. Neither he nor you have any legal rights over any of the goods, furniture etc contained within the said property. The only things your father owned were the clothes he stood up in, together with a few personal possessions, which he took with him when he vacated the said property three months ago. Since then, the owner has decided to sell, together with the contents. There is, however, a few stocks and shares; if you require any further information regarding this matter, then we would require legal documentation stating you are allowed access to his affairs. You are, however, always at liberty to seek legal counsel from another chamber."

With this revelation, her face starts to turn the same colour as her lipstick. Her mouth opens to the full extent that the fillers allow and she screams.

Smithy's eyes rise up to his fellow solicitors, half expecting their portraits to now show their hands clasped over their ears to block out the noise emanating from the banshee. Silky smooth he asks, "May I offer you a glass of water as it appears you have had a shock?" He now feels like a mouse playing with the cat and loving every minute of it.

A hissing, "Ahh!" is all she can muster.

When she gains an element of composure, Smithy believes it's now time to implement the standard solicitor idiom for 'off you go now, we are done'. "Unless you have any questions, I do believe this meeting is concluded." Not waiting for a reply, he lifts the handset of the internal telephone.

Pressing the button marked 'Henry', the call is immediately answered with a well-practised, "Yes, sir?"

"Will you please escort the lady in my office off the premises?"

"With the greatest of pleasure, sir." It is registered by the solicitor that the response is said too enthusiastically.

And with the command given, Smithy rises, comes round to her side of the desk and proceeds to the door, which he opens. He graciously nods to her in such a way that her unwelcome interruption is now very much at an end. As she haughtily walks from the room, she turns her head to face him and scowls. He braces himself, expecting to receive her saliva. He gives silent thanks to the gods when none is forthcoming.

Smithy observes, not only is Henry waiting impatiently to rid the chambers of her, but also, out of sight of the visitor, he is rubbing his thumb and first finger together in the sign of money. The solicitor latches on to what is meant by this signal – *are we paying her fare back to the railway station?*

A discrete negative wag of his head is given in response. A smirk crosses Henry's face as Smithy addresses him formally. "If you would be so kind as to show…" he cannot find the correct words to now describe the ex-client – by her actions she is definitely no lady – so he reverts to gender neutral, "this person out. Thank you, Henry. Oh! Please lock the main door on their departure, as the office will be closed for the rest of the day." He inwardly thinks, *I don't want her coming back and spoiling the rest of my boring day.*

He is not ready to sit at his desk but moves instead to the window overlooking the road. From this vantage point, he is able to see, unnoticed, what is taking place outside the chambers. He catches a glimpse of Madam on the pavement below. He jumps back in alarm when he thinks she is about to look up. He lets out a long-held sigh when she moves a few paces away from their establishment. He sees Henry wave to a taxi that does a U-turn and pulls up beside Madam after his clerk points towards her. It would appear his clerk has done all he is prepared to do, by the way he darts back into the office. "Good boy, Henry," he says as a wide smile crosses his face.

So, with the vixen out of his rooms, the street door firmly shut, and locked, with head held high, he starts to hum a tune heard on the radio that morning. The internal telephone rings, and a familiar voice is on the other end, his father Smyth-Tompkins senior. "Hi, Dad, when did you get into the office?"

"Minutes before your fancy woman walked in. What's up with Henry? He's acting like he's had too many coffees – he's buzzing."

"Pop up and I will tell all, but give me two minutes first?"

"Okay, and then I will take you for a late lunch at the Randolph."

"Thanks, Dad, I would like that. Two minutes though." He returns the handset to its cradle.

Still standing, he extracts his mobile from his desk drawer and presses a speed dial number. It rings four times before the call is picked up without any acknowledgement. Smithy takes a deep breath and then speaks, "Done." The line goes dead. Erasing all evidence of the call, he throws the phone back in the drawer. Sitting down in his chair, resting his elbows on the desk, putting his fingers together like a tent, he cannot stop a broad smile appearing on his boyish face.

*

Just over forty miles away, another man sits behind his desk in an equally comfortable chair, resting his arms in front of him, placing his fingers together like a tent, but he does not smile. Barely audible and speaking to himself in a low, gruff way, "Well, that didn't take long, and now it starts." He then sighs a deep, long sigh. "Let's hope they are all up to the task in hand." Looking down, he sighs again. He picks up the mobile on his desk, scrolls down to contacts, finds the name he needs, presses the green telephone icon and waits. It goes straight to voicemail, which he had expected. He has already prepared what he needs to say and now is his chance, once the phone blips to let him leave his desired message. "Need you home, and don't fart arse about getting here." Red button pressed, end of call. He then places the, now silent, phone on his desk.

He wipes his slightly damp palms on his trousers before standing, allowing the now obsolete desk chair to slide majestically across the wood floor. Turning towards his closed study door, he bellows like some deranged bull, "Trish, is lunch ready? And I need a glass of wine with it."

*

In Smithy's office with the two minutes up, the door swings open and in walks his father. Taking in the sight of the middle-aged man before him, he comments without a moment of hesitation, "Been to the gym, I see, casual dress today and looking refreshed. Was it a good one?"

Smiling at this remark, he answers back just as quick, "Not bad, not bad at all. So, what do you have to tell me?" as his father takes his rest in one of the leather chairs.

Smithy relays what took place in the last half an hour. He doesn't leave any element of the meeting out, including the practice picking up her taxi fare. Stating also his mind-numbing discomfort of being in the same room as a vacuous, self-serving bimbo.

He thought that his dad would laugh, but he doesn't, causing him to question his actions. "Dad, did I do something wrong? Tell me please." Seeing the concern in his son's eyes, the senior solicitor takes a very deep breath and decides now is the time to tell his story.

Patting the empty leather chair, he says, "Please sit, not behind desk but here, and I will be grateful if you could just listen." He waits until they are both are ensconced in their seats before he carefully and calmly begins his tale.

"You were at university, at the other place, Cambridge;

sorry, but it was much to the disappointment of the family, who had hoped that you would attend my college here in Oxford. However, getting back to the issue in hand. I had been introduced to a government minister, at some local function, and he had been impressed with the work we were undertaking and how the practice was growing. He was a man who had all the talk, and he assured me, all the right connections. Over the next few months, he threw a few crumbs of business our way, nothing earth-shattering, but it paid well. It was mainly purchasing and selling of buildings and land, in Oxfordshire and the neighbouring counties, on behalf of the British Government. Grandad and I were well versed in the conveyancing side of law, so we saw it as easy work for not a bad return. But, as you know, I wanted to branch out into court work, my specialist area, dropping the conveyancing side altogether. This was never an option at that time, as our court work alone was not sufficient to keep the business afloat, and Grandad loved the joy he gave people when they bought a new property. So, it was agreed that I would carry on doing the Government work, on a short-term basis, while Grandad continued to look after our loyal, local clients." Steadying himself for what he needs to get off his chest, a big, long-held secret, he breathes in and then out a couple of times before continuing.

"So, I prepared the paperwork, Whitehall signed off and we were paid; the few deals I did for the minister, Nigel Trevisa, sailed through without question. End of story, you might think, but oh no. I got slapped in the face with a Failure to Disclose; it would have ruined our reputation, our business and ergo our family name, your name. It would have been us against the British Government. Not for one minute did I think I had made a schoolboy error of not checking all the paperwork was complete, in order and all documentation signed off by all the parties concerned. As you can imagine, I played out everything that happened with the case in question. Over and over in my head, every detail, every bit of paperwork that passed through my hands, even down to what the weather had been like, what I had been wearing and who I met, on the days in question."

Smithy, realising the distress in his father's voice, places a reassuring hand on his arm and waits for his usually unflappable father to resume.

With a weak smile, his dad continues warily, "I could feel in my very bones what was coming, so I persuaded your grandparents to get out of town before all hell let loose."

As a memory of that time floats into his head, Smithy nods at his father while making an observation. "I remember now, I wanted to come home before my exams, but Mum told me to stay in Cambridge and enjoy myself with my friends. She said it might be the last time we are all together. Sorry, Dad, I interrupted you."

Now it's Senior's turn to place his hand on his son's arm. "No, it is okay, son. Well, all I could think was, during one of our Whitehall sessions together, I had to leave the minister's office to use the bathroom, leaving the signed paperwork with him. That's when it must have happened; he took a vital part of the document. I felt the world was closing in on me; who would believe me against the word of a minister? Everyone I met or saw in the street I assumed knew my business; I became paranoid. At my lowest point, out of the blue, a friend came to my rescue. One person, whom I had been to college with across the road, he believed my story when others didn't. I felt the office wasn't safe, so we had to meet in secret at an old college friend's family home, which is not far from here. You've been there many times, and we must go again soon, but I digress. What I found strange is, when I told him, this person, my tale, he didn't seem shocked. If anything, he was overjoyed.

Can still see the look of unremitting happiness on his face, and this is a person who doesn't show his emotions very often. Not sure you will enjoy his company as much, although you have communicated with him today." When Smithy looks at his father with a puzzled expression, all he receives is another tap on the arm.

"But don't worry on that score; you will be meeting him, soon. Well, the missing documentation and signed paperwork reappeared like magic; it was established the minister had it all along. At the time, I was never able to ascertain where it was found or by whom. Although I did have my suspicions that were later confirmed. However, what the minister's little game was, or if it was some form of vendetta against our family, I was never able to get to the bottom of. It made Grandad and I very wary of undertaking Government work again. As for the college friend, he asked a big favour of me in return, that involved the minister, and to my horror, I agreed. As for the green-eyed monster who turned up today, she is the minister's daughter, cut from the same cloth. And as noted in the front of the family file, when the daughter came sniffing around regarding her father's property, you were to ring a number that I had programmed into your mobile and say the code word 'done'. You did everything you were instructed to do; thank you, my son."

Looking at his watch and noting the time, the senior solicitor murmurs, "I will pause the story there and take you and Henry to lunch, but no business is to be discussed. Come on, get your coat; I think we both deserve a glass of wine, water for Henry."

Before leaving the office, Smithy has one last thing to do. Acknowledging Henry waiting for them at the bottom of the grand staircase, Smithy, with great gusto, instructs the clerk of the chambers on one final task of the day, "Henry, can you please archive this file, in-house for the moment. Diarise, to go to our off-site store in one year's time. You will be pleased to know, my father is treating us both to lunch." Placing his hand on the clerk's shoulder, saying , "Sorry, old man, but its only water for you."

Once Henry has locked the file in the strong room, they all head out towards the Randolph for a late lunch, but not before ensuring Madam is not lurking in the locale, waiting to pounce.

CHAPTER 4

MONDAY

It has been barely seven hours since I received the summons from my father to drop what I was doing and return to the family home in Northamptonshire. Somehow, Sir George Khan, the world-renowned cardio thoracic surgeon, understood, without enquiry, when I asked to put on hold my placement. Although my secondment has been brief, six months rather than a year, it has been both an honour and a privilege to be taken under his wing. It has been made easier as I have been able to stay at my parents' London flat, as Dad cannot officially live in Northamptonshire, working for the London Metropolitan Police Service.

At just before 9:20pm, Sir George steps out of his office, narrowly missing me as I attempt to rush past. He asks, "Eleanor, why are you still here?"

I reply without hesitation but a little breathless. "Just finished my last shift, Sir George, and heading out to catch my train home." Something I have never witnessed before, a smile, just a faint one, flickers across his face. Looking at me in a manner I can only describe as paternal, he continues to speak in his soft, lilting way, which causes the feeling to grow.

"My driver is outside; I hope you will accept a lift to the station; it's the least I can do for all your hard work over the last six months. I am sorry you have to break your placement halfway through. We have been very lucky to have you working for us. No, working for me. I hope you will look favourably on coming back to continue your training and then maybe take up a permanent position on my staff?" Barely audible, he continues, "But, in the meantime, if I can be of any assistance to you or your family, please do not hesitate to contact me."

I know, to say no to the former is not going to be an acceptable response. I am, however, confused by the latter remark, in a similar way I was to his wholehearted agreement to my request to break my training. I hope my face doesn't betray my bewilderment. So, with great thanks, I accept a lift to London Euston Railway Station.

Sitting silently in the back of a lavish car, I cannot easily dismiss the comment regarding future assistance as just good manners on his part. This feeling is enhanced when, just before I alight from his car, he takes both my hands in his and wishes me luck. This is not some throwaway line but heartfelt. What's going on? I feel a bit discombobulated; does he know my family personally? What happens subsequently brings me back to earth with a bump as, the next thing I know, I'm standing on the pavement, with my ride quickly disappearing round a corner.

Walking, downhearted, into Euston Station, I check the time and platform of the train I need to take me home. I have ten minutes to reach my platform and climb on board before it departs for Long Buckby. Seated, out of habit, I count the number of stops before mine, displayed on the overhead monitor, and give a little inwards sigh at this constant reminder of the length of my journey.

On the small grey table in front of me is a bottle of still

water, a snack bar of dubious content that I grabbed from the staff room, my wireless ear buds still in their container and my mobile. Running through my head is a tidal wave of questions needing answering.

Am I the only member of the family to be called home? Why has Sir George been so accommodating? Does Dad or Mum know Sir George? And what is so urgent? Knowing there are no ready answers, I lay back, put my wireless ear buds in my ears, put the music on my mobile and let the sounds of London Grammar wash over me like a comfort blanket.

A calm voice utters the long-awaited announcement, "The next station is Long Buckby, Long Buckby. Please remember to take your luggage and mind the gap." It prattles on about something else that I ignore. The train comes to a halt, the 'OPEN' button flashes, which I touch impatiently. The door slides to one side and I step down, taking in the smells of my home county, Northamptonshire. I do not move off straight away, just stand and wait in the moment, serene, at one with myself. The guard gives me a cheery wave as he departs. I sigh as my train disappears into the distance. Signals have now turned red, and the electric hum running through the tracks cease. Both platforms are refreshingly empty. The only sounds I hear are not those of farm animals in the fields beyond but a couple of very annoying dogs barking. From my vantage point, the village is spread out before me, long and narrow. The central part of this rural idyll may be less than half a mile away, however, it is invisible to me as the line has been constructed in a dip, running parallel to the Grand Union Canal. Also, my vista is not helped by a new housing estate that appears to have sprung up overnight.

Blue flashing lights, but no 'twos' cut through the air. Automatically, I think *village's Fire and Rescue team must be going out on a shout*, a common occurrence being so close to the M1, M45, the A5 and the A14. Needing to get on, I slowly walk towards the exit. Glancing over at the drop-off area, Freddo, who is my best friend and tonight my personal taxi driver, is waiting for me.

Freddo, real name Fredrick, and I go back a long way, all the way back to junior school. He didn't have many friends back then, as his mum was our headteacher, but for some reason we clicked. We both went to the same senior school, sitting when possible next to each other. We progressed from friends to a couple and then, to my great sadness, to a sister/brother relationship when we both realised I wasn't his type. After sixth form, we eventually went our separate ways; I went to medical school, and he went to university and then the police service. If he had failed, a modelling career would be waiting, as there is no getting away from it, he is one drop-dead gorgeous man. Although he has a boyfriend, he is the love of my life until Mr Wonderful turns up.

Reaching the car park, he sweeps me up in a much-needed bear hug and bestows sweet brotherly kisses. Reluctantly releasing me, he instinctively grabs my hand and asks in his softly spoken way, "Do you want to go round to mine or home to your parents?" Continuing playfully, sounding like the child catcher, he says, "I have food, coffee, heating at mine."

When I don't immediately reply, his jocular tone changes to one of annoyance as he fixes me with a stern look. "Oh, and thanks for your email an hour ago, with your pitiful plea to be picked up at this godforsaken time of night, after I had only just got into bed. I do shift work as well, and long hours."

Ignoring him, I automatically head for the front passenger seat, leaving him to mutter into thin air, "So then, it's maybe my house, maybe to your parents' – where does the 'Great Doctor' want to be chauffeured to?"

I cannot help but chuckle at his posturing. Once in his

sports car and seat belt on, I automatically recline the leather bucket seat to give me a more comfortable snoozing position. By the time Freddo gets in, I've closed my eyes and am starting to drift off.

My nap doesn't last long as, mercifully, I'm abruptly woken when the low-slung car fails to avoid a divot in the pothole-ridden road just outside the library. The blue flashing lights, which I took to be the local fire brigade, are actually emanating from two police vehicles. Slowing down, it is obvious that one is deliberately placed to straddle the junction, between Market Place and Station Road, stopping vehicles turning into the adjacent lane. Two very bored-looking police offices are on sentry duty, while the second car, parked in an equally questionable way, is unmarked with a detachable blue light on top, pulsating blue strobe lighting circulating underneath like a pimpmobile.

Freddo cannot resist stopping the car in order to find out what is going on. A cold blast enters the car as my window goes down and he shouts across me. "Hi, lads, what's up?"

The skinny officer slowly ambles over, placing his elbows on the open window before leaning into the car. I'm expecting a 'move along, nothing to see here', but the officer recognises Freddo and his whole demeanour changes from official to friendly.

"Hi, Fred, had a tip-off that there are drugs at number 10, Mr Patel's."

A laughing Freddo responds, "Did you find anything?"

Continuing the light-hearted banter, the young officer answers, "Yes, blood pressure, diabetes and a few others you expect an eighty-year-old man to have. Hard drugs? Leave it out, but the boys have got to do their job to satisfy the Drug Squad. Never know, I may plant something to make Mr Patel's neighbours and the local magistrate smile." And with that, they both laugh. Up to this point, I have been invisible.

"Wow," the young officer exclaims, looking straight at me, "Fred, you're punching above your weight with this one."

Two things come immediately to mind: he cannot be a true local, otherwise he would know me, my father's rank and would now be shitting his pants. Secondly, that's my house they're raiding.

Thankfully, Freddo lets the comment sail over his head as he raises my window, causing the officer to jump back. A quick wave of goodbye between both men and we're back on our way. Sensing something is amiss, Freddo speaks in a tentative way, "Did I do something wrong?"

Don't know if he expects a 'no' response, but all I can say is, "Shit, shit, shit."

Shocked, his brotherly instinct kicks in. "What? Tell me."

"Number 10, you idiot, they are raiding my house. Knowing I was going to be in London for a year, the Patels, you know, who run the local newsagents, asked if their father could use my house. This is an under-the-counter agreement between us; no one knows, only Mum and Dad. It was only on a short-term basis while they finish converting their garage into an independent living space for him – *shit.*"

Thinking quickly, and trying to keep both my body and voice calm, I speak, while trying to keep my eyes focused on the road ahead, "Sorry, Freddo, should have said, any chance you can take me to my parents?" And in a blink of an eye, we leave the village behind.

With my request barely off my lips, it seems not only does Freddo become a different person, but also his body becomes part of the car. Noticeably, he is more focused, as a clear, unlit road opens up before us. Adjusting his seat, he sits more upright, while also pushing his back and bottom into the leather. He moves his head slightly to both the left and then right, checking his wing mirrors. The fingers on his right hand open, resting gently on the steering wheel, while his left palm caresses the gear stick. He opens his window slightly. Not sure why, maybe it's for the cooling breeze, or to hear the outside world?

We haven't travelled more than half a mile, on one of the village's unlit back roads, when, checking his internal mirror to ensure no one is following, he turns off the car lights. Gripping my seat belt and with a slight panic in my voice, I ask, "What are you doing?"

He softly taps my knee. Even in the darkness of the car, I can tell he is smiling. We continue on our journey for another four hundred metres, with only the light from the night sky to guide us. With great aplomb, he manoeuvres the car through the open gates of his house, which lead onto a large, gravelled drive. In one swift movement, he stops the car behind a double garage, slides out, before quickly returning to the front of the property. He closes the tall, wooden gates shielding us from the road. Leaving a bewildered me in the car, I hear the sound of another vehicle, his Range Rover, before I see it.

Not a word is exchanged when he opens my door. Putting his hand on my shoulder, he motions me out of the car. Before I move one inch, he puts a finger to my lips. As I said previously, the car is low slung, so you cannot get out of it in a very glamorous way. So, trying not to fall flat on my face, I just go for it in not a very dignified way. Landing on all fours, I quickly stand up and grab my handbag and laptop from the well of the car. Rightly believing we are changing vehicles, I'm somewhat surprised when one of the rear doors of the car opens and Freddo jerks his head from me to the back of the vehicle.

After reopening the front gates, he comes to my side of the car. He kisses me, in a tender way, on the cheek and then cocoons me in the back of a Chelsea tractor, with a purposeful walk Freddo moves to the driver's seat.

There is something about talking in the dark that releases built-in inhibitions, no facial expressions to give you away. Leaning slightly forward to be closer to his left ear, I ask, "Freddo, why do you think my cottage is being raided? There is no way the Patels are pushing drugs. This is beyond weird. Is this why you switched off your car lights and changed to the Range Rover?"

Still mindful he is driving, he answers while looking ahead, "Back there, don't know why, but I knew it was your place they were raiding. Thankfully, they didn't know you and they thought you were my girlfriend. As for the lights and the change of vehicle, well, yes, this was needed to check we weren't followed. Had a feeling, you know, that gut reaction that someone is watching; you can't put a finger on why or see anyone hanging around, but the sensation doesn't go away. Did I do the right thing?"

"Yes, thanks. But they said nothing was found – do you think they have finished searching?"

"Well, on reflection, it seems they are still looking."

"Is it possible this has been done to unsettle me? Because it has. Bloody hell, am I being watched?" Freddo remains silent, as though unable to answer me. I look out the window to seek out familiar landmarks on our journey.

While I keep a house in Long Buckby, my family home is only a fifteen-minute drive away, situated in a small village of very expensive and exclusive properties, The Bramptons. You can understand why people want to live there. Surrounded, like a barrier to urban life, by two private golf courses, paddock upon paddock of horses grazing and a wide expanse of fields of various crops. It also has a church, a small primary school and two public houses, one of which is situated next to the Brampton Valley Way. This is the old, disused railway line between Northampton and Market Harborough; a part of it has been lovingly restored and stream trains are operated over a two-mile section by dedicated enthusiasts. It is also a popular walking, cycling and jogging venue as it is off the beaten track.

Incomers regularly pay over a million plus for a property and then swiftly demolish it. Often in its place, some monstrosity will be built that has all the appeal of yesterday's pizza. That line in 'Ozymandias' comes to mind…. 'Look on my works, ye Mighty and despair!'.

In contrast to these new builds, my family home has perfect symmetry and style. The house sits behind high wrought ironworks atop a metre-high honey Northampton stonewall. In order to gain access, you must pass through a pair of tall ornate iron gates. Two sets of oversized double garages have been cleverly blended into the façade so as not to lose its beauty. Many times, I have witnessed a passing dog walker stand and admire the house, much to the delight of my mother, but to my father's despair. This is a functioning family home for the twenty first century, and it contains everything modern living dictates.

Freddo is one of the very few people who is trusted with the key code to the gates. It helps that his parents live next door, the Macs – his teacher mum and army recruitment officer dad. On pressing in the correct sequence of numbers and letters, the gates obey his command and spring, seamlessly, open. He rolls the car slowly towards one of the now open garage doors, as the gates return to the closed and locked position. Lights inserted into the drive illuminate our way. Once we have passed through the open mouth of the garage, its door, like magic, closes gently and barely audibly behind us. It is not until we are enclosed, sealed inside, that an automatic light come on. My driver, as if by remote control, puts the handbrake on, the car into neutral and switches the engine off, which is followed by the extinguishing of the car lights. It is only then that Freddo removes his left hand from the gear stick. He now releases me from the back as he deactivates the door locks.

Moving from the back, and opening the front passenger door, the car's internal light comes on, showing me the empty packaging of various meal deals occupying the seat. "So, this is why I was chucked into the back? Gross." It is all that I can think of to say.

After removing the rubbish to the well of the car, I gingerly take the passenger seat. We both look straight ahead of us silently and into nothingness. Freddo's left hand travels behind my neck to my left shoulder and, in one swift movement, he pulls me towards him.

This brotherly concern lasts less than three seconds. "What are you doing home early? You still have six months to go. Does your dad know?"

I know it isn't going to work, but I attempt the little-girl-lost routine anyway; however, it comes out as hard-nose, cynical bitch face. Trying, with difficulty, to control my increasing temper, without much success, my reply comes out like rapid gunfire. "My father ordered, yes ordered, me home. Happy? If not, I don't care as it would appear we are both in the dark as to why I am in Northamptonshire and not in London."

Continuing with my diatribe, "It would seem a shit storm has either happened or is about to, and I am a participant, maybe you too. How much I am involved and why I may be a target is a mystery. Is that good enough for you, or do you want to take it outside?"

Before I could carry on, a door at the far side of the double garage opens and basking in the light is my father. He cannot resist placing clenched fists on his hips and making a very fatherly comment in a growling manner. "Hope you two are not making out in here, or I might have to set the dog on you." He cannot help himself but burst into a rare guttural laugh.

For me, this just makes matters worse. Firstly, he knows we are just friends and, secondly, we don't own a dog.

Between his tears of laughter, which are so out of character, he motions us into the house. As we pass, now in control, he whispers, "Mum's in the kitchen and, Fredrick, your parents are on their way over."

The plot just thickened. Only need my brother, who is a major in the army, to turn up, and we will have a full house.

CHAPTER 5

TUESDAY

Regardless of the number of rooms and their functions, it is the main kitchen in the cellar that is the family's go-to area. For whatever life throws at my family, two things are certain: this is our safe place, where we can be open with each other, and the kettle always seemed to be on with the biscuit tin open, filled with our favourites. Sometimes it's just to crash out on one of the two well-worn, well-loved sofas, with their numerous mismatched cushions, that invariably end up on the floor. There is also seating for four at the breakfast bar or, if the mood takes, then you can assemble round the oversized granite-topped kitchen island, which fits perfectly in the opulent, large area. No matter what, be it social, business or pleasure, this is definitely the epicentre of our home.

On entering this cavernous area, a few minutes after midnight, my mother looks up from her busyness. With a sparkle in her eyes and a smile on her lips, she greets me as only a mother can, "Hello, sweet pea." She moves quickly towards me and sweeps me up in her arms like I'm a lost child who needs reclaiming.

Over her shoulder I notice she has already filled teapots. Mugs, spoons, small plates together with a sugar bowl, milk jug and an assortment of snacks are arranged on trays.

Prising myself from her *mummy bear* grip, I give her a pleasing smile I know she wants to see before I plant a soft but heartfelt kiss on her cheek. In the lightest of ways, I greet her, "Hi, Mum, how are you?"

Her reply is equally light. "So-so. Glad you are home." As she says this, she gently touches my face with her fingertips, with their lovely manicured nails.

As I look at my surroundings, I cannot fail to notice the island's granite surface covered in paperwork. Trying to act nonchalant, I prowl. On closer inspection, there is a small, neat pile of official-looking documents, and a number of Ordnance Survey maps of Wales. To keep them immobile, various condiments have been strategically placed; the herb and spice rack is now empty.

Hearing the sound of voices getting louder, Dad enters, hand placed in a friendly way on the shoulder of our next-door neighbour Mac, Freddo's father. Freddo follows with his mum. Smiles and nods are exchanged.

Once we are all seated, Dad takes up his role of waiter. He pours out the tea for each of us, and then hands out plates, while doing the rounds with the snacks. Placing the now emptier trays on the coffee table in front of the sofas, he sinks down with a thud and a sigh next to Mum, taking her hand in his and giving it a squeeze. The only conversation at this point is the politeness of small talk; people are waiting for the 'show' to begin. It doesn't matter who says what, but it cuts through the silence that is threatening to hang in the room.

"Another cupper, Mac?"

"Can make a bacon sandwich?"

"I think we have cake if you prefer?"

"No thanks."

"Yes please."

"A top-up would be great."

"Lovely snacks."

"Did say on the radio we might have rain by morning."

This easy-going chatter is now beginning to put my nerves on edge. Ignoring Freddo, seated next to me at the breakfast bar, who is happily munching his way through a small heap of snacks, I look over at Dad and can see he is now getting ready to bring the meeting to order.

He places his empty mug on the table and wriggles in his seat to obtain a better position. While looking at each one of us in turn, he clears his throat and begins his deliberation. "I'll get straight to the point."

I cannot help but think, *about time too, and then we can all go to bed as it's past midnight.*

Continuing in a manner which doesn't allow for questions or interruptions, he starts to tell his story.

"As a somewhat, green around the gills, young police officer, I was put on temporary attachment to the Home Office. This was at the request of the father of a friend I was at school with. The father, of my friend, held the position of Private Secretary to a government minister. I had been invited to the family seat on many occasions and had become indoctrinated into his family circle. Holding such high position both in State and socially, the father had made sure he was well acquainted with both my family's background and mine. I was aware that, over my formative years at school, Oxford and then in the Metropolitan Police Service, he had been keeping a close eye on my career. Therefore, it came as no surprise when I was approached to undertake a clandestine operation for him. I took it as read; he was satisfied that I would not be an embarrassment to him, or his department, and I could keep my mouth shut.

"The 'Person of interest' was a minister, the Minister of Cultural Affairs. On the surface, my duties were straightforward – look, learn, listen and, above all else, keep out the way, basically stay in the shadows. In essence, I was there as eyes and ears for my friend's father. If the minister asked, which he did, my cover story for him was different; I was on protection duty. I was even given a gun; no bullets, just a gun. This was a time of heightened tensions, both at home and aboard, with various extremist organisations seen as posing a real threat to our sovereignty. He seemed satisfied at this explanation.

"If anyone looked closely, they would note my 'day-to-day' tasks were irrelevant; I was just pushing paperwork from one side of the desk to the other and back again. However, soon I was charged with monitoring incoming and outgoing telecommunication traffic in the minister's department. What better position could there be in order to snoop? For you young ones, electronic communications, as you know it today, was in its infancy then; we had mobiles the size of bricks; landlines were still very common, as were telephones in telephone boxes; facsimile machines and telex were still the norm. Yes, we had personal computers, but these were big, bulky and, at times, unreliable and slow. If you are not sure what any of these things are, Google."

Getting back to the matter in hand, he continues, "I never asked verbally *why*. I told myself that it was not my position to ask the question *why*. I was there to monitor this minister and report on any unusual activity to the private secretary and no one else. I had total faith in what was asked of me by my friend's father; however, the minister became an enigma. I monitored and reported information I deemed 'of national importance'. I did this via his son, whom I saw on a regular basis for a drink, a meal and the occasional round of golf, so to the outside world it was normal. But whatever I found, the status quo in the office had to remain in order not to give the game away.

"Two things happened during this period; the first was, the minister had a propensity for taking advantage of young junior female staff. A matter I confronted him about, but he just laughed. I then brought it to the attention of my superiors. Naively, I was persuaded to let them deal with the matter; they did not.

"Secondly, this task I had been set become an itch that I needed to scratch. So, I started to gather information surreptitiously. When I returned to my police duties, the data gathering continued, at a pace. Only a handful of trusted people knew what I was doing.

"Sometime later, our paths crossed again, the minister and I. I heard rumours that the minister was now displaying sexual predator tendencies, picking out those who would give in to his lecherous way without causing waves. Delving down into these allegations, in order to establish the validity of the accusations, I soon reached the conclusion that they were well founded. However, unlike the time before, I was now of a rank, which allowed me to assert a greater degree of authority. With the full support of ministerial officials, the minister was gently persuaded he should sign over his family home in lieu of good behaviour or a full-blown investigation would take place and would be leaked to the papers. A member of my family was placed on the land registry. He was told, to save face, he would be permitted to remain in his properties until either his body was found face down in the gutter, he was locked up in jail or placed in a care home. I had a friendly solicitor who did the honours for me. It was all above board; it had to be." With this last statement, he touches his nose in a telling way.

Looking round the room, I can see we are all gripped, taking in the revelation that has just been laid before us. Dad stands up, picks up the tea things and decides to make a fresh brew. No one speaks, frightened to break the spell. The mugs, plates and spoons are stacked in the dishwasher. Teapots rinsed out. Leftover snacks that can't go back in the fridge are deposited in the small cream canister marked 'Food Waste'. This last act is much to the annoyance of Freddo, whose personal motto is 'eat when you can, especially if it's free'. The tea ritual begins again; kettle is filled with freshly drawn water before the process of bringing to the boil and topping up the milk jug. With the reemployed teapots, clean mugs and spoons, the obligatory biscuit tin is taken to the coffee table.

After taking a sip of his tea, he continues in a calm, flat voice, now standing with his back to the island. "I had helped him, the senior partner of the law firm, some years previously. It was in a very awkward situation he managed to get into. I hasten to add it was a schoolboy error on his part, which took a turn for the worse. If it was not for our college connections and my negotiation skills, it would have seen him disbarred and possibly jailed with his family name tarnished. He had a son who was just about to enter the profession, hence the need to look for a solution to his problem. Once the dust had settled, he owed me a debt, which had no time limit on it. Since the incident, our paths have crossed on numerous occasions; neither of us ever mention our past history, nor does anyone know of our bargain." He paused to give us time to take in the disclosure of the last few minutes.

On my part, while my attention is fully engaged, I can't tell what anyone else is thinking, but I'm certainly intrigued.

Giving a small cough, Dad breathes in and continues as though giving a lecture. "So, a few years later, I once again walked into a very frightening situation – this time the minister had a graduate trainee up against the wall in his office. He had become more audacious as he had the girl by the throat with one hand and the other up her skirt. I can still see the look on her face, which was one of sheer terror. His trousers and pants were round his ankles, and you didn't need to look to see he was aroused. As I already said, this was not the first time I had caught him with his pants down, but it was definitely going to be his last. I invoked the legal agreement from years back. I think the shock of his predicament resulted, two weeks later, in him suffering not only a heart attack but a stoke, rushed into hospital and operated on by the number-one heart surgeon. His lecherous days were over, thank goodness. It wasn't until later that I found out it was the surgeon's daughter, who would take her own life, who was his victim." He looks directly at me. "And earlier this year, you were going to work for him – small world."

A muffled sound comes from Freddo, desperate to ask a question, but before he can, Dad drops the bombshell.

"So, you may be asking yourself who in my family officially owns the minister's properties?" His eyes come to rest on me, while his hand reaches behind him to pick up the pile of legal documents. "Sorry, sweet pea, it's you." Bringing his paperwork-filled hand to the front, he walks slowly towards me.

I know astonishment is written across my face. *So, it's me who is in receipt of the poisoned chalice, or should I say a ream of official documents.* I don't look at the legal gobbledygook but go straight to the back where the signatures are. I can't believe my eyes for there it is, my signature. I cannot help it, but my mouth engages before my brain has fully processed the story.

"When were you going to tell me that I'm in the middle of one gigantic fraud, the number-one suspect? All these documents have my name plastered over them with my signature. *My signature.*" Throwing the paperwork on the floor in order to distance myself from the lies, but indicating to the documents in a haphazard way with my hands, I continue in the same vitriol tone, now turning my attention full on to my father. "Let me point out that I didn't sign any of these documents and the forgeries are so good that I would have a hard job persuading the authorities. And yes, I do mean the police, if not one of those secret organisations you rub shoulders with all the time, and don't think I don't know because I do." Trying to suppress a sneer and now shouting, "It will be *my* career going down the drain, not yours. What were you thinking, or didn't it enter your head the consequences to me? And what about fraud, money laundering, inheritance tax and any other tax the Government loves to slap on people? Oh, I see, as long as you are high and dry. Your own daughter." I need air and a place to think; running through my head, *I need to go to my special place. How to escape this toxic environment? I have done nothing wrong and definitely don't warrant this level of manipulation, especially behind my back.*

Turning on my heels to look at the blank faces before me, my voice now becomes sarcastic and high-pitched. "I'm going to bed if that is okay with everyone, or do you want to add your two pennies worth in?" Their faces go from me to Dad, the Alpha Dog, and all he does is shrug his shoulders, as though I'm having a hissy fit. And with that, I storm out the room. Want to slam the door behind me, but it's on soft hinges – *even the house is against me.* I stomp up the stairs like a petulant teenager.

In my bedroom I put on a pair of black trainers. I'm already wearing black jogging bottoms and a black top, so my outfit is perfect for a night stalk, although bed would be a better option. Silently I come down the stairs. Unlocking the side door, as quietly as possible, I enter the back garden, shutting the door, equally quietly. Now in the open, I run to the left-hand corner where I know there is a small gap under the privet hedge. On all fours I crawl, army fashion, onto the golf course behind the house. Thankfully, there is still enough light from the moon to illuminate my way, as the clouds have not obliterated fully the night sky. Moving unassumingly to my favourite spot – the bunker on the fifteenth green – I lie down in the sand, giving out a small sigh. I refuse to give way to crying, but I do feel nauseous.

Lying here, in the soft, but slightly damp, cold sand, my hearing becomes more acute as I tune into the noises of night creatures, the odd bit of traffic, even people walking their dogs on the far side of the golf course. I'm invisible, just breathing in and out with the minimal amount of sound and movement, trying to act detached from my family. Picking up a familiar noise, there is no surprise when Freddo joins me.

Bending down on the rim of the bunker and trying to speak as quietly as possible, he says, "Before you ask, I left our parents in conference and yes, I knew where you would be going. So here I am. Do you want to talk?"

After I tell him yes, he climbs down and snuggles close. We don't speak, just focus on the display of magical twinkling lights high above us, happy to be with each other.

It hasn't been ten minutes when I hear another set of footsteps. The steps stop only metres from where we are. My leg brushes against Freddo's, more in reassurance. With a sudden burst of light illuminating the bunker, instinctively I roll towards Freddo to firmly grab him. I only have to move halfway as Freddo is doing the same movement towards me.

With relief, Dad is looking down on us. Talking in a friendly way as though my recent outburst didn't happen, he speaks in a low, soft tone. "Come on, you two, I haven't finished, and," turning away from us to look over his shoulder, "don't bring any sand in the house." Releasing ourselves from each other's grip, our next task is to get out of the bunker. After a few failed attempts, we leave an untidy mess – *the grounds keeper is not going to be pleased when he does his morning rounds.*

As our little band heads back to the house, Freddo takes great pleasure in slapping my behind, rather than brushing the sand off my back with a gentle pat.

After a few more steps, I pull at my uncomfortable, sand-filled underwear. At my actions, Freddo laughs in a knowing way as he loops his arm through mine. I don't join in his laughter as my mind is now starting to brace itself for round two of this nasty little saga.

*

Entering the house, I release myself from Freddo's arm when Dad closes the front door behind us. I turn to face my father, putting a hand up to stop him in his tracks, before he has a chance to rejoin Mum and the Macs. Over my shoulder, aware of what my next task is going to be, I motion to Freddo to give us some privacy.

I can see he is desperate to say something, but seeing the *don't go there* expression on my face, he just mouths, 'okay' and, with slumped shoulders, leaves.

Once we're alone, I say, "Dad, a strange thing happened on the way home from Long Buckby tonight, so much so, it has rattled me. The drug squad raided my cottage in the village. My house, they raided my house, Dad. Do you know anything about this? Is it connected to your story?" Putting my hand up again to stop my father from commenting, I carry on, "There is more I must say before I lose the thread. Freddo spoke to one of the officers who confirmed nothing was found at the property, no drugs, nothing. When we left the scene, Freddo started to act all weird and, when I asked, he said that he had a feeling we were being followed. No, Dad, I *was* being followed. He had picked me up from the station in the Porsche, then changed cars at his place, before coming here. Dad, I'm scared – should I be?"

Taking my hand, the tone of his voice relays how shocked he is. "Did they recognise you, the police officers, and did you see anyone else out on the street?"

Closing my eyes, I calmly try to recall the incident, although my stomach is doing summersaults. "No, new officers to the area by how they reacted to me. Only recognised Freddo, thought I was his girlfriend, and there was no one about, that I saw. You know how it is, Dad, the neighbourhood net curtain brigade would be looking out, but they are the locals. There was no one on the street. Up to that point, I didn't think too much about it, about anything, I had just woken up when we hit a bump in the road. Why should I worry anyway? I live in sleepy Northamptonshire, not in the back streets of some crime-ridden city."

Reverting to his more even voice, my father replies, "I'll speak to Fred, find out why this feeling has taken root. Also, I need to know if he saw anything, maybe at the station car park while waiting for you."

Initially, I feel reassured by his reaction. "Thanks, Dad, sorry to act panicky, don't do this at work, but at the moment I feel I cannot control F all. What if it's not just me; what if it's Mum, you, the Macs?"

I don't immediately move as Dad moves close enough to whisper in my ear. "Please trust me when I say I don't know anything about this, the raid. As to the second question, based on what you just said, more than possible. I think for the time being it may be best if we keep this little discussion to ourselves; your mum will only worry. As I said, I will talk to Fred when I can get him on his own."

I amaze myself, agreeing with his decision.

However, it would seem he hasn't finished, as the whispering continues. "This family, and I do include the Macs, has found itself in the middle of a shitstorm. This storm has been dormant, waiting for the right moment and conditions to appear, and it would seem that it is now time for it to emerge. I understand you have every reason to be worried, and angry with me. I assure you, although it doesn't look that way, our involvement in all this is above board. We have done nothing wrong, hand on heart." Placing his hand, the one holding mine, on his heart. he carries on, "I will protect you, and in the end, the truth will out. I hope this helps?" And with that, he nods at me as he waits for my reply.

Without hesitation, I nod back and then rush into his arms to receive a long overdue fatherly hug. When he releases me, I notice a tear forming in the corner of his eye, mirroring the reaction of my own eyes. I cannot help but think, *he is under some pressure with all this*. We both give each other lopsided smiles before joining Mum and the Macs in the cellar kitchen.

Entering the kitchen, tea things have disappeared and the paperwork, which I threw on the floor, is now back on the granite surface, in its original neat pile. Four bowed heads of different colours look down, and all with the same objective; nobody wants to make eye contact with us as we join them around the island.

Dad clears his throat and begins to discuss what is going to happen next and what part the maps have to play. "Before we start on the maps, Fredrick, am I correct in saying you are back on shift tomorrow night? Sorry, tonight."

Freddo nods. "Yes but no. I am meant to be off tomorrow, today, whatever, but agreed to cover the day shift, today and tomorrow, as we are short at the moment. Then I have a few days owing so I will be off until next Monday, unless an emergency crops up."

The commander continues speaking to the young police

officer, "Good, very good as it gets you to where I need you to be. You must go back to work today, as you agreed, but I do need you to keep your ears to the ground, discreetly of course. I know I have only told you part of the story, this is for your own safety, but I now need you to be aware of anything. I repeat, anything that you would have previously dismissed as insignificant, which may be of value to me now. You may ask what. You are an intelligent person, so I will leave it to your judgement. Text your dad." Turning his attention quickly to his neighbour and friend, he checks, "Okay, Mac?" who just nods in agreement. Turning back to Freddo, he continues, "As I said, if you hear or see anything that may have a bearing on what you have heard tonight, let Mac know, but once it is sent, clear your mobile and, above all else, don't tell anyone what I have tasked you to do. Just go about your day to day activities and your police duty." Freddo nods again.

To Mrs Mac, he repeats a similar directive. "School for you today, well, in a few hours, after we have finished up here. Sorry, but a modicum of normality must be maintained so as not to bring attention to us all. You will just have to get through the day on limited sleep." Like her son, Mrs Mac nods without comment. Mac puts an arm round his wife's waist, pulling her towards him in a comforting way before planting a soft kiss on her cheek, in the manner of a thank you.

Looking at his watch and then to the clock on the wall, in order to check the two correspond, he turns his attention to me. All in the room cannot help but notice me yawning. *I have been up... I cannot even do this basic calculation, but I did do a double shift before I left the hospital.*

Dad is acutely aware by the way he gently speaks to me. "I know it has been a very long night, but I'm sorry it's not finished yet. You and I have an early morning breakfast meeting with an old friend and his son. So, I want you, in a minute, to go to your room and take a nice lingering hot shower, five minutes tops will do it. Put on something really nice for our meeting, a dress rather than jeans," he points to my face, "and cover up those black lines under your eyes with a bit of make-up and get ready to hear from someone who has a piece of the jigsaw."

I cannot help it, but when I'm tired, I become sarcastic. My response to my father is prickly. "And do you know what the picture is on the box of this jigsaw?" He just smiles, not prepared to bite on my comment, just turning his attention to the maps.

Sweeping his hand over the island, he goes on, "Wales is our target area. The red circle indicates the location of the mansion we are interested in and where it sits in the region. Over the last couple of years, Mac and I have undertaken numerous walks in the area. So, we are conversant with the terrain and the idiosyncrasy of the Welsh weather in the locale. One moment it is clear and the next you cannot see a hand in front of your face. The terrain is similar, changing from grasslands to shale, hence the slate mines, forests, shrub and bracken. Likewise, due to it being such a mountainous location, cutting a swath between the sea to the west and farmland to the east, it ends up having a fair share of rain. So," looking at me, "we will have our prearranged breakfast meeting. Then, once I have concluded that element of our business, and before you ask it is closely intertwined with what is erupting, we will return back here. By the time we get back, Mac and Mum will have already left for Wales, to the mansion."

He moves away from the island to his jacket that has been on the back of a chair, unworn since I've been home. Delving into one of the pockets, he pulls out a large set of keys and a small piece of paper. He hands them over to Mac; no words are exchanged between the two men. Mac quickly glances at the note before placing it in his trouser pocket.

After that little show, I give my full attention to what is laid out in front of me. Although I am nowhere near as good at map reading as Mac, Dad and my brother, I do make a point of registering the topography of the surrounding area – roads, rivers that head out to sea, lakes, the odd village and the elevation of the surrounding peaks.

Mac points out a few other geographical features. His hands move beyond the immediate area of the mansion towards the north with its low-lying farmland and forests, which make way for barren mountains, and then west towards rivers and then the sea.

Mac, noticing Dad looking once again at his watch, comments, "I think I'm finished for now; I'll give a further briefing when all those going to Wales are ensconced in the mansion."

Eyes now move back to my father. "Once we meet up at the mansion, I will let you know what we need to do next if you have been unfortunate in your endeavours."

Now looking directly at Mac while tapping the map, my father says, "This is our entry point An early warning system needs to be set up. Sorry to teach you to suck eggs Mac – move all equipment you need into the house and park the car, out of sight in one of the adjacent garages or barns. Just hide it." A knowing look is exchanged between the two friends; no words are needed.

Dad bows his head towards me, so I am the only one to hear what he has to say. There is no laughter in his voice; he is dead serious. "The picture on the jigsaw box is 'shit hitting a fan'. Mum will take the clothes and equipment you need. A change of clothes will be laid out on your bed. Once ready, we can get on our way to join her and Mac."

Straightening up, now addressing Freddo, he continues, "Fred, I will need your car. Don't worry, it will be back in my garage for you so you can get to work later today. You may have to fill her up on the way, and I don't mean with food wrappers. How can you live in such a pigsty?" Whatever is meant by the utterance, and by the tone used, is understood completely by the owner of the Range Rover. "Or are you going to use the Porsche, which you always keep immaculate? Don't understand it myself. Once we have all gone, can you please ensure all the documents are placed in the main safe and the house is secure? Mac will take the maps with him."

Dad nods his thanks to Fred and then moves to Mrs Mac to give her arm a small squeeze before turning to me and pointing to the ceiling. "Shower."

CHAPTER 6

TUESDAY

Looking in my full-length bedroom mirror, I am pleased with what I see. It seems an age since I have put on anything that made me believe I am special, dare I say, sexy. I have always loved the dress I'm wearing and cannot help but give a little twirl while smiling inanely. Who would guess that an invigorating shower, taking extra time to style my hair and putting on a bit of make-up, could change me into something resembling my old self? Or should I say young self? Oh! And what did Dad say to do? Cover the black marks under my eyes, which I've done with concealer. Have to agree with him that they were noticeable. I check the top of the bed for the things I need to take with me: handbag, fully charged mobile, lippy, brush, purse, hankie x2 – one for blowing, one for giving – notebook and pen. *Are you ready, you gorgeous creature?* Glancing around the room, which looks like an explosion in a clothes shop has taken place, I answer myself, *yes, I am*.

Slowly ascending our wide staircase, as though I'm the belle of the ball and Prince Charming will be waiting for me, I notice instead it's the Macs and Mum, watching me proudly.

Reaching the bottom step I curtsy, trying not to show my knickers, and then stick out my tongue.

"Not very ladylike," Mum says haughtily before everyone laughs. "You look especially lovely, and you are wearing your favourite dress." Fighting back a tear, she continues, "Go on, away with you; your father is waiting outside. Don't forget his bark is worse than his bite."

As though off to a glamorous party and already drunk on half a bottle of wine, I shout merrily, "See you all later. Love you, Mum." I turn to leave before the waterworks start, Mum's not mine.

I amble out to the front of the house to where a smartly dressed Dad is waiting beside Freddo's Range Rover. Although I have been given the once-over by the group, Dad cannot resist giving me a quick look up and down.

With clenched fists on his hips, and his back resting against the car, he declares, "Yep, you'll do."

Forever the gentleman, he opens the passenger door. I hesitate, as I know what has been taking up residency in the front seat only hours before. Thankfully, Freddo's food waste has been removed. I still run a hand over the seat just to make sure there is nothing sticky. Happy, I reach up, with my left hand, to the overhead handgrip above the door, placing my right hand on the seat. Slowly, I bring my right leg up, followed by my left, to be as ladylike as possible, now I am in a short, tight dress and high heels. I had decided in the shower that maybe it would be better if I allowed myself to be managed, at least for the moment. Slamming the door shut, my father moves to the driver's side to take up chauffeuring duties.

With seat belts on, he starts the car. Lights on, car into first gear, handbrake off, gates swing open and away we go. Clenching my hands, forming them into fists, I have to ask as calmly as possible, "Where are we going, and who are we are meeting?"

"We are going to Oxford, the Randolph Hotel; a parking space on the premises has been arranged. As to whom we are meeting. You will be happy to know it's the solicitor, who drew up the legal documents you so graciously threw on the floor, and his son. We should be there in about forty-five minutes, as I don't expect to come up against too much traffic at this time of night. So, take forty winks, you could do with it." And with that, the conversation ends as he concentrates on the road ahead, and I try to take a nap.

"Come on, sleepy head, wake up." Not sure I had forty winks but somehow, we are entering Oxford via the Woodstock Road. As Dad turns down Beaumont Street, the Randolph Hotel, with its flags waving outside, and our parking destination, opposite the wonderful Ashmolean Museum, awaits us. I have spent many a relaxing hour in the museum; the Ashmolean has been a very calming influence in my life. Not least because of its rooftop restaurant. When life has kicked me in the teeth, I have sat on the terrace, regardless of weather, and taken in the views until I'm relaxed. Tea and cake do help to add to the ambience and aid recovery I have found. Looking at my mobile to check the time, I cannot help but think, we are way too early for the type of breakfast I have been gearing myself up for, extra-large full English with plenty of toast and tea.

Hearing my sigh, Dad knows instinctively what I'm moaning about. "You don't have to worry; you'll get a hot breakfast. You just need to know how to pull strings." And with that, he turns into the hotel's car park. Stopping in front of the yellow and black barrier, the security guard, noting the car's registration number, indicates to a parking spot. He then brings his right hand up and touches his forelock in a mild salute as he raises the obstruction with his left in order to allow us in.

Reaching reception, via the front of the hotel, a neatly turned-out night porter is waiting for us. "Good morning, madam, sir, welcome to the Randolph Hotel. I'm Chris; my colleague David and I will be looking after you. Your guests are waiting for you; please come this way." He says this in a very official but warm way. Turning on his well-polished heels, we follow obediently.

We enter the mainly plush pink, *Alice in Wonderland* themed dining area, which has been laid for breakfast, but not for us. The stunning chandeliers adorning this large room momentarily strike me dumb. Beautiful pink leather seating, pictures of *Alice's Adventures* enhancing the walls; I'm pointing without speaking at the Mad Hatter, White Rabbit, eat me, drink me, the twins – *what are their names*? Looping his arm through mine, Dad steers me clear of a table, thereby saving me from embarrassing myself.

He whispers in my ear, while looking up to the ceiling, "Wouldn't fit in the car if you were thinking of pinching one of them."

Chris must have the hearing of a bat as he picks up on what Dad said. He jovially comments, "Yes, lovely, aren't they? I don't think even between the four of us we could remove them from their lofty position. If you would like to continue to follow me?"

I resist the temptation to giggle as we are guided, expertly, on our short walk towards the right-hand side of the glittering bar area. A very much smaller and pleasingly intimate, richly decorated room awaits us. It is striking and so vastly different to the room we have just passed through. Decked out, including the ceiling, with wallpaper that is festooned with red, orange and yellow flora on a black background. The velvet seating is soft cherry red in colour; small, round, marble-topped tables, smoky yellow wall lights and red-shaded table lamps finish the decor.

As we approach, two gentlemen immediately stand up in acknowledgement of our arrival. *I'm all for women's lib but strangely I do enjoy these little acts of common etiquette from a man, or in this case men.* Even just giving them a cursory glance, you cannot mistake them for being anything other than father and son. Viewing their appearance, I now understand why Dad insisted that I was dressed smartly, and I am thankful he did. It would appear they are off to the city after our meeting finishes.

The night porters, it seems, will now become our chef and waiter. "May I take your order, madam, sirs?" asks an equally polite David. I know, like me, Dad will have the 'works', but I'm taken aback when our other two table companions agree to the same. With their physique, I'm flabbergasted that anything fatty passes their lips – *gosh they are* fit. I'm pretty sure that I blush as that thought runs through my head. *Good job the lights are low.* Touching my hair in a nervous gesture, I tell myself, *act calm even if you don't feel it.* Another giveaway sign is that I pull at my dress. *Should have gone for something full length. Why didn't anyone say that before we left?*

Once the 'waiter' has removed himself, Dad introduces me in a proud way. "This is my daughter Eleanor, the doctor. Ellie, this is Mr Smyth-Tompkins senior and his son Smithy." Not saying any more, Dad holds out a hand, which is shaken in greeting, first by the father and then the son. This done, he now addresses the young man in a friendly way, "Smithy, we spoke yesterday, or should I say you spoke and I listened?"

All eyes turn to me; I smile politely at Mr Smyth-Tompkins who responds in kind, but for some unfathomable reason, I positively beam at his son like some adolescent teenager. I definitely blush; I can feel my face heat up as though standing under a very powerful sun lamp. When he smiles back at me, it is with such intensity it reaches up to his ears. Realising what he has just done, I cannot fail to notice he bends his head down quickly to hide his embarrassment. In this light I cannot tell if he is also blushing. *Easy, El. Oh! Good, saved by the drinks order.*

Trying to defuse the situation, I give our waiter one of my polite, professional smiles before adding, "Thank you, Chris." Don't know why, but I take it upon myself to pour the tea; they can add their own milk and sugar if required. No one speaks; for my part, I keep my eyes fully focused on tea-pouring duties, frightened to look at Smithy just in case I give anything away. I cannot help but wonder, *has he got a girlfriend? Should have with his looks. Can't have by the way he just smiled at me.* Once again saved, but this time by the food order. The well-trained waiter once again discretely leaves the room when he is satisfied we are all content with the food and we need nothing else.

Not waiting for us to finish eating, as though time is of the essence, Mr Smyth-Tompkins' ability to come straight to the point mirrors my father's. "I'm sorry, Ellie, if I might be so informal?"

"Yes, please continue," I mumble between bites of very welcome hot food, not daring to look at Smithy, although I can feel his eyes on me as he also attacks his breakfast.

"Borne out of necessity, you have been placed in a precarious position; you are a pawn in an important game that the opposition must not be allowed to win."

Why is it professional people love to talk in riddles? It's a very annoying habit.

"I have been assured, by your father," nodding encouragingly at Dad before continuing in a tone unique to solicitors, "you have been made aware, you are the owner of a mansion in Wales. My firm of solicitors, here in Oxford, on your behalf, have sold the property to a branch of the Government, who now have legal ownership of said property. The residue from the sale has been placed in trust for you to do with as you wish under the guidance of the trustees. It has been agreed that you are allowed twenty-four hours," glancing at his watch, before continuing, "from now to take anything from the said property. Do you understand?"

While Dad also looks at his watch to confirm the time, I'm somewhat at a loss as to the implication or the significance of what has just been revealed. Catching the gaze of Smithy studying me, I get the impression his father's disclosure also mystifies him.

All I can say is, "Well, no!"

Surprised by my negativity, Smyth-Tompkins senior murmurs, "Please clarify?"

Before I can reply, Dad jumps in. "Twenty-four hours is very generous, Tommy. Yes, very generous. I take it your firm will keep all the necessary paperwork and my daughter will have contact with your son, regarding this and any other matters that may arise in the foreseeable future?"

It would appear the two senior men are on very intimate terms, and I also surmise my loving father is fully clued up on the whole shooting match. *When we get back in the car, we are going to have a very long talk. And as to the last part, contact with your son.* I look at my father first and then at a now visibly blushing Smithy, who has just interpreted my dad's veiled comment the same as me. *We have just been set up on a date. I don't know the man, but we are both consenting adults, roughly the same age. It has been some time since I have been out with a guy on a date. Why not? It may be fun...*

Touching Mr Smyth-Tompkins on the arm, Dad enquires of him, "Tommy, may I have a word, and it may be best if we move over there?" He indicates with a flick of his head to the small adjacent dining area to the right. Taking their teacups with them, they excuse themselves, leaving us alone.

Not seeing the point of beating about the bush, I look Smithy in his lovely dark brown eyes and go for it. "Sorry about that, but I think my dad is trying to matchmake?"

"Yes, I got the message, so what do you say? Next Saturday? I can pick you up from your parents in Northamptonshire and we can go out for the day, get to know each other? Never know, we might even get to like each other?" And with that, he gives a shy laugh as he reaches for the last piece of toast.

"Okay. Just tell me what time and what I should wear?" I hold out my hand for him to shake, but he leans across the table and plants a chased kiss on my cheek. We both giggle.

In the small dining room, the conversation is conducted in no more than a whisper, with the commander taking the lead. "Tommy, does your son know?"

"I told him, some of it, yesterday after he told me he contacted you. I can assure you I didn't want to, but with Nigel Trevisa's daughter turning up at the office like she did, I felt I had no option. I must say it opened some very deep wounds. I haven't told my father or my wife, Katie, yet; I think they will also be shocked. Heaven help us, Alpha, as this whole episode in our life has just resurfaced. We knew it would happen one day, but it still has come as a bolt from the blue. When I told the boy, I wasn't sure how he would take it, as he was out of the picture, thank God, when it happened. If he had been studying at our old college, he might have been dragged into the mire with me, just through association. You know how it works, better than I do. From Ellie's reaction, and I must say she is a lovely young lady, and smart too, I take it she knows nothing about any of this? Or what tomorrow brings? I curse the day that man walked into my family's life, my life. Sorry, but that horrid man and his daughter... what did the fellow from the 'other place, Cambridge' say, you know Tennyson?"

From deep in the recesses of his brain, Alpha takes great pleasure in being asked to recite a poem, as though a party trick. "What? 'Half a league, half a league, half a league onward, all in the valley of Death rode the six hundred'."

"No, the other one about Camelot, you idiot."

"Oh! You mean, 'She looked down to Camelot; out flew the web and floated wide. The mirror cracked from side to side, "The curse is come upon me," cried the Lady of Shalott'."

"You were always a jammy bastard at school; I could never remember poems. I think you had a touch of the Cyrano de Bergerac about you even back then to woo the girls; you were ugly enough." With that, the tension breaks and the two men smile.

Putting a steadying hand on Tommy's shoulder, while looking into the other room, the commander responds in a reassuring way, so to convey to his friend he is not alone in all this. "Well, like you told some of the story to your son – can I say that we have come up trumps with our children, and not forgetting our wives – I told Eleanor some of the story, after making her come back from London. I was thankful that she was under the tutelage of George Khan, whose daughter died tragically due to the actions of Trevisa, may his body rest in hell. I was able to get her home without too many questions. The appearance of Cassandra Trevisa will hopefully help us to finally find out what her father was truly up to all those years ago and maybe allow us all to move on. I hasten to add that Ellie is unaware of the true extent of your family's involvement other than what you told her tonight, this morning or whatever time zone we are in at present. To her, you are only the solicitor who drew up the original documentation and then those to sign over ownership on the mansion. By the way, she didn't like that her signature had been forged. It was only to be expected, but she is a smart cookie who will eventually put two and two together. Speaking of putting two and two together, those two appear to have clicked. Is your lad a free agent? Ellie is not seeing anyone at present, much to Trish's disappointment. Neither of us can understand how medics can surround her all day and she cannot bag one for herself. What is wrong with the girl? Look at her. I'm not just saying this as her father, but she could never be described as plain. Just like her mother Trish, long blonde hair and beautiful."

"I agree with you, last thing I would call her is plain, and yes, my wife, Katie is the same with Tolly. I think she has pushed every available girl in Oxford and the surrounding area at the boy. I keep telling her the right person will come along one day, leave him alone and he may surprise us yet. I didn't think the girl in question would turn up with her dad in tow." At this last comment they both laugh again while looking furtively at the young couple conversing tête-à-tête. "So, may I ask, what is our next step?"

"My next step is to go to Wales with Ellie and find out what I can in the twenty-four hours we have been afforded. You can go about your day-to-day business, but I might have to call on Smithy's services any time from now if plans have to be adapted. I cannot say when specifically, only it may be today, tomorrow or the day after. Tell him he must keep his tank full and his mobile by his side at all times, day and night. I take it you are happy for him to drop his work at a moment's notice, in order to safeguard your family?"

"Yes, anything you need, Alpha. This is getting very 'cloak and dagger', and when did you last wear a cloak?"

"Went as Count Dracula to a Halloween party once, cloak and teeth?"

"What did Trish go as?"

"Don't know, was so blotto that I didn't notice, but I think it was something that involved fishnets?"

"You are incorrigible."

"Thank you for dissing my good name."

"Don't have to, my friend; you can do that all on your own."

With that last observation, the two school friends embrace in a brotherly way. Standing back, they face each other but still have physical contact, now just with extended hands on arms, as though frightened to let go of the special bond and with the knowledge that it's going to get worse before it gets better. The commander falls back on Tennyson once more. "'Twilight and evening bell, and after that the dark! And may there be no sadness of farewell, when I embark'."

"Come on, you will have me in tears at this rate." Taking in his surroundings, with its strong *Alice in Wonderland* theme, the solicitor cannot resist quoting one of the few lines of poetry he can remember. "'Beware the Jabberwock, my son! The jaws that bite, the claws that catch! Beware the Jubjub bird, and shun the frumious Bandersnatch!'."

Stunned by his friend's recall, the commander exclaims, "Tommy, bravo, and yes, I will beware other fearsome creatures as well. I think we have left those two for far too long. Don't want them to get tired of each other's company before the romance has started. Trish and Katie will never forgive us."

With breakfast finished, Dad and Mr Smyth-Tompkins return to the table, formally shake hands and say their farewells. Whatever was said or agreed to in the other room is not for my ears. Smithy and I push back our chairs in unison and join our respective parent, but not before exchanging kisses in the French way, left cheek then right. I cannot help but take in his cologne, exquisite. Like the good girl I am, I thank Mr Smyth-Tompkins for his kindness, and in return he gives me a very open smile. Dad catches the eye of an attentive Chris who shows the pair of us a side passage, thereby avoiding the restaurant.

Pushing me towards the reception area, I can tell Dad is now in a hurry to leave. "Come on, slowcoach, clock is ticking," he says, tapping his watch impatiently.

"Okay, I get it, but can I go to the lavatory first?" Chris points me towards the ladies'.

"Yes, and be quick; I'll be in the car." David escorts my father to the garage.

Coming back into the reception, only Chris is there, and he takes it upon himself to accompany me to Freddo's car, enquiring as we walk, "I hope Madam enjoyed her breakfast and will visit us another time, to enjoy the hospitality of our hotel at a more conducive hour?"

"Thank you, Chris, my meal was excellent, as was the service. I will be back. What time do you usually serve breakfast to your guests?"

Knowing that this is pure banter on my part, he grins and then whispers, "Any time our guests request it to be served. May we expect your young man to accompany you?"

With that last comment ringing in my head, I think it's best I leave without answering. Chris opens the internal connecting door to the garage and bids me a good night.

Walking over to the idling car, I remember, *yes, and now for that long talk.*

CHAPTER 7

TUESDAY

Leaving the display of college flags – including Dad's – festooning the reception at the Randolph, I am now sitting somewhat perplexed in the passenger seat of Freddo's car. Dad has returned to chauffeur duties, but I'm unable to relax. Questions are bubbling away in the recesses of my brain, a receptacle that is getting progressively filled. Also, I cannot shake the image of Smithy, coupled with the wonderful breakfast we shared; it was like *Lady and the Tramp* but with toast not spaghetti. Noticing me deep in thought, Dad stretches out a hand and touches my leg, simultaneously asking, "Okay, sweet pea, soon be home. Did you enjoy your breakfast? And the company of the Smyth-Tompkins?"

Taken by surprise, borne out of tiredness, I can only muster a softly spoken, "Yes, breakfast was very nice, and Mr Smyth-Tompkins and his son were a pleasant surprise. Dad, how do you know Mr Smyth-Tompkins senior as you two seemed to be very relaxed in each other's company? I noticed you called each other by nicknames." He gives me a quick disapproving glance, before concentrating on driving. "Don't look at me like that; I wasn't imagining it – I'm a grown woman, not a teenager who you can brush off with any old story."

"We were at school and then college together."

And that is the sum of it, a single sentence, however, I'm not finished. "I take it Mum also knows him, being at college with you?"

I can tell he is trying hard to not sound annoyed, and maybe I have pushed him too far, especially at this ungodly hour of the morning. "Yes, your mother knows him, and can we leave it for now?" With that pronouncement ringing in my ears, silence prevails. Mile upon mile is quickly covered, then the large, 'Welcome to Northamptonshire' sign appears, and I break the silence once again.

Tentatively, I ask, "Dad?"

"Yes?" He doesn't take his eyes off the road, that is only just starting to get busy with the first of the day's commuters heading to work.

"Smithy has invited me out this coming Saturday," speaking like I'm sixteen years old again and asking my parents if it is okay.

"I know."

"Err! You do? Were you and his father listening in on our conversation?" I cannot hide the surprise in my voice.

"Nice man, just your type."

Didn't know my dad took so much interest in my type or that I give off that sort of vibe.

He continues in this light-hearted way that the conversation between us is taking. "He is tall, dark, handsome, well-educated and has a good career with excellent prospects, nice family too."

Sounding offended, I retort, "Dad, such a cliché. I'm not that shallow."

Trying to sound brusque, he replies, "*Oh! Sorry – really?*", unable to contain the belly laugh which started to form at the beginning of the Smithy conversation. And with it, I note he is becoming insufferable as he continues, "He's not short of a bob or two, as you may have noticed? I take it you did notice? Of course you did, by the way you had your eyes locked on his. Dresses well too; those shoes are not cheap. Takes care of himself that one. Play your cards right, could be a keeper."

"Dad, stop it; it's only one date, doubt there will be two. Thought you would be pleased as you and Mum keep going on about me being left on the shelf." *With what has taken place over the last couple of hours, I would love to be on a shelf with the condiments.* I start to think that I've made the point too furiously, as the hole I'm digging is just getting bigger. Furtively looking at him, I cannot help but notice his face, in the last half hour, has taken on a relaxed countenance, the first time since I've been home.

Trying to deflect the conversation away from me, I venture, "Dad, do you mind if I put the radio on?"

"No, a nice bit of background noise would chivvy our journey along."

I press the radio knob, and mellow tunes fill the car.

On reaching the Towcester roundabout, sitting astride the A5, I inwardly rejoice that we are getting ever closer to home. The last traces of the darkness of the night are starting to lift to reveal a glorious sunrise. It is worth the early hour of the morning just to be able to enjoy this beautiful sight. When we reach the outskirts of Northampton, serious father returns; the respite from the intensity of what is taking place vanishes into the ether. Eventually swinging the car onto the lane side of our drive, he activates the mechanism to wind down the driver's window. Leaning across to the gate control and punching in the required numbers and letters, the gates obey, acknowledging our presence. Once both gates and garage open, the vehicle is driven smoothly onto the driveway into the awaiting space, where Freddo had parked this Range Rover previously. We both remain in our seats until first the main gates, and then the garage door, close.

My driver does all the normal motoring safety checks – handbrake on, gears into neutral, engine off and then lights off – but not before the car bleeps to say that they're on. Dad jumps out, moving to the connecting door between garage and house. He initially turns a key in the lock, then presses another set of numbers and letters before we are able to gain entry. No noise, as our alarm is silent. Deactivated, we can now move freely through the house. The house is hushed other than the tick of clocks and hum of electric appliances. Mum and Mac have already gone to Wales to await our arrival.

Hovering in the hall, somewhat restlessly after such a prolonged period of inactivity for me, I wonder what I should be doing. At the hospital, the staff never get the luxury of standing around idyll, but lately, at home, here and now, well, it's been a different ball game. Ushered towards the stairs, I soon find out what my next task is to be.

Dad gives me my orders. "Change. The clothes you need should be laid out on your bed. You don't need to take anything with you when we leave, and I mean anything, as Mum has dealt with that side of it. On reflection, you can take your mobile, but switch it off, and your handbag. Stay away from the bedroom windows, no lights, and be quick."

Upstairs, I enter my room, and Dad enters his. In the blink of an eye, he is at my open bedroom door waiting. He has changed into rambling clothes, including his dark green combat trousers. Looking intensely at his watch, and then me, not able to keep the impatience out of his voice, he says, "Come on, come on, clock's ticking."

Managing to pull my pigtail through the loop at the back of the cap I am now wearing, I triumphantly say, "Done." And with that, we retrace our route back downstairs but deviate at the bottom, as it would appear that we need to go to the garages at the other side of the house. Another change of car; this time it is to be Mum's – *it would break my heart to part with* – Mini Countryman.

Just before he has a chance to unlock the connecting door, his mobile pings to indicate an incoming message. Swearing while giving daggers to the text, I sense a man who needs to pass on instruction to others, and fast. My next proposition could help us both, as I need to alleviate my ennui by being occupied and he needs to bark out orders to some poor soul.

Trying hard to sound upbeat, I suggest, "Dad, would you like me to drive? At least for some of the way? Happy to help."

His response is somewhat half-hearted. "Yes, good idea, A5 to Wales. Once I've dealt with this," waving his mobile in the air, "I'll take over and you can have a catnap?"

"That will be brill, thanks." We are soon on our way. As we pass through Long Buckby to join the A5, I allow myself a moment of reflection. *Was it only last night that I arrived at the railway station there? Or was it a dream? Of course not, as you have to sleep to dream.* Focusing on the here and now, I start to tick off the towns and villages we pass. As we do, I calculate how long in time till the next place, and whether we've travelled a quarter, half, three quarters of the journey to where England ends and Wales starts. My next thought is, *need to fill up, and a cup of tea would go down well and, dare I say it, a comfort break.*

I turned my thoughts into words. "Driver could do with a break. Café coming up, can also put some gas in the tank, keep her topped up?"

Not taking his eyes off the road in front, he answers as though the question has broken unwelcomely into his thoughts. "Yeah, okay, tea and something to eat, but has to be on the move though. Take it you need the little girls' room?

You do what you have to do, and I'll get the refreshments. Meet you back at the car." Looking down at the fuel situation, he continues, "Good idea about the need for gas. Yes, once back here, we will swing over to the forecourt for fuel."

Jumping back into the driver's seat, after my pit stop, I swing over to the pumps. While Dad fills the car up, I munch on a cheese and pickle roll, not the best, but it hits the spot, seems an age since breakfast. My tea, in one of those recyclable cups, will have to wait as it's far too hot to drink at the moment. I know what will happen – I will forget about it and end up drinking it cold. Occupational hazard as I've lost count of how many teas and coffees I have drunk cold; you get used to it, but hot is best.

I watch, reflected in my wing mirror, Dad finish filling up the car, pay at the petrol pump then slip the receipt into his pocket, along with his wallet, which now contains the bank card used. As part of a routine, he replaces the petrol cap, locks it and then closes the little outer door. Wipes his hands on a sheet of kitchen roll hanging down from the side of the pump, throwing the used sheet into the waste bin.

Returning to the passenger seat, he passes over the car keys, enquiring gently, "Are you still okay to drive?"

Tapping the steering wheel happily, I reply, "Yes, refreshed, happy to carry on for a few more miles." I wipe the crumbs from my jumper before taking a sip of my tea, *yep, still too hot*. I already have my seat belt on, just waiting for Dad to do the same.

Sitting comfortably, he starts to fish in a brown paper bag for his snack; he has the audacity to bring out two large ham rolls, like a magic act. Placing them on his lap, together with a large bar of chocolate, with his tea already in the cup holder, he happily sits back with a sigh and signals ahead with a wave of his hands. Impatiently, he says, "Go on then, we'll change over driving duty once in Wales. You should have a full tank?"

He doesn't eat immediately but checks his watch, something he has been constantly doing since leaving Oxford. Even with his head bowed, I can tell he is calculating the time passed since the twenty-four hours given to us by Mr Smyth-Tompkins. I hazard a guess that this specific time period is critical. I decide it's not worth asking why; no doubt when the twenty-four-hour mark is reached I will find out.

Trying to be as jovial as possible, I answer, "Yes, sir." I switch the car on and wait to see if the petrol dial is registering full. Yes it is. First gear, handbrake off, mirror and signal, and away we go back onto the A5. As agreed, we change driving duties just before the border, and it cannot come a moment too soon as I try to stifle a yawn.

My siesta does not last long as, in a blink of a very sleepy eye, I receive the unwelcome call, "Wake up, sleepy head – we're nearly there."

Drowsily, I ask, "What's the time?" This is more to tell him I'm awake rather than actually wanting to know the time. The reply is non-verbal but a tap on the clock on the car's display by the driver. It would help if my eyes could focus, so I just say, "Oh."

It is still morning when our destination comes into view and *wow*. I'm blown away by the property, the land surrounding it and views beyond, Snowden and Cadair Idris. I resist the temptation to google the details, namely how much it was sold for, as I didn't dare ask Mr Smyth-Tompkins earlier. However, as we get closer, I change my mind. What a dump – I've been to many heritage sites with buildings which have no roof and half the walls missing and they are in a better state of repair than this.

Sensing my disappointment, Dad laughs. "Be thankful it's not yours as you signed over ownership to the Government. Beauty is only skin deep; by the end of the day, I may give you cause to think she is actually the most gorgeous girl in the whole of Wales."

Pulling up in front of the locked gates, reassuringly, Mac appears from the side of the building. He doesn't come towards us immediately.

After checking the area hastily, he unlocks the gates, but before he opens them fully, he comes to Dad's side of the car. The driver's window goes down. I get a welcoming nod before Mac bends down and whispers a few brief words in Father's ear.

There is no reply – *yet another conversation I'm not privy too*. Mac nods again and then moves to the gates in order to open them wide enough for us to pass. Dad quickly swings the car behind the mansion, stopping at the entrance to a waiting shed.

Not making eye contact with me, he speaks in a way which doesn't welcome argument. "Sorry, sweet pea, but this is going to be a tight squeeze, so jump out, but don't go far."

"Okay." I alight Mum's car and stand obediently to one side.

Mac joins me, after relocking the main gates. Putting a hand gently on my shoulder, he gives me a soft kiss on my head. "Don't worry, I'll wait for Alpha to park the car. Your mum's in the kitchen," looking at the dirty green back door, "go."

I don't need to be told twice as I cannot wait to see her. Entering the kitchen, I find Mum checking floor-level cupboards. On my approach, she turns to me with a relieved look on her face. I cannot hide my feelings when I speak quickly and somewhat disjointedly, "Mum, have you been crawling on the floor? You're filthy. Dad's parking the car, thank goodness you and Mac are safe. Have you seen this place? It's a dump. Anything still standing looks like it's going to collapse any minute. I'm sure if I sneeze, another piece of masonry will fall off. I can imagine this was once a very grand property, but what more can I say? And yes, Dad did say, be thankful it's not mine. Tell you what happened this morning later. Dad is full of surprises, but you already know that?"

Standing up from her kneeling position on the floor, she holds out her arms so we can embrace. Without breaking her motherly hold, I know that Dad has just walked in by how she shifts in my arms. I kiss her lightly on the cheek and let go so she can embrace my father. Mac enters the room behind him, with a less than convincing smile on his face.

My parents hug in a manner that shows each is glad a small part of our family is, for the moment, together. Releasing each other while still holding hands, be it by fingertips, Dad's voice is calm when he speaks to Mac, not worried I am party to the conversation. "Have you set the motion detectors?"

"Yes, if each is triggered, I estimate six minutes and then three, based on worst-case scenario. Will be tight, but it is workable. As you noticed travelling down, the main road, and especially the lane, neither are in very good condition, which should work in our favour."

"Thanks, Mac, now to get on." After releasing Mum's hand, Dad and Mac look at their watches, and then nod in agreement.

A military operation has just swung into action, and I know I'm not going to like it.

CHAPTER 8

TUESDAY

All standing in the kitchen, Dad tells us a bit more of his story. "It is believed by senior ministerial officials, my masters, the now deceased retired MP Nigel Trevisa had adopted technology and placed all his nefarious actives onto a computer USB stick. Our job is to see if we can locate it." Regulating his tone to little more than a whisper as though in a library, he continues, "Now we are all back together, we need to think like the minister – if I was a man with limited mobility, and this precious commodity, because that is what it is, has to be easily accessible, where would I put it?"

Mum speaks, also in a whisper, "Wouldn't the daughter already have taken it by now? Mac and I have been round the property and, as far as I can see, the house has been cleaned out. Only a few odds and ends that look like they have no value are left. Doubt if a charity shop would accept what remains. Pictures here and there in cheap frames, dilapidated furniture only good for firewood, cups and plates from a cut-price store. By the marks on the floors and walls, the good stuff has flown. Surely, whatever we are looking for is with the taken items?"

Moving his head so their eyes meet, Dad answers the question, as though they are the only two in the room. "No, because she needed to gain access to the property. All the locks for the house, gates and outbuildings have been changed and electronic security stepped up. I gave Mac the codes and keys before you left home. When she went to Tommy's chambers, it confirmed my suspicions that she hadn't been in the house. Now, we need to get on. Mac, you have the floor."

The commander gives way to Mac, who may now be an army recruitment officer but was a brilliant army tactician. "Right, as already highlighted, the minister had a debilitating stroke and heart condition, which affected his mobility. The house is far too large to search everywhere, and it's my considered opinion he would not have used the whole property. This was a man who was so smug and snobbish, it was enough for him to own it. Trish and I have done a quick sweep of the property, including the garages and outbuildings. You can tell a number of booted and gloved people, I estimate between six and nine, have been in this property very recently, as indicated by dust patterns. On the surface, the place has been picked dry of anything of value; only the crap remains. Before you ask, a professional Government removal company did the honours. From previous experience, having dealings with these people, they wouldn't hang about doing the job, a quick in and out. This helps us, as on the upside, in their haste, they left many telltale signs behind, which will make our job of eliminating rooms and areas slightly easier. We too do not have the luxury of time so, while waiting for you two to turn up, I have made a set of rough plans of the layout of each floor." Reaching into his combat trousers map pocket, he brings out a notepad and a multicolour retractable pen. Seeing intrigued glances, he is happy to tell us, "Christmas present from Freddo, handy bit of kit." He then demonstrates the different colours available to him.

Alpha looks at his watch, which is becoming a very annoying habit. Mac notices this action and speeds up with his presentation. Pointing to the first page of a book of sketches, Mac begins to tell the group what he found and what is to happen next. "Okay, starting with the attic. Floorboards are undisturbed, number of empty packing boxes, some of them the old wooden type, tea chests. Although there is a staircase to this area, I witnessed no footprints other than those of army-issued boots. Plenty of cobwebs, thick dust and a couple of wasp nests." With that disclosure, he puts a red cross through the area.

"Moving on down to the second floor, which contains a number of bedrooms. It appears these haven't been used since the coronation of the Queen, Victoria not Elizabeth." With this remark, he gives a nervous laugh. "Similar with the bathrooms on this floor, which could do with being ripped out, you would have to be desperate to want to use them. No sign of occupation by members of the family." Another cross is put through this area's sketch.

Turning over the page to show the first-floor rooms, he goes on, "Once again moving down the house, we have a sitting room, which shows evidence of use, three bedrooms – only one used by how clean it is compared to the others. The large bedroom also has a recently used en-suite. These three rooms need to be searched. Now to the floor we are on, the ground floor. All rooms, I can confirm, show indication of occupation and therefore will also need to be searched. I have checked the basement, which goes on forever. My initial reaction is, you will break your neck if you go too far into this cavernous zone. The area is covered in undisturbed cobwebs and long-abandoned detritus. It would appear the removal team didn't believe anything of value was in this area, as the footprints go no further than the entrance. If there is still wine down there, it has long since turned to vinegar, which you wouldn't want to put on your chips. Cannot see the minister venturing into this zone of the house, so a red cross for the basement. In conclusion, the search areas are: first floor – bedroom, en-suite and sitting room and the cupboards on the landing; ground floor – sitting room, drawing room, study and cloakroom. Kitchen and dining room have been checked and are clear. I suggest Ellie and I take the first floor. Alpha and Trish, you have this floor; sing out if you find something – we will come and join you if necessary."

Looking at the commander, he throws an earlier remark back in his face, "Sorry to teach your granny to suck eggs, but you must look before entering the area to be searched. You proceed with the utmost caution. It has to be treated like a crime scene. It is bad enough a herd of elephants have been in. May I point out, the electric is switched off and we only have a few hours of daylight, so be thorough and speedy as I would rather not search with torches. Go, go, go, people."

Turning to me, "Come on, you do the en-suite; I'll do the bedroom and then we will both do the sitting room, if need be. But I must have a word with Alpha first." Mac and Dad move away from Mum and I, to have yet another secret conversation. Whatever is discussed, Dad's face is grave as he sets about his task. Mac and I leave my parents and bound up the stairs, our mission to find this tiny item, if it exists.

Inspecting the bathroom from the door, I initially do as I've been told: look before entering. Taps have hospital handles, so you touch them with your wrists not your hands. Shallow Belfast sink, not the kitchen type, sitting on a very nice chrome stand but with dirty towels dangling off of it. The lavatory has the water tank high up on the wall and a chain pull to flush, cool, very retro. Lastly, a mirrored cabinet, on inspection, has nothing inside – *that's strange!*

I shout, "Mac?" whilst continuing to scan the area. I'm waiting for Mac to answer when he appears beside me instead.

"You bellowed, so what's the problem?" he asks evenly.

Pointing first to the cabinet and then to the cistern, I explain, "Need to check the top of the cabinet and the water tank – can you lift me up? Not sure how tall the minister was so he could have been able to reach up."

Before I can finish, he moves to the toilet seat, puts the lid down and stands on it in order to check the tank. Passing an eye and a hand over the ceramic top, he declares, "Clean, same with the top of the cabinet. Good call, Ellie, I'll leave you to finish up here; not much left , so no hanging about."

I cannot resist tapping the walls covered in large, expensive, creamy white Italian tiles, floor covered in Italian cream marble tiles; *they may look glorious, but I bet it's cold when you need to go for a pee in the middle of the night*. Similarly, on hands and knees, I check the floor. I know it's going to be a meaningless exercise, but I do it anyway, before calling out to Mac, "All clear in here. How you doing?"

Efficiently, he replies, "Yep, all clear with me, so sitting room, meet you at the door."

Meanwhile on the ground floor, Trish washes her hands and face in cold water, as she feels so dirty. Not being able to find anything to wipe them on, she resorts to the T-shirt she is wearing under her jumper, which has been spared the worst of the muck. She knows her husband is in the sitting room and would have called if he needed her. The next room on her list is the cloakroom. Moving into the hall, it is easy to picture who has been in the area by the pattern of footprints on the floor.

A disappointing nothing. Turning round, her crestfallen husband is in front of her. "Okay? So, with the sitting room done, I will move to the study, and you can have the drawing room. It would appear the two upstairs are having as much luck as us," he says as he shrugs his shoulders and moves away.

After an hour of all of us being in headless chicken mode, Dad bellows from downstairs, "*Stop...*" For a brief moment, pandemonium sets in as we all hurry to join him.

On entering the study, it looks like a war zone. Dad is sitting on a chair he has rescued from the kitchen. He has placed it in the same spot where the minister's study chair would have been, indicated by the marks on the floor. Seeing us, he sits up fully with a boyish grin on his face. Despite knowing our search has been futile, he does want verbal confirmation.

Mac answers for the both of us, "Nothing."

Mum, "Nothing."

And then, trying not to sound too downbeat, I ask, "What's next?"

No reply is forthcoming to my enquiry; his only response is to raise an arm and then extend his hand towards the multicoloured drabbed wall opposite. For a brief moment, it seems he has lost his way and his mind with it.

As though telling us what he saw on tele last night, he begins, "I remember seeing a Tom Hanks film, forget the name of it, but there was a bit in it that dealt with encryption."

Somewhat perplexed, I have to ask, "Aren't we looking for a USB stick?"

As I look round at my other searchers, I witness our collective reaction of *eureka, can we go home now?* turn to *shit, the old man's lost his marbles.* I can sense Mum wants to give him a big hug; however, she knows it is neither the time nor the place. For my part, I hate to see Dad looking so negative. He is the one constant in my world; he is the one with the big shoulders who carries the family problems. He is our rock that cannot be broken, which makes it possible for our family to stand tall and proud.

Wow, that was close. In the blink of an eye, I'm pleased to report positive Alpha Dog is back, as he is only ruminating on our next move. I know it is going to be useless to ask why *and who, so I will not. What did Granny say at times like this? Save your breath for your porridge. Yep! Good saying.*

Dad is going into Plan B mode, and here he is again, the man with all the authority. "Mac, do you have that stud finder in your car?"

"Yes, I'll go and grab it, will be two ticks." With that, Mac runs out the room and through the kitchen into the backyard; to his car also in one of the sheds.

Coming back in no time at all, he hands Dad a small box-like piece of equipment. Moving from his sitting position, trying not to trip over the rubbish, he moves to the wall with the multicoloured daubs on. Turning it on, he waits for it to stop clicking, then runs it over a small piece of the uneven plasterwork. Answering no one in particular, but not taking his eyes off the wall, he says, "Yes, Ellie, we are still after the USB; however, I believe we have stumbled upon something unexpected – dare I say, an effing bonus." Mac stands stock-still while both Mum and I shrug our shoulders.

Like a teacher trying to wheedle information out of a less-than-bright student, he goes on, "Tell me what you see, Ellie?"

I always hate being put on the spot, but here goes, "Well, someone who cannot decide what colour to paint his wall by the number of paint swatches on it. I count six colours, and that bit of wall is a bit ropey, would have to be replastered."

He reaches into his jacket pocket to retrieve his phone, acknowledging my observation. "Correct. Just need to send a couple of messages, and while I am doing this, you can get a bit of shuteye. Trish, you may want to do the same, will wake you when we need to go. Mac and I will finish up here."

Being slowly edged out the room by Mum, I give Dad a

less-than-pleased look before asking, "Are you going to tell us what is going on?"

"Sorry, Ellie, rather wait to see if my hunch is correct." He moves to Mum, kisses her sweetly and winks, a knowing wink which says plenty; it is a language only known to the two participants.

Alone in the room, the two men get to their task. With photos of the painted wall taken and sent, the commander retrieves a penknife from his pocket and starts to dig into the plaster where the stud detector reacted. It does not take much effort to expose what he is looking for. A metal ring appears, no bigger than a ten pence piece. Motioning with his head to the item now appearing through the dust, he whispers to Mac, who is standing at his shoulder, "Here we go. Can you grab that, Mac? Careful, don't want it to break or drop down the back."

A concentrating Mac, intent on getting it right, mutters, reaching for the object delicately, "Got it – is this what we have been looking for?" He cannot help but show how shocked he is that an item so tiny might contain years of data.

A relieved commander takes it from Mac, wraps it in a hankie and places it safely in an inner jacket pocket. "Thankfully, we only have to deliver it; we are allowed to wonder what is in it, but it is for others to analyse its content. So, my next task is to arrange delivery and then return home. Not sure if Ellie was needed after all, but don't tell her. Right, so we can start packing up the few bits we brought with us into the two cars." Checking the time once more, he continues, "Yep, a couple of hours, then give the girls a shake and we can get moving while it is still dark. Get clear of this place within the twenty-four hours, okay, Mac?"

"Yes, I agree…" He is just about to say something else, but the first motion sensor goes off. As he starts his stopwatch, he changes tack, taking the lead without being asked. "I'll get the girls. Leave the cars, need to move fast. Bags and clothes we need are in the hall; get into your outdoor clothes and get ready to help the girls. Go, go, go." With that, Mac moves into action and races up the stairs to wake the girls to ensure the four of them get out before being trapped by whatever is coming down the road.

CHAPTER 9

TUESDAY

At the same time father and daughter are about to leave the family home for their breakfast meeting in Oxford, equally early in the morning an attachment to the British Army, near Sennybridge in Wales, is getting ready to undertake a five-day training exercise. All equipment has been unloaded from their All-Terrain Vehicles (ATV). Although meticulously checked at barracks, the soldiers now ensure they have all their own equipment. Once done, they are called to muster. The officer in charge, Ellie's major brother James junior, prepares to give the final orders, but there is a moment of hesitation. Reaching into a jacket pocket, while turning away from the expectant group, he quickly retrieves his mobile. Placing it to his ear, he listens intensely to the message. Whatever the message was, when he turns back his face is emotionless.

Without missing a beat, he speaks in an authoritative way, "Captain." The second in command looks up from his position talking to a small group of soldiers. Joining the major, the two senior men deliberately move out of earshot of the rest of the company. Whatever is going to be said is not for general circulation. "I am instructed to return to base; I will take a driver with me. The exercise is to be continued uninterrupted, so resume with the orders. No doubt I will be able to join you later."

Looking around the assembled group he spots, through the darkness, the person he wants who is squashed between two men who would make Thor appear small. Ensuring he keeps a commanding note in his voice, he speaks directly to the acknowledged soldier, "Corporal, you're with me – fall out and get your kit." He nods to the captain in a knowing way, but deep down, he's envious that he will not have five days of fresh Welsh air pumping through his lungs and experiencing endorphins coursing through his body, bringing him a high through rigorous exercise.

A hubbub ensues with the major's pronouncement. The captain needs to impose his authority to bring the noise quickly to a halt. "Quiet, eyes front; we are not here to have a picnic – we are here to work, to sharpen our skills."

With the need to get going, the major runs towards the smallest ATV, slinging his pack onto his back in a single, fluid movement. For the corporal, it is like the parting of the waves, as a path is cleared for her as she races to catch up. She resists the temptation to glance around at her colleagues.

Reaching the vehicle, the major is already behind the wheel, with engine and lights on. He taps his fingers on the steering wheel impatiently, while the corporal climbs into the passenger side, placing her kitbag between her legs.

Neither speaks as the vehicle is slowly manoeuvred from its parking place on the grass back onto the unofficial dirt track. The ride downhill is at a steady ten miles an hour, as water-filled potholes have to be dealt with. Only an off-road vehicle could manage to negotiate this type of environment; anything less would be shaken, bumped and rattled into a thousand pieces. Eventually, after a bone-crushing drive, they finally reach a half-decent tarmac road.

The corporal takes a swig of water, deciding she needs to break the tension starting to build in the cab. "Major, why did you pick me? I was looking forward to a lovely walk through the rugged mountains of Wales up to my knees in mud during the day and face down in sheep poo at night. Oh! And let's not forget the weather, rain followed by even more rain, and don't say all this is good for the complexion." She doesn't have to look at him to know he is grinning.

At the first convenient spot, the ATV is pulled off the road. While keeping the engine running, after putting the handbrake on and the gearbox into neutral, the major has decided now is the time to begin the process of letting her in on what is taking place. But first, he needs to contact a couple of people. Turning his body slightly towards his passenger, he speaks in a friendly tone. "I need to make a few calls, and then I will explain what will happen next. I will keep the engine running; it will keep the cab warm." With that, he jumps down from the driver's side and moves to where he can get a small amount of respite from the weather and away from the noise of the idling engine.

Anyone listening in on his phone call would think it is to be a boys' night. The upbeat way he speaks adds to the effect when the call is connected. "Hi, all set for tonight? How are your teeth after having a tooth pulled? Oh! Don't forget it's black suits, we're going to push the 'boat' out and then bring the 'house' down. Got two girls lined up for us two boys; get ready to kick up a storm, my son. Then if all goes to Plan B, in bed by midnight in their arms. What do you say?"

The response by the person on the other end is equally cheerful. "Great, teeth okay. Can I bring a friend to the party?"

"Sure, as long as they don't rock the boat."

"Will meet you at the house? Crash out at the beach hut after, always good for a breakfast before we part."

"Yep, I'm coming straight from work – can you pick up my suit? Don't want the gang to think I'm slacking."

"Sure, bye." And with that, the line goes dead.

The recipient of the call untangles what has just been said – *Plan B, if needed, is extraction at midnight from the boathouse with four people – two male, two female – take down coast to beach hut to arrive by dawn. Major coming with us, need wetsuits and expect trouble, looking forward to it, should be fun.*

Pressing a pre-programmed number, the major doesn't have to wait long – four rings and the phone connects and a mature voice answers, "Hello?"

"Hi, Dad, transport if needed will be waiting for you at the agreed time and place. May I point out that the tide is a most important factor in getting you all away? If we are not needed, let me know."

"Thank you, my son."

"Love you, Dad."

"Back at you," and with that, the call ends.

With this element concluded, he rejoins the corporal in a nice warm cab. Once settled in his seat, he turns to look at his passenger. He speaks seriously, looking into her eyes. "Don't let my rank fool you – I might be a major, but I am higher up the food chain than you might think." The corporal goes to say something, but he puts up his hand to stop her. He continues in the same vein, "Firstly, you are the ideal candidate to help me with what is to follow. Secondly, whatever happens in the next forty-eight hours, for the rest of your life the events that are to take place never happened. You cannot commit anything to paper or discuss it with friends, colleagues or partners, a bit Bletchley Park. Thirdly, I am in a position to offer you anything in the army that will not generate too many questions. Have you thought about a posting to a warmer climate, with a promotion to sergeant? Or I can ask you to get out the vehicle and walk back to your colleagues, where, no doubt, they will ask too many questions and spread whatever rumours they like. What do you say?"

She doesn't answer immediately, pondering on what has just been said. *There has always been something about this man I can never put my finger on. He is not like any of the other senior officers who have crossed my path. This one is given respect from the lower ranks, as would be expected, but also from those in command of the regiment. I have witnessed it first hand when top brass have, metaphorically, thrown themselves at his feet. They are not frightened by him but somehow are intrigued, overwhelmed by his charisma, an allure which is bestowed on the chosen ones. Who cares? It's Christmas.*

If the corporal were acquainted with the major's family, she would know, like father, like son – the apple hasn't fallen far from the Sutherland tree.

After a moment of weighing up the situation and the implications, the corporal replies, if somewhat too enthusiastically, "Yes, please and thank you, sir. A warmer climate would be nice, and sergeant, wow. So, what is next?"

Although he cannot help but smile at her easy compliance, he decides drip-feeding her information is the best option. "You will take a nap, whether you need one or not, while I drive, and before you ask, we are not returning to base. We will, however, return to the unit, be it towards the end of the exercise, and so it will still be rations." And with that, the vehicle is put into gear, lights switched on and manoeuvred gingerly back onto the road, direction and destination known only to the driver.

The corporal wakes from her imposed doze. Checking her watch, she calculates that one hour and forty-five minutes have passed. Taking a refreshing drink of water, she stares out the window to try to establish their location.

"Welcome back, Corporal, we will be stopping soon as I would like to stretch my legs; no doubt you want to do the same?"

"Yes, thank you, sir."

"Good. Do you by any chance have anything edible?"

"Yes, sir, I have a bar of chocolate – would you like a piece?"

"That would be wonderful, if you don't mind me sharing the treat you hoped to keep to yourself?"

"No, sir; happy to share, sir." Delving into one of the outer pockets of her kitbag, she fishes out a medium-sized bar of white chocolate. Taking the wrapper off and carefully stowing the paper and foil coverings back into the pocket they came out of, she breaks the bar in two. It snaps with the expectation of a wonderful taste to come. She hands one half over to the driver, who grabs it eagerly, while she bites into the other part, giving out a sigh of deep satisfaction.

Talking with a chocolate-filled mouth, he comments, "Lay-by coming up, army pulls into this one all the time so shouldn't be a problem for us. Toilets in the café. Don't speak to anyone regarding anything army. When you get back, I'll go and grab us a couple of hot drinks, some additional water, so is it tea or coffee?"

"Tea please, sir, milk no sugar."

The promise of a much-needed mug of hot tea sees the corporal move quickly to use the café's facilities. The major waits patiently for her return; once she is back in the vehicle, he strides with intent to also use the lavatory and then get tea for them both. She cannot help but notice he is returning with a cardboard holder containing two large mugs of, hopefully, piping hot tea and a large paper bag containing, what?

Opening up her side of the cab, he passes up the tea before closing the door and then moves to his side of the vehicle. Climbing back into his seat, placing the bag on the area in front of the windscreen, he addresses his passenger. "Took the liberty of buying us some food to go with the tea. Pasties, muffins and crisps okay with you?" He believes it's only right as she gave him half her chocolate.

"Better than rations any day."

"We all need a little treat from time to time, and thank you for the chocolate, just returning the favour, hope you don't mind?"

"No, sir, yes, sir. Oh! Very welcome. Would you like your tea?" she says in a befuddled manner.

"Thank you, Corporal." He takes his drink from her before continuing, "I think it's time to tell you want is to happen next while we eat. Our first destination is another hour away. When we get there, you are to leave me and travel to a point – I will give you the co-ordinates for later. There is fuel in the back if needed. Don't stop until you reach your destination. Right now, eat, no questions."

Putting all the empty bits from their food break into the paper bag, after he has extracted two bottles of water, he casually murmurs, "Just get rid of the rubbish and we can be on our way. Next stop, you will have to wait and see, no point in getting ahead of ourselves." With that, he opens his door, jumps down and walks briskly to the waste bin where he deposits their waste. Returning, he is constantly scanning the area for anything which could spell danger. As he climbs back behind the wheel, he absent-mindedly let's slip something she has wondered about since being plucked from her buddies. "Area appears clear – we can proceed." With that observation, he slips into silence. The corporal undertakes a yoga breathing exercise to bring a sense of calm to an intriguing state of affairs.

With the promised hour up, the ATV is reversed a hundred metres up a side lane. Large, mature trees obscure its presence from the road. Happy with his driving technique, the vehicle is parked with its engine switched off. Reaching into a trouser pocket, the major pulls out a map that shows the topography of a large expansion of the area. Unfolding and then refolding to show the section that is about to be discussed, he places it between the two of them. "We are here. You are to travel to here. These are the co-ordinates. There will already be two vehicles parked outside a beach hut, the only building in this remote area, you will need to park as close as possible to them. Remember to face this monster back up the lane, easier to do when you arrive than struggle later. You will stay with this vehicle at all times, lock yourself in and don't leave this cab even if someone is dying on the beach. If you need a pee, it's down to you to work out how you achieve it. You already have food and extra water. I'm only going to take the things I immediately need; all the rest will stay with you, which I will retrieve when we meet up. If all goes well, it will be dawn tomorrow; we will be coming from the sea. Oh! There's a guy living in the beach hut – this is him," showing her a mobile phone picture, "believes he has a touch of the Brad Pitt about him; cannot see it myself. He is expecting you but will not approach; he is there as our lookout. You may ask questions now, Corporal."

"What if I am stopped by the military?"

"Nearly forgot," drawing an official piece of paper from another pocket, "here are your orders, and you will note they are signed by our commanding officer."

A little shocked at the gravity of it all, she responds, "Oh! Gosh, I will keep these safe."

"If you don't mind, Corporal, as I will need them back, so no giving them away or keeping them as a souvenir. Do I have your word on that point?"

"Yes, sir, of course, sir."

"Right then, let's get going, you on your travels and me on mine."

CHAPTER 10

WEDNESDAY

Unknown to Eleanor, the phone calls her father had been making and receiving have been done in order to pre-empt what is just about to go down. While Alpha had told himself it was just a precaution, with the first motion alarm activating, he is glad there is an operational Plan B.

*

Given the instruction to get some sleep, I slowly walk up the dusty stairs of the mansion, reflecting on my situation. *Cannot believe I returned home very late Monday night and here I am somewhere in Wales. Oh, and in the middle of a shitstorm. Gosh, I'm tired; hopefully the bed is soft.* But my slumbers don't last long, as a cold rush of air wakes me. I soon realise that my sleeping bag, which I was too tired to get into, has been thrown back, and Mac's hands are pushing down on my makeshift mattress.

"Quick, get dressed, outdoor clothes downstairs waiting – go now! You have one minute, and don't put on your torch. Now *move*." And with that, he is gone.

Rushing down the stairs, I find my outdoor clothes waiting for me in the hall, together with fully kitted-out parents. Only the light from the moon illuminates the passageway.

Usually, Dad is in charge, but Mac is calling the shots. "Trish, we practised this escape route earlier, but while we have been inside, it has rained; the surrounding area is going to be a bit muddy – take this into consideration. So, out the back door, run over to the left where you will pick up the path to the outer gate and the mountain beyond. I've unlocked the gate – go through and then follow the path up to the forest line. We'll be close behind; keep down, no talking and no lights. Whatever happens, keep moving, as we need to get clear of the mansion. No looking back, girls, just keep going. Don't worry – help is on the way."

Help? What help? And why is it that when people say, 'don't worry', the first thing you do is worry? I'm a bit confused. "We have cars, so why aren't we taking them?"

Mac replies with authority, "Not safe. Now be off with you." As he says this, his phone starts to buzz like an early morning wake-up call – it's the second warning device on the road to the mansion being tripped. "Go, people, go."

With that, Dad kisses Mum and pushes us towards the back door, leaving him and Mac in the house.

The cold hasn't hit me yet, as I'm still warm from being in bed only minutes ago; all I can think of is *I should have had a pee before we left.*

Mum and I move swiftly into the back courtyard with its outbuildings containing our cars. With great confidence, my mother strides to the back wall with me staying close. There is no attempt by either of us to muffle the noise of our feet on the shingle as we head, as instructed, to the unlocked gate which leads to the mountain beyond. A barely audible command is given, "Through."

I don't need to be told twice as Mum quickly takes up her position as our leader once more. As my eyes adjust to the darkness, an upwards path is visible leading up to where the bracken meets the tree line. Turfs of grass brush my legs as we race onwards and upwards.

Spoke too soon as progress has just become laborious. The heavy rain has made the path, bracken and tree roots slippery as Mac said it would. Small streams are criss-crossing our way and cannot be avoided. *If I survive this day, I'm going to write to the manufacturers of waterproof boots to tell them they let in water.*

We reach a point on the lower part of the mountain where we have sight of the front of the house and the lane leading to it. Mum assures me we are far enough away from the mansion, in a place where Mac and Dad will find us. From my hiding position between the sodden bracken and the forest line, I can just make out the headlights of two cars snaking round the valley floor in our direction. My eyes are keeping track of the fast-approaching vehicles, while my ears are listening for Dad.

A hand lightly touches my arm. "Keep down – where is Mum?" the low, familiar voice whispers. Frightened to speak, I just point. A faint click is heard, and Dad moves towards it. I remain fixed on the approaching menace. I now pick up the sound of the speeding motors. The headlights are dancing over the road as every bump, hole or mud-splattered surface is found; there is no attempt by either driver to slow down. Stupid really, as I've seen the bobbing lights come to a halt more than once. *Festina lente* – 'make haste slowly'. However, it would seem for these mad drivers, it's destination the mansion and nowhere else. Don't like the look of it, but I have to keep looking.

"Quickly, tell me what you see." Another shadowy figure appears, crouching beside me. It's Mac.

Relaying the information as if giving a patient's diagnosis to a colleague, "Two dark cars have pulled up a little way from the front of the house. Four men got out of the first vehicle, three out of the second, no – wait – another person has just got out the second vehicle. I can see by the car headlights he is giving the orders. Two are moving towards the locked gates."

Placing a reassuring hand on my shoulder and speaking equally reassuringly, Mac says, "Keep watching and keep down."

No sounds are heard, but I can see the flash of gunfire as I assume they are attempting to break the lock. As the gates swing open, the cars move to the front of the house. Mac whispers in a calm measured way, "Okay, nearly time for you to go into the forest; cover your ears." And with that command, the earth beneath my feet moves; the night sky turns to day. The sound of an explosion echoes off the valley walls; the sleeping Welsh mountain dragon is now awake and no doubt its roar can be heard in Cardiff.

"Keep low and let's go and join your parents."

But I'm rooted to the spot, still observing. "Wait, someone is getting something from the boot of the car not under a pile of masonry. You are not going to believe me, but I think it's a massive drone."

There wasn't panic in Mac's voice. "Right, quick, into the trees. We must get out of its path and into a cave just up above us."

Led by the hand by Mac, I'm now sitting as best I can in the near darkness of the cave.

Mum is the first to break the unbearable silence. Feeling for my hands, when finding them, she gives me a water bottle. "Here – take small sips; breathe gently; try and relax."

I cannot help but speak in a slightly shaky, high-pitched voice, as nothing in my medical training has prepared me for what has just taken place. "Relax, relax, what happened? Why did they attack the mansion? No, scratch that – why did they blow up the place?"

Mac, in a matter-of-fact way, interrupts, "Well, actually, it was timed to go up in six hours' time, but I overrode the timer. Hence bash, bosh, bang...."

I don't have to see him to know that he is smiling in a self-satisfied way and shrugging his shoulders. His tone of voice is so annoying, as if it's an everyday occurrence. My reply is one of disbelief. "I'm sorry, are you saying that all the time I have been in that place, half an hour of which, according to my mobile, I was asleep, I was only metres from a load of explosives? Dad, Mum, did you know?" I don't give anyone a chance to respond. "Of course, you knew." As I start to come to terms with the calmness of the people around me, the penny drops. "Oh! I get it now – twenty-four hours, and the basement was a no-go area for checking as it was full of explosives that the removal men had dumped and primed. Silly me, as for one brief moment, I thought I had fallen down a rabbit hole, and it would turn out to be a dream, bloody nightmare more like."

It doesn't matter how old you are – I'm thankful when Mum moves close to give me a parent's reassurance. She puts an arm round me, strokes my hair lovingly and then tells me, "Dad and Mac are just going to check if the drone is coming this way." I sometimes forget how strong a woman my mother is.

Mac returns and once again takes charge. "It's okay – my monitor hasn't picked up anything. Sorry about all this, Ellie, but Alpha co-ordinated an emergency evacuation point earlier this morning for if we were rumbled and our escape by road was blocked. So, we need to get to the boathouse on the estuary. I pointed out this feature to you back in Northamptonshire. We don't have much time, as we need the tide in our favour, so chop-chop, people."

Before we leave, Dad brings out a small box from deep within the cave; it is about the size of two shoeboxes. Breaking the seal with his knife, he stuffs some of the contents into his rucksack but not all. I notice he unwraps a gun and places it in his jacket; he hands another one to Mac.

Visualising in my mind's eye the topography from the maps that were on our kitchen island, I calculate that the boathouse is about four miles away. Spring day on a flat surface, with a small backpack, would take twenty-five to forty minutes tops to jog/chat/run, but we have to go up, round, down while staying clear of any bad guys. So, it would seem we are being taken out of the area by boat, down the river and then into the sea, hugging the coast.

Dad gives the last of our orders. "Ellie, you're in the middle. No stopping unless I indicate. Keep your ears open and your mouth shut – be as quiet as possible. Let's go."

Leaving the cave, I pull my hat further down and then check my outer coat is tight against my body. It is not only the wet conditions making progress slow; we are also hampered by having to keep well into the forest. I am told it will make it harder for the drone to spot us; hopefully it doesn't have thermal imagery. More than once, I'm whacked in the face by branches and stumble over roots and vegetation. Luckily, I don't fall, but I can tell I'm not the flavour of the day with my parents or Mac. The cover of trees is quickly running out. We are coming near to the point where we must start to climb and then descend the rest of the mountain across open land. Dad raises a clenched fist. I tell myself, *stop dead, El, crouch down and hold your breath.*

Further up on the ridge, I spot two people, *friend or foe, who can tell?* What I do know is that I'm fighting the urge to shake in fear. I close my eyes and hope that if I can't see them, then they can't see me. I know it's weird logic, but I still do it, well, for a couple of seconds.

"The drone is about – bunch up." From his rucksack, I

notice Dad produce a groundsheet. "Get underneath, you two," meaning Mum and I, "make sure you're covered."

Read about it but never seen it, a cloth that stops heat signatures being picked up, and I'm using it. Any other time I would feel excited, but all I know is, I'm terrified. Time is ticking, but it's meaningless under the present situation. I can hear the distinct noise of the multi propellers of the drone, like the buzzing sound of very annoyed bees. Thankfully, it doesn't hover overhead but moves quickly on up to the ridge of the mountain.

I can see, from a slightly raised edge of the material, Mac is tracking it.

"Drone has moved away, but I need to see what is going on. Stay put till I get back." And with that, he is gone.

While we wait, the weather begins to change yet again. The moon is now trying to disappear behind wispy clouds. With any luck, a large area of the ridge will be covered before too long. A single *click* is heard. Mum replies with a double *click* and, as if by magic, our party is now back to four.

Mac reports, "From what I can make out, those two are ramblers, doing a night walk. Lucky for us, our visitors would not have known there are four of us." He whispers something so softly to Dad that he makes it impossible for me to hear, but I guess it is to do with them walking into danger.

Rapidly, the area has become enveloped by drizzly cloud and with it the whole topography of the mountain has also changed. For safety, three of us are attached to each other by cord, an arm's length apart; thankfully, I'm still in the middle. Mac is flying solo.

Going is a bit quicker but not a lot. *This is going to be one hell of a long night as we are only just coming off the ridge and must still have two- or so miles to go.*

Other than the weather, shale is now our next problem –

loose, wet and various sizes of slate mean that you don't have firm ground underfoot. Any moment, you can twist an ankle or a knee. It is also a noisy material to walk on. Fortunately, the cloud cover will deaden the sound, but rather be going up than down on this stuff. After being dragged by Dad and pushed by Mum, it is such a relief to stand on the lower part of the mountain, with its grassy bank.

Catching his breath, Dad speaks quietly, while undoing my reins, "Need to do a check as the cloud is getting lighter, and we need to take stock of the area and make sure the drone is not following us. So, ears and eyes as you sweep the area, people. Trish?"

"Clear."

"El?"

"Clear."

"Mac?"

"Clear."

"Good, but we are going to have to run the last mile in a record-breaking time."

We run like our lives depend on it, which they do. Reaching the boathouse, the tide is now on the turn as debris is now heading for the open sea. We hear *click, click*.

Mum's reply is, *click*.

Three shadowy, black-clad figures emerge from nowhere. "Hi, Mac, hear you and the family need a lift?"

With that, I'm lifted into an equally black boat – like the ones used by the inshore lifeboat crews – then pushed down low inside. Mac and my parents follow. There is no engine noise; the crew just let the river take the boat out to sea and only then do they start a very quiet electric motor. As I previously thought, we now hug the coast heading south; no one speaks. I lay cold and exhausted on the wet floor of the boat. Every time I attempt to lift my head to see if I can pick out the coast, to get my bearings, a strong hand pushes me down. Still, no one speaks or moves other than to gain their balance when a wave hits. With the movement of the sea and exhaustion, I fall asleep. Awaked by a different type of motion, we are now on dry land with the first signs of morning starting to appear. However, the sun is absent as the beach is covered in a sea mist.

Slightly disorientated, someone out of my vision gives an order, "Out, move."

Not sure if it is aimed at me, I'm grabbed, unceremoniously, like a rag doll and dumped on the sand. I can feel my brain trying to go from fuzzy to overdrive quicker than an F1 driver. I'm in no condition to think clearly, but I know that I need to obey orders, especially if someone has a gun and is telling you to move. I know it's not much, but I'm reassured my parents are living this nightmare with me. As this black-clad mini army sweeps me up again, balance is the next problem – sea legs and tiredness – as they dump me on the nearby lane.

Trying to brush off more sand from my bum, I look over at my armed guard and I don't believe it. I recognise that stance, as it belongs to my big brother. *I think I'll go over and have a little chat; it's only polite.* Before I can move, a hand grabs my arm.

Reacting angrily, I exclaim, "Ay, what you doing?" Turning to my restrainer I come face to face with Mum, who is not letting go.

Talking between her clenched teeth, I'm put in my place. "Keep your nose out – if he wants to acknowledge us, he will. So, for now, be pleased you are in one piece, and keep your mouth shut, be savvy?"

What is it with everyone giving orders? Crestfallen, I reply, "Okay, you win." Then, under my breath, "For now."

"What did you say, young lady?"

"Nothing, just clearing my throat."

Standing cold and shivering on the narrow lane, I notice Dad and my brother are deep in conversation, while Mac is on his mobile.

I have witnessed that look many times on the wards. *Something is not quite right.*

As I scan the area, there is an army ATV, which is having a partially deflated boat pushed into its rear, together with an assortment of equipment. There are also two other vehicles: a van and a car. Walking towards me is a young female solider who wears a stern look on her face. She takes me to the front of the ATV before leaving me alone. My wet clothes are sticking to me. No amount of tugging with numb fingers is able to draw the fabric away from my cold skin.

I'm stopped in my challenging state by a softly spoken voice. "Hi." Taken aback by this heartening, single word of welcome from my brother, I can sense that tears are forming in the corners of my salty eyes.

His warm breath brushes my face as he comes even closer in order to speak privately. In a low, soft, reassuring tone, he says, "The task force is unaware of our relationship. To them you are just a party that needs to be evacuated, and I would like to keep it that way."

Between chattering teeth, I manage an, "Okay."

Still just the two of us, he signals to the corporal to join us. "Corporal."

"Yes, sir?"

"You will find a dry bag under the driver's side rear passenger seat of the Polo. Take this lady with you, and after you've collected the bag, move yourselves behind the van. Give her your fatigues, including boots, you will need her shoes. You will find a change of outfit for you in the bag. Put her wet clothes in the dry bag and return it to under the seat. No need to retrieve your kit; you will not need it as you are not coming with me – you will be driving the van with Mac as your passenger. Once you are on the road, he will tell you where you are going. Oh! I will need your ID; it will be returned."

While he spoke to the soldier in an officious tone, when he focuses his attention on me, his cadence holds a chuckle. "Sorry, there is no change of underwear, so you will have to go commando."

It seems an age since I had a reason to smile. Not only does one play on my face, but if it weren't for the fact that the family is under the cloak of anonymity, he would receive a well-aimed sisterly punch. Quickly followed by a big hug, no – scrap that – I will give him the biggest of all hugs if we survive whatever is taking place.

After having to ask for female help with my transformation from civilian to soldier, I'm now in a warm and surprisingly comfortable outfit, alas minus my knickers and socks. However, even in the half-light of morning, I can tell the corporal sports a puzzled look on her face. I take it it's about his inappropriate, somewhat personal, remark to me and my bemused reaction.

Oh! I see – she has the hots for him. Wonder if it's reciprocated? No wonder she is giving me the evil eye and is reluctant to help me out of my wet things. If she isn't happy now, she definitely will not be ecstatic with what happens next: the assignment of the other vehicles and the travellers in each.

Hovering by the ATV, I cannot help but notice that Dad has just finished a mobile phone call and is now talking to my brother. A handshake ensues before he heads towards the Polo with Mum and two escorts, now in mufti. My parents do not give me a second glance. James junior is still in military fatigues and is going to drive the ATV, with Doctor Ellie as Corporal Eleanor. The real corporal is accompanying Mac to somewhere I'm not privy to. While she waits in the driver's seat for the order for her and Mac to proceed, I cannot help but pick up on the vibe from my doppelganger. Her evil eyes keep looking at my throat as through she cannot wait to strangle me.

My brother nods a farewell to each driver in turn before telling me to 'get in' the cab of the ATV. Once the two vehicles disappear down the lane, he reaches up to take his seat behind the wheel. "We need to wait for our signal." The beach hut man comes into view, gives a thumbs up, followed by a wave of goodbye, and then darts back from where he came. "We can go." The engine roars into life.

We slowly move down the less-than-forgiving beach lane. *Why is it I cannot shake off the feeling my father has thrown me to the lions in order to achieve closure for his spooky friends? Cannot see why I'm here. Also, why am I wondering if I will be back in time for my date on Saturday, with a man I had breakfast with in the company of our fathers? The mind boggles.*

CHAPTER 11

WEDNESDAY

Mac has never been a good passenger, he would rather drive, and today is no exception, as he needs to be occupied. Bundled into a waiting van on the Welsh beach, before noon, he is now being driven back to Northamptonshire. This was not part of the initial plan; however, contingency is always change and adapt whenever the unexpected arises, and this is just that.

When they landed on the beach his mobile signal kicked in, he noticed he has missed his wife's call; his blood ran cold. For a split second, his mask of composure had slipped. It was not until his friend and neighbour placed his hand on his shoulder asking, "What's wrong?" did he realise he was standing oblivious, to what was taking place around him.

Over and over again silently in his head, Mac remembers his reply ."It's Fred – he is in A & E at the local hospital. Been hit by a car, the wife is in meltdown."

The thought of Fred is pushed to one side as he remembers, vividly, what his wife told him about that fateful day when his firstborn, Michael, died. He knows Michael was murdered; he just doesn't know why. As a serving member of the armed forces and now in recruitment, Mac has seen death, of colleagues and friends, but he never expected to have to deal with one of his adult children losing their life before him. Like his wife, he lives that day every day, hoping the outcome will be different, but this is not a film – there is never going to be a happy ending. In the presence of his family, he has taught himself to hold his emotions tight. He consciously tries not to wrap Fred in cotton wool. Although he has his army recruits and his wife has her schoolchildren, it is not the same; they are not their flesh and blood. Every day, in his heart, he lights a candle for his son and says a silent pray.

That ill-fated day started well, when Mrs Mac was happy to agree to drive her pilot son Michael to Cranfield, as he didn't want to leave his brand-new car at the airport. Cranfield is one of many small commercial airfields dotted around the country. However, unlike Gatwick or Heathrow, it has one major advantage over its big cousins: discretion. Professional pilots are attached to private airlines that ferry A-list stars, heads of state and diplomats around the world. No fuss, no interference from the media or fans, clients can come and go in relative secrecy. On his return he knew, a quick phone call and Mum would always come and pick him up, regardless of distance or time of night. It was a non-school day; Mac was away from home and Fred was at police college on yet another course, so she was happy to spend some time with her favourite son, although she never said it in so many words.

Although willing to drive, Mrs Mac was happy for Michael to undertake the task. As he slowly pulled off the drive, saying in an upbeat manner to his mother, "Plenty of time for a nice steady drive to work. I'll treat you to coffee and breakfast, then I will be all set for a mid-morning briefing and lunchtime flight." And that's what it was, an enjoyable trip. But some idiot dropped a load of stones on the road which resulted in a cracked windscreen. "Sorry, Mum, an inconvenience but no problem. I'll see if one of the garage staff can arrange a new windscreen while we are having coffee."

Michael had no problem parking the car near the terminal building, but it would have to be moved to the workshop once he had contacted them with his windscreen request. The duty security manager was there to meet them only because she had slipped out to have a fag in a restricted area. Hiding the half-smoked cigarette behind her back, she gave a morning greeting to Michael and Mrs Mac, which came out shrouded in a fog of tobacco-heavy air.

Blushing like a schoolgirl caught behind the bike shed, she tried to cover her indiscretion. "I hear it's briefing in forty-five minutes, so I will leave you to it as just got a couple of jobs to do. Have a good trip and will see you on your return." And with that, she hurried quickly away.

Michael loved the briefing room as it overlooked the runway. It was one of those places that he would be happy to sit, with a cup of coffee, and just watch the comings and goings of small aircrafts and ground staff all day. He was taken aback as he entered the room as it was usually empty, but on this occasion, it already contained another crew. "Hi, Chris and Steve, what are you doing here?"

Steve's reply was somewhat messy as he was talking with a mouthful of a breakfast sandwich, while trying to stop the runny egg oozing out the bread. "Didn't the boss tell you we are coming with you on your trip? The old romantic, Chris is whizzing me off for a dirty few days for our anniversary, and as you are going our way, thought we might thumb a lift. I'm your designated co-pilot by the way. Trip has been logged; paperwork has been checked against cargo by customs and we are clear for take-off at the scheduled time; initial checks on the plane are done. I know you will do your own checks, but aren't I good to you?"

"Oh, you can return the favour of the lift, Steve. Can my mother borrow your car as she now has a cracked windscreen which was picked up on the way here? Just spoken to the guys in the garage; they are going to deal with it but cannot get hold of a new screen till tomorrow and Mum needs to get back home today."

Steve sighed, trying to stifle a smile. "My car? You'll want my bank card and pin number next."

"Only if you insist." Mac junior laughed at the suggestion.

Now laughing as well, Steve threw his car keys on the table while Chris handed over the necessary documentation, including the logged flight plan for today's trip to Europe. Michael knew the itinerary as he had undertaken the route many times. His cargo was always the same: two large document storage boxes – the kind you would find in any office stored under the desk – and a crate, which varied in size but was usually the width, depth and height of a flat-packed kitchen table. He never saw who dropped them off at Cranfield, but the same person at his destination collected them in a small white van. Michael had told his father about this strange monthly occurrence, as he knew Mac was always interested in out-of-the-ordinary events. During these father and son tête-à-têtes, Michael would sometimes put on a very good impression of a cabbie with a cockney accent, saying, "You wouldn't believe who I had in the back of my taxi today, gov," before dropping the name of some A-list celebrity whom he knew his dad didn't know. Politician yes, rapper no.

Kissing her son and acknowledging Steve and his wife with a nod, she spoke as a mother does to her children, "Michael, pilot safely. Steve, Chris, have a great time, and I will expect a nice present, no tat. Steve, if you could drop off my car once repaired, I can return yours?" And with that, Mrs M left the room; within ten minutes, she had left the site, driving Steve's sports car lid down, wind howling round her ears, not realising that she would never see any of them again.

'The same day, late afternoon, the following news bulletin was broadcast on the radio:

> *BREAKING NEWS:*
> *We have reports coming in that earlier today a light aircraft exploded on take-off from a small commercial airport on the Bedfordshire/Northamptonshire border, crashing into a nearby field. We have no details at present of how many fatalities or injures other than it has been confirmed that the pilot and co-pilot were killed in the incident. The Civil Aviation Authority together with the emergency services from the surrounding counties are at the scene, and local hospitals are on standby. Will bring you more information later.'*

From that day she could never listen to the radio again, fearing what might be said on the hourly news bulletin; she stuck to music CDs instead. Family and friends were surprised at how well Mrs Mac was dealing with the situation; Mac knew this was a front, for like a clown, she was smiling on the outside, crying on the inside. He waited, knowing it would not be long before the dam on her emotions broke.

When the forest-thick CAA report was broken down, it apportioned blame to mechanical failure of a critical part of the plane's engine. Mac wasn't convinced at this conclusion as Michael was meticulous in his checks. He was not a person to check once but as many times as needed. He had piloted the same plane on many occasions and had said to his father that he was well aware of all her idiosyncrasies; he knew how she would perform in the wet, the cold and the heat. He instinctively knew when she was poorly and needed cosseting and when she was revved up, raring to go. Mac believed his son garnished the same love, care and attention on that plane as he did on his car, his clothes and girlfriends. There was no mincing his words, for Mac was adamant his son was murdered, but he had no idea why or by whom.

Mac rejected the offer of someone in the Cranfield office bagging up Michael's possessions; Mac wanted to do it as he knew how it went far better than them. He had been charged on a few occasions to both have the dubious honour as well as the privilege of undertaking this task for his fallen comrades. While other officers may write a brief note of condolences to the bereaved, Mac's outpouring of sorrow would take up pages on the character of the dead and what their loss meant to him and the unit. For he had always made the point of knowing everyone in his unit as though family: their likes, dislikes, friends, partners, children and pets. One of the deeply religious lads once said of Mac, "If he wasn't in the army, he would have made a brilliant priest. I'd be happy to go to confession and would joyfully wait to see what penitence he bestowed on me." But when it came to Michael's locker at Cranfield, it contained nothing of any use or value to anyone other than his parents. Any clues as to why or who felt the need to kill him was elusive.

After the memorial service had taken place (due to the intensity of the crash, nothing that could constitute a body to bury remained), Mrs Mac's health went into free fall. Mac had managed to secure a leave of absence with the support of army welfare and an understanding senior officer, whose son had died on active service and knew of the devastating ramifications this would have on the family.

"Take your time, Mac, the army and I are with you and the wife every step of the way. Call me day or night." But he knew the support he needed was closer to home; this was when they took their neighbour, the commander and his wife Trish, into their confidence.

＊

Coming back to the here and now, Mac needs to take control of the situation, but he wonders if what happened to Michael is in some way part of this mess and if Alpha is expecting Fred to dig up evidence to provide this. Or is this purely conjecture on his part, as at no point, before we left for Wales did Alpha say, in his presence, what Fred should be looking for. Shaking off this thought, he says, "Corporal, when we get to Northampton, I need you to drive to the Drill Hall," (area headquarters of the Royal Anglian Regiment, home of the Territorial Army [TA]), "where I will leave the van. I've arranged storage on site. I will give you directions nearer the time on how to get there. Don't worry, you will be picked up and taken back to a prearranged point to liaise with the major and his passenger. Once there, you will be briefed on the next stage, as you will have to return to your army duties, namely the exercise your company is presently engaged in. I know you have already been told, but I must reiterate that this is a secret mission, and it must not be discussed with anyone, ever."

"Yes, Sergeant. Thank you for having confidence in me," while thinking, *that will be me soon, an army Sergeant, if the major keeps his promise. He will because his that type of guy, a man who keeps his word. So watch out world, it will be me giving the orders for others to follow.*

As a man used to reeling off vast amounts of data by rote, he does the same with the route the corporal needs to take back to Northampton and then to the Drill Hall.

Parked in a side street in sight of the Drill Hall, Smithy is waiting and watching for a white VW van to turn up. He didn't realise so many people drove the same type of commercial vehicle. Time ticks slowly by, so he plays out once again in his mind the events of the morning that resulted in him being here, in the heart of Northampton town centre:

A call came in just after dawn from his father, relaying an urgent message from Ellie's dad. He surprised himself by his positive reaction to be part of the 'gang' in Freddo's absence, who is now languishing in the local hospital. The role he was assigned was 'wheelman', as though he was going to do a bank heist. Before parking his Range Rover near to the TA centre, his first task was to go to the Northampton General Hospital to take over the driving baton from Mac's son, the injured Freddo. Although Freddo was waiting to go down to surgery, and somewhat relaxed due to the pre-med, he still managed to not only pass on instructions but also to tell him about his relationship with Ellie; she being his best friend. Lastly, in not many words, what he was going to do to him, physically, once he was up and running again. For nothing more than not liking his face.

Smithy recalls the parting gift he gave the patient:

Deep from his trouser pocket, he brought out a softly clenched hand with only the second finger raised, saying, "Swing on that?" and then made a hasty retreat, quickly walking back to his car, laughing like a loon.

The instructions were: "Wait patiently just outside the TA centre in Northampton for a van registration… it will contain my dad, Mac," picture shown, "and a young female solider, description unknown. Mac will make himself known, so stay in the car and he will ask you a couple of questions. You will know the answers, so don't worry. Once the correct answers are given, Mac will give you further orders. What happens to Mac after that is not your concern."

As the striking, nineteenth-century, Grade-Two-listed TA centre comes into sight, Mac starts muttering, "Check the make and model plus registration of cars parked in Clare Street. Is he here? Check if it's the driver who is expecting us? Ask the question: what are you doing this Saturday and with whom?" With a calm voice, Mac points out to the corporal he has spotted Smithy's Range Rover and requests she pulls over so he can check all is okay.

The corporal parks a little further down the road than she would have liked. Once a brief scan of the area by Mac all is clear, he alights the van, alone. As he walks towards the car, Smithy lets down the driver's window ready to speak to Mac, whom he has already checked out against the picture on his phone.

The young solicitor initiates the conversation, after checking his watch to see if it is still morning or the day has slipped past noon. "Good afternoon, sir, do you have something you would like to ask me?"

Taken aback momentarily by the young man's manner, he proceeds with the questions. "What are you doing this Saturday? And who with?"

Speaking in a very uptight way, Smithy replies, "I will start with the second question first: Eleanor, the commander's daughter. As to what we are doing this Saturday, it is my secret; as it will be our first date, I would rather tell her than you what I have planned. Have I passed the test?"

Used to summing up recruits, it is easy for Mac to get a handle on this person's character, now that he has met him in the flesh, coupled with what the commander has told him. He has come to the conclusion, *yep, the type of guy Ellie needs in her life, hope it works out.* "Yes, thank you." Motioning to the van to signal all is well, Mac gives Smithy his orders. "You are to take the corporal," nodding to the van's driver, "to the outskirts of Salisbury Plain, no satnav; here is the map you need, and I have indicated the lay-by you need wait in and the time you must arrive. The time is critical, as it must coincide with the arrival of another vehicle. An army ATV will turn up with a very familiar person in it: Ellie. Don't get out your car; let the driver come to you – he will recognise the corporal. You will then exchange passengers. Out of recent experience, don't expect to enjoy the corporal's company, best if you two keep the talking to a minimum. Before I go, I have a personal favour to ask."

"Yes, please ask."

"Don't tell her, Ellie, about Fred until tomorrow? This is so my wife and I can deal with the situation. Also, can you take Els somewhere safe so she can sleep? That girl is running on empty."

"Yes of course. I did speak to Fred earlier before I came here; he was very much 'on the ball' waiting to go into surgery. Oh! Do you need a lift to the hospital? I am more than happy to swing round and pick up Mrs Mac."

"No thank you, I have a task to undertake here with the van and then I can walk down to the hospital to meet up with Mrs Mac, who I have been informed is waiting for me. Thankfully, a few of Fred's colleagues are with her lending support."

The corporal has alighted from the van but has made sure she is far enough away not to overhear their conversation.

Mac continues now with a small smile appearing on his face. "Yep, the commander is right, upset Ellie and you will have to deal with a very angry father. Now I've met you, make that two to deal with, and that is without having the company of Fred and the major, El's big brother." Noting Smithy hasn't flinched at this threat, he continues, "You will do, my son. Keep our girl safe and see you soon. Would you like me to give Fred your love? Maybe not, as I can imagine what he said earlier, knowing you're hanging about with his best friend."

"Thank you for the offer but no; however, may I ask a favour of you?" Without waiting for a reply, he goes on, "Tell Fred I will send him pictures from our date on Saturday; I'm sure this will help him make a speedy recovery."

With that, Mac taps the top of the Range Rover, motioning to the corporal to join them. As though talking to a comrade, he says, "Goodbye, Smithy, glad to meet you, and when you see your father, say hello to Tommy for me."

Before a surprised Smithy can reply, the corporal is standing next to the car. "This gentleman will take you back to continue with your army duties." Passing over the keys to Mac, she moves to the passenger side and takes her seat for the duration of the forthcoming journey to Wiltshire.

Without a sideways glance, Mac's next task is to hide the van in the Drill Hall. Having an office in the very distinctive building, his actions will not be questioned. With the van safely stowed away in one of the outbuildings, he can now exit through the main gates. He looks over to the now vacant parking spot, then mutters, "Drive carefully, Smithy, my son, and bring our girl back safely to us." He shrugs his shoulders, trying to dislodge the weight of the world that has climbed onto them since he heard the crushing news. Shaking his head, he gives a little silent prayer, *Michael watch over your little brother and your mother. Big hug, son, miss you every minute of every day.* Walking with purpose, he calculates ten minutes and he can be with the love of his life and his scatterbrain of a son, whom he equally loves to bits. But he cannot stop his mind wandering back to that dark time.

While waiting for Steve's car to be picked up by his family, Mac had to move it to a neighbour's garage as he often found Mrs Mac sitting in the sports car, rocking and crying uncontrollably. Then poor Fred was bombarded with his mother's phone calls of love and concern all times of the day and night whether at work or not. *You will keep safe? Don't put yourself in danger; drive carefully; you're not taking the motorway job, are you? Ring me when you get home and when you leave for work; are you eating? What are you eating? I'll cook you something and bring it over and sit with you while you eat.* The list of things the lad was subjected to seemed to be endless. However, at least she was talking; not much of it was cohesive or satisfied her need to protect, but it was a respite from the crying. Guilt entered the fray, the overbearing feeling of blame that the boys were her responsibility and she let them down by not protecting them. She punished herself for loving Michael more than her youngest. Pleaded, gut-wrenchingly so, with Fred, begging him to forgive her for not loving him enough, saying she was a bad mother and would make it right. How this was to be achieved, nobody knew, least of all her. She was wallowing in treacle, not able to grab the hands that were reaching out to her. While all this was going on, Mac's world was also imploding.

This evokes a memory of a conversation he had with his senior officer; it was more that Mac listened and the officer spoke:

"Sorry Mac but grief doesn't go away, as I know. I see mental health, my mental health, as a very expensive vase, which has been knocked onto the floor and broken into large pieces. No matter how careful you are at repairing the damage, and to the outside world it looks like the same

vase, you look for the cracks because you know where the glue has been applied. You notice a small, tiny piece of porcelain is missing that you cannot find, you will never find. The trick is to not break the vase again, for the next time the pieces are smaller, and more are lost. Family, friends, colleagues carefully, lovingly, move the vase to one side so it's not knocked."

Mac could relate to the analogy; he was suffering the beginning of his own breakdown. His one saving grace was that he was aware of it, and the techniques used to control the downwards spiral, through seeing it in others.

Pushing the darkness to one side, he smiles. The first time Mrs Mac laughed again, it was like a ray of sunshine poking through a cloudy sky. When this beam of laugher hit the ground, it was with such intensity it split into a thousand colourful bubbles of pure joy. At that moment, Mac understood why he loves his wife so much.

—
*

He lifts up his head, eyes forward, and strides the last couple of hundred metres towards A & E, avoiding the waiting ambulances and the milling smokers standing just outside the perimeter of the hospital grounds. A colleague of Fred's, who has been waiting diligently, stops him in his tracks as he reaches the main doors. "Mac, boys have been with Mrs Mac since Fred was brought in. I've made sure she hasn't been left on her own. A couple of the girls came as well, both had Mrs Mac as a teacher. Now Fred has come round from the operation to reset his leg and pin his ankle, he can have visitors. I was just waiting for you and now I'm popping down to the hospital shop to get Fred some squash and a bar of chocolate – do you want anything? Should I pick up a sandwich and a coffee for the wife?"

"Coffee for us both would be great, flat white, no sugar and a couple of sandwiches would be very welcome. Before you ask, anything in the way of a sandwich is fine, brown or white bread doesn't matter. How did the accident happen, do you know?"

"Sorry, Mac don't know anything, wasn't the officer on the scene, came straight from home when I got a call from the commander ordering me to 'pick up Mrs Mac and then get to the hospital fast, and above all else don't leave her alone'. Rallied the officers she knows and therefore would feel comfortable with. Knew you were not going to get here for some time, so we all jumped in to help, like you would do for us and our families." With that, the off-duty police officer tells Mac were to find his family, before going downstairs to the shop.

Alone, Mac pushes open the door and then checks the route to Fred's ward on the notice board. Once satisfied with the directions, with hands in his pockets, he strides down a very long corridor. Not knowing what he is going to be walking into, his mind is made up that the family will deal with today's struggles head on. If professional help is needed for him, the wife, Fred, then so be it.

CHAPTER 12

WEDNESDAY

A road sign informs Smithy to 'Drive carefully', while another bids him 'Welcome' into the next county, as he is now leaving Northamptonshire. Him and his passenger travel in silence; the only noise is the steady hum of the engine and the soft whirl of heated air being pushed around, keeping the two occupants warm. Mile upon mile is slowly ticked off, as they pass through county after county to their destination. He is looking forward, as Mac had said, to a more agreeable companion on his return journey. Coming from another direction, Ellie and her brother in the ATV are enjoying being in each other's company. Passing town names and signposts, the direction of travel for both is Salisbury and its plain, home of military exercises. Nobody will notice one extra military vehicle there; it will be like a single tree in a forest.

*

We are still on the outskirts of Salisbury when my brother gives a very audible breath out followed by an element of triumph.

"Great when a plan comes together." Coming up fast is a lay-by to our left. Slowing down, he gives the car, stationary in the lay-by, a quick flash of our headlights. The driver moves the Range Rover forward, giving us enough space to park the beast behind.

Now stationary, James barks out an order in as if it's a reflex, "Wait," then, with an afterthought, "please." While I try to watch what is going on outside, through a very mucky windscreen, I don't immediately notice that my brother has left the cab. My line of vision is taken by something playing out in front of me.

What do we have here? Alighting from the passenger side of the Range Rover is the real corporal. *I bet you want my brother to run to you, take you in his arms and whisper sweet nothings in your ear – "Oh, Corporal I have missed you. Let's run off into the sunset, leave this life behind us, never to wear khaki again." "Oh, Major, wrap me in your strong embrace." Pass the bucket; I want to be sick. It's all in your dreams, my dear corporal, as he is ignoring you and is to talking to the driver.*

By my brother's demeanour, I can tell the conversation is purely business, not social. *Well, that was a quick chat*, I think as he lifts himself back into the driver's seat. As he turns to me, I cannot help but think, *oh, that's not a happy face – who has upset you?*

I can tell he is trying hard to suppress feelings of fury when he speaks. "I want you and the corporal to move to the side of this vehicle, in the shadows, and change clothes. Then go to the vehicle in front; the driver has instructions to take you home to Northamptonshire. Quick, I haven't got all day."

Trying to smooth over the cracks which seem to be forming between us, for some unknown reason, I reply, "Thank you for being my guardian. Shall I give Mum and Dad your love?"

Grabbing my elbow firmly, he says, "Give Mum a kiss and hug from me. Tell Dad," he hesitates before continuing, "tell Dad everything is okay in my world, and we will catch up soon. Maybe get in a round or two of golf, but drinks will be on him." Before a wave of something washes over him, he lets go and looks forward. "Go on, off with you and remember, I love you, smelly Ellie with the big fat belly, my little ellie-phant."

I cannot help myself. "You soppy sod. Love you." Before tears run down my face, I jump out of the beast and move into the shadows to change back into Doctor Ellie.

Moving to the passenger side of the beast, I come face to face with another beast. Looking at me with utter contempt, which is followed by a single raised finger, is one very pissed-off corporal. "I'll have my uniform, boots and my ID and, here, you can have these things. Sorry they're not your things; your wet rags are in a waste bin in Wales, bitch."

For my trouble I get a pair of trousers, a less-than-flattering T-shirt, a hoodie and my shoes all thrown at me, and not in a nice way, but I will be the adult in this situation.

"Thanks," I say, really thinking, *up yours also, bitch*. Although uncomfortable in this latest clothes change, I move to the waiting car more in anticipation than hope. I open the door, and all I can say is, "Oh, it's you." Now I know why my brother's face was like thunder, he was expecting Freddo.

My driver's reply is more articulate. "Am I glad to see you! Jump in and I'll get you safely home." And with those few words, we both smile.

Getting settled into a much nicer car seat, I ask in a matter-of-fact way, "Do you mind if I open the window as it smells of army and I have had my fill of that organisation to last me a lifetime?" We both laugh joyfully at being in each other's company, before I carry on, "If you want me to help with the driving, you just need to say," adding, "I do have fully comprehensive insurance and a clean driving license."

At ease in each other's company, while pulling out onto the road, he replies, "I know you are good for a very nice new car if you smash this one up. Remember I now take care of your trust fund. I may take you up on sharing the driving; however, you look like shit."

For some unfathomable reason, considering we have only known each other in minutes rather than days, I reach across to touch his arm.

Taking his right hand off the steering wheel, he momentarily touches my hand, simultaneously smiling, then asks, "I would like it if we can just talk. Nothing heavy, maybe films, music, food you enjoy. What you do at work, holidays you've been on or would like to take one day, or you can tell me how you ended up here?"

"Get the picture. Are you being nosy? Is it a solicitor thing or a Smithy thing, and what is your real name? Smithy doesn't sound right."

"My given name is Ptolemy. Yes, I know, but I have got used to it. The family call me Tolly for short, unless I have done something really bad; I would like it if you could use my given name as well?"

Uplifted, I find that I'm looking forward to our journey from Salisbury to Northamptonshire. "Tolly?"

"Yes?"

"Will we be stopping for food on the way?"

"Food, comfort break, gas, whatever you want, but just keep talking."

"Deal." Yet another smile appears on my face, but this one stretches from ear to ear, mirroring the one on Tolly's. However, as we both seem to be embroiled in a world miles away from our own, I feel that it is only right I tell Tolly about my recent journey from Wales to Salisbury. It may be best if Mac or my dad fills him in on what took place at the now flattened mansion.

So, with a deep breath, I start my tale, from leaving the Welsh beach with my brother, to arriving at the lay-by only moments ago. If a relationship between the two of us is going to end before it gets going then so be it, but here it comes, warts and all.

"You may wonder how I ended up in an army ATV dressed as a soldier. Can we leave that part of my story out for now?" I receive a nod from my driver. Happy, I continue, "I will start from early this Wednesday morning. So, alone in the ATV with my brother, whom you have just met, I was hoping to speak openly with him about what was happening around me because I didn't, and still don't, have a scooby. So, I shot off the opening volley, 'Where are we going? And, in case you haven't noticed, we are going to stick out like a sore thumb in this green monster truck.'

"He replied, 'No, not really as we are going to an army base in the area, as I have orders to report ASAP.'

"I could tell the conversation was going to be like pulling teeth, but I continued, 'If it hasn't escaped your attention, I am, and have never been, a serving member of your army. How do you think you are going to pass me off as a soldier, let alone a corporal?'

"He came straight back with, 'You just need balls. I assure you that it can be done.'

"I knew what he was talking about as I've seen my dad walk into a room with so much confidence that he had senior men eating out of his hand in a blink of an eye, but I don't have this ability. I told my brother this. 'I hope that you are talking metaphorically, because the last time I looked, I didn't have any, balls that is.'

"That's when I was taken aback by his reply. 'Yes you do. You've always had them. This has nothing to do with your looks but your intellect. You use the English language as a weapon and also the comprehensive knowledge that no one is better than you, regardless of gender or social standing. You have the inbuilt ability to fight your own corner and protect those who are not strong enough to protect themselves. So don't tell me you have no balls. Because, my dear sister, my dear doctor, if you want to be castrated, then give up your calling as a physician and get yourself a soul-destroying job rather than have a fulfilling career.'

"Tolly, I hope you don't think me big-headed, but his declaration came as a great surprise, as in the last couple of days I've felt like I was way out of my depth, thrown into my dad's world, a world I knew nothing about. "

Trying hard to both stave off fatigue and concentrate on his driving, Tolly speaks softly, "Ellie, you are lucky to have a brother who looks both out for and up to you; I don't have such luxury as I'm an only child." Reaching for my hand, he asks gently, "Please continue, as I'm now even more intrigued."

Diving back into where I left off, I continue, "I remember, I drew in a big gulp of air, sat up straight, squared my shoulders, planted my borrowed boots firmly on the floor, rubbed my hands on my knees and became the soldier I was dressed to be. I then asked him, 'Where is this base? And what do you need me to do once we get there?' "With that, James turned all military, telling me," 'We will have to pass a series of checkpoints, but *they* are expecting us.'

"He continued, anticipating my next question, 'The corporal was picked because you two look very similar, hence you have her on-loan army ID. Security checks will be done, mainly on the driver's side, when we enter base. There will be a vehicle check but only on the outside, including the underneath. Although it would be customary for a junior rank to drive me, I will continue to undertake this duty. Only I will speak, and whatever orders I bark at you, you must obey without answer. Once we get the all-clear to proceed onto the base, you must remain with me at all times. Never walk in front or alongside; half a stride behind is okay. Treat me as though I'm one of your high and mighty surgeons, instead of your high and mighty brother. You will be required to salute. I will brush your leg or give a little cough to prompt you to do so. You can salute?' In your short meeting with my brother, you can imagine the frown on his face when he said it?"

Tolly's reply comes out as a knowing snigger.

"Don't laugh as I soon found out that I was useless, so I received a crash course on saluting."

Trying to sound like my army brother, I explain, "With right hand, give a well-practised, crisp, straight finger, open-hand salute before bringing it down, unwavering to the side of your right hip, in readiness to go again. The movement for a soldier is automatic, a reflex, done without thinking; it happens. But if you do it wrong, or don't do it when required, it will be noticed, noted and punished. Remember, it's long way up and short way down. Let me see you practise, and don't hit me on the way up, or down."

Like an adolescent schoolboy, Tolly enthusiastically cries, "Show me?"

After a couple of goes, I think I have done a good job, but my driver has a different opinion on my efforts. "Maybe it will look a bit better if you stop sticking your tongue out while you're doing it. Oh, I'm enjoying this part of your story."

"Stop laughing, Ptolemy. Have you ever tried saluting sitting down? My salute didn't look anything like those seen on a parade ground. At one point I wondered if adequate was okay, but we are talking army, so the answer was no."

His rowdy laugher only stops when I give him a playful punch on the arm so that I can continue with my tale. Attempting to sound serious, I go on, "So I practised, as I didn't want to embarrass my brother. He came over all strange when he grabbed my hand, as Dad did only the other day, and placed it on his heart. Bizarrely, he spoke the same words: 'I will protect you, and in the end, the truth will out.' He looked deep into my eyes, making me truly believe him. A thought entered my head that I knew would break the tension; I asked if I would be back home by Saturday as I had a date with a guy, you."

At this part of my story, a most glorious smile appears on Tolly's lips and his eyes twinkle like stars.

While I hesitate, thinking of my brother's reply, not sure I can tell him the next part, Tolly speaks knowingly. "I can guess the major's response."

"Yes." I squirm in my seat, knowing I have said too much, but have to carry on. "He asked, 'Who is this idiot? Spill the beans or I will be joining you as chaperone and beating the information out of him. I can be very persuasive.' I quipped back, 'Wouldn't you prefer spending time with the lovely corporal? Or is fraternisation between ranks frowned on?' "Touché, but I could tell he didn't like my observation. However, he was not letting go of enquiring about you. Hope you don't mind?"

Tolly shrugs his shoulders in a non-committal way.

"Told him we are about the same age, you are a solicitor in the family's firm in Oxford and our dads introduced us. He said that he would check, adding in, and sorry about this next bit, 'Gosh Dad must be desperate to get you married off. And what does our Fredrick say to you dating? Before you say anything, I do know he has a boyfriend, but he likes to look after you in my absence, and I am thankful to him for that. But, El, you are dating an Oxford solicitor; Mum will have the banns read before the week's out. I take it that Dad is holding back on this nugget of gossip?'"

No sooner than the words are out my mouth, I can feel myself blushing at recalling the subject of marriage, not daring to look at Tolly. Returning to the job in hand, I realise that this is part of the tableau and had to be included regardless of my embarrassment. "Told my brother, 'Neither Fred nor Mum knows. Please don't tell them. If there is a second date, I may tell them, but no guarantees.'

"He said we had been royally set up. Tolly, have we?" I'm sure he can hear the concern in my voice.

"No, as I wanted to ask you out from the moment I saw you."

Relieved but trying not to sound too enthusiastic, I reply, "I'm glad you did as I'm looking forward to Saturday. However, as we are being honest, my brother said, 'If you want me to keep quiet and stop Mum from booking the church, then you own me big time.' With that, he broke into a tone-deaf version of 'Get Me to the Church on Time' from *My Fair Lady*."

With us both smiling inanely and thankful the intimate part of my story is told, we pull into a service station.

After stopping just long enough to grab food, gas and pay a visit to the lavatory, we are back on the road. My refreshed handsome driver asks, "So, why were you dressed in army clothes and in an ATV with your brother?"

Now in a happier place after our stop, I playfully reply, "Oh! I thought we would talk about films and holidays?"

With mocking annoyance, he responds, "No! You are on your way to the base. Now give."

Relenting joyfully to his demand, I explain, "As you may have guessed, the base was not far from the lay-by. Once on base after all the security checks, the ATV was manoeuvred in a well-practised manner to a car park where an assortment of army vehicles, in various military colours were lined up as though awaiting an inspection by some bigwig. I waited in the cab while

James jumped down to talk to a man. He then passed over the ATV's keys to him. After I was back on solid ground, he walked purposefully; I just followed in his wake to a very non-descript grey building among many. With no malice intended, pointing to a building, he said, 'That's our destination, and remember you are an insignificant person, just a body in a uniform. Just follow my lead.' Pushing the half-windowed, battleship-grey door open, he walked in first; at least he didn't let the door swing back so it smacked me in the face. No sooner were we in the building than we were stopped in our tracks by a man in civvies. Drifting back, I leaned against the wall, remembering I was to keep to the shadows. Satisfied, we proceeded, but only to another man further down the hall, also in civvies. Once again, a positive reaction and then we were instructed to go to yet another guard. At this point, I wasn't sure if all this security was for the building or for the person we were about to meet. Well, I definitely couldn't see it being for us. Reaching a door with the moniker 'Adjutant', James gave it an understated tap. By how swift the door was unlocked, the person's bodyguard must have had their back against it. With the door barely open, we were ushered in, without a word spoken. Before us was an unremarkable man in a dark three-piece business suit, sitting statesman-like behind the adjutant's desk. I quickly summed up the bigwig in the chair – enigmatic career civil servant, and a man who, after meeting him, you cannot remember what he looked like or whether or not you did meet him. That Mearns poem came to mind:

> 'Yesterday, upon the stair,
> I met a man who wasn't there.
> He wasn't there again today,
> I wish, I wish he'd go away'…

"The next thing, the 'suit' extracted himself from his chair to quickly greet us as though we were long lost kin. I could tell you that neither of us was taken in by the antics of this man. Our father taught us well on many things, one of them being, in a situation like this, play along. If only to discover what is going on, and above all else, keep your guard up. He also said lead with your left, punch with your right; that's okay if you are a boxer, I suppose."

While I take a drink of water, Tolly fills the void, "From the tales my father told me about his schooldays, he said your dad is a handy guy to have on your side in a fight."

"My dad has always been a close shop when it comes to school and college days. I now know that your father is a friend, but I started to wonder if the 'suit' was also one, and I will tell you why. So, getting back to this morning. The bodyguard left to give the three of us some privacy. The conversation opened up in a very easy manner, if one-sided on the part of the 'suit'. Remaining standing, but leaning on the desk in a possessive way, running his hands along its edge, he smiled then asked, 'How are you, Major?' Rhetorical rather than a genuine enquiry as he carried on, not waiting for a reply. Looking directly at me, 'Corporal,' he said with a raised eyebrow and a more serious face, 'you may be wondering why you have been called here? The reason is that I wish for you to convey this highly sensitive piece of information back to your father. Only then are you permitted to read the contents.' As he said this, he passed me a small sealed white envelope. Taking it, I could tell, just by running a finger over the surface, that all it contained was something no bigger or thicker than a playing card. Written on the front was my name with my accreditation in bold typing. This was not an afterthought. He must have known my need for answers, but he stood motionless. Why he couldn't put an address and a stamp on the envelope and send it via Royal Mail, rather than this entire cloak and dagger stuff, beats me.

Our host then speedily changed tack. 'As the major and you have been vetted, it was agreed that it was more expeditious for us, 'the Government', to pull you off your training.' Creepily, he winked at me."

"Did he now?" my knight in shining armour comments.

"Then the 'suit' thanked me on behalf of his colleagues, saying, '*They* do appreciate your help in this matter. Please take care, for none of us know what tomorrow will bring.'

"Reaching behind him to pick up a long, thin brown envelope, the 'suit' then presented it to my brother. 'Thank you, Major, you are now dismissed. Here are your orders, stating you attended this base, as requested by your company commander. I have taken the liberty of having your vehicle's content replaced with a couple of cases of fine wine and a few bottles of his favourite tipple.'

"My brother nodded. As you can imagine, I'm utterly confused by going all that way for a ten-minute meeting, for what? Departing, the 'suit' took my brother's hand. Thankfully, I got a curt nod.

"What was strange was that when James thanked our host, he said, 'I will let our father know we have met, if that is agreeable, sir?' A flash of a happy memory showed in his eyes, while his voice broke with emotion. 'I would like that,' he said. We were then shown out the building, and off the base. Once settled backed in the ATV, keys already in the ignition, my brother spoke calmly, 'Right, I need to get you out the army and have my corporal returned to me.'

"I cannot tell you how happy I was to relinquish my military role." Now glancing at a confused Tolly, I add in, "And with that, we headed out of the base to goodness knows where – down a rabbit hole for all I cared. But as you know, we pulled in behind your car in the lay-by." With my story coming to an end, we sit in silence and to my surprise about to enter Oxfordshire.

CHAPTER 13

WEDNESDAY

Sitting in the back of the VW Polo, Trish has intertwined her fingers with those of her husband's. She gives his hand a little squeeze before whispering in his ear, "So, where are we going?"

The squeeze is reciprocated before he turns his head to face her. In a similar vein, he keeps his voice low, ever mindful of others in the car, although he is fully aware they can hear the conversation. "To see an acquaintance, a hacker, and in his case, an ethical one. You'll like his office very much. You're in for a very pleasant surprise." With that, he smiles and then resumes gazing out the window, not looking but thinking.

Seeing his reflection in the car window, Trish realises his need to work out how to clear a path through the fog that is engulfing the family. When the four people in the car do talk, it's light-hearted topics – the weather, sport, food and the state of the roads and traffic. And in all this, Trish holds on to the belief all will be well.

Driving into the city centre – their destination – the transformation of the skyline is very noticeable; Trish cannot hide her surprise. "Coventry has changed massively since I was here last. Any possibility we can visit the cathedral if we have time? I hear that the tapestry of *Christ in Glory* by Graham Sutherland is breathtaking, and then there is the Baptistery Window? Can't wait to see them for myself."

Smiling, trying not to laugh when he speaks, he replies, "Whatever your heart desires. Sorry, but must tell the lads where to park." Leaning over between the two front headrests, the commander gives the driver his instructions, before relaxing back in his seat.

Slowly, the car is manoeuvred into a parking bay reserved for the cathedral's dean; Trish cannot contain her horror at what has just taken place. "We cannot park here – the car will be towed away! It's sacrilegious."

Tapping his wife's leg, the commander says, "Stop worrying – the lads will stay with it; coffee and food has been arranged for them, and permission has been granted by those 'on high'. Anyway, the dean is away on business and the space would only go to waste." Addressing their guardians, he continues, "No doubt you heard all that? Refreshments will be brought to you so no need to leave the car unattended. This is a restricted area, so nobody should bother you; if questions are asked, wave those fake IDs you carry. Be on your guard, but try not to kill or maim anyone; remember that all and sundry have a camera these days." Looking at his watch before continuing the short brief, he says, "I reckon an hour tops. When you see us returning, if all is well, tap on the roof. If not, you two pull away, and we will shift for ourselves. Thanks, lads."

Being the gentleman he is, the commander alights the car first and moves to the opposite side to help his wife. Tucking her arm in his, they move to the entrance of Coventry Cathedral like a couple of eager tourists.

Trying not to sound too impatient, Trish says, "Darling, I only want a quick look, then we can be on our way. Now that we have left the kids in the car, is this person 'on high' an old school friend by any chance? Or is this a 'don't ask questions and I will tell you no lies' time?"

He cannot help but think how he has missed this light-hearted banter between the two of them the last few days. Cheerfully, he answers, "How long have we been married, and you are only just catching on?"

Standing at the imposing glass screen that welcomes worshipers and tourists, the commander, although in a hurry, cannot help but allow his wife the enjoyment of beholding Coventry Cathedral for the first time. While he has been here many times – a point that she doesn't know – he is happy to bathe in her reactions as though only now seeing its exceptional beauty.

Trish is like a rabbit caught in the headlights of a car. "How did they do that? Where did they get the ideas? Oh! The design and the expanse of glass, the wood."

He makes a suggestion, in the hope it will chivvy her along, "I will purchase a guidebook, and you can read it on our way home."

With an approving nod, they enter the consecrated ground. However, it doesn't stop Trish pointing, looking up, down and around, frightened that the smallest piece of this holy cavernous wonderland will be missed. She also cannot resist a moment of piety, murmuring, "I would like to light a candle."

Realising he should have proposed it, he agrees to the request. "Yes of course. I will join you, if that is okay?"

"Don't be silly; of course you can, as we both need to remember our families and friends, reflect and be thankful for the joy and the sorrow we receive." With this last comment, he quickly turns towards her with a surprised look on his face. Seeing this, she clarifies what her observation means. "You cannot have one without the other; it's the same with love and hate, yin and yang, so when you experience times of wretchedness, which we seem to be having by the bucket load, you appreciate those moments of happiness more."

He waits, head bowed, for her to light her candle, reciting in his head parts of the sacred vow he made to her: for better for worse, in sickness and in health, to love and cherish. He lightly kisses her hand and whispers so only her and God can hear, "I promise we will come back, and not just as tourists, but now we must go downstairs."

"What's downstairs?"

He does not answer, moving nonchalantly to a staircase to one side of the chancel so they can descend into the area below, which has various private rooms leading off of it. Checking his watch, waiting for the correct time to be reached, he then knocks on one of the doors.

It swings open with the greeting, "In." With the door shut and locked, a tallish, scruffy young man in his twenties gives a fuller welcome. "Hello ,you two, nice journey from Wales? And do you have something for me?" He holds out a waiting hand.

The commander reluctantly hands over the USB that has been burning a hole in his jacket pocket since it was dug out of the study wall of the now deceased mansion. Not being technically savvy, he has to ask a couple of questions: "Did you get the pictures I sent and can you decode them? Will anyone know that you have accessed the USB data? Can I have a copy of the data? And I need the original stick back. I don't have the password – is this going to be a problem? And lastly, no taking copies as a souvenir."

The young man's passion for technology is clear by his measured response. He ticks off each point on his fingers. First finger: "Well, let's start with the basics – yes, I did receive the pictures, and although you slept through most of it, that Tom Hanks film wasn't wasted on you I see. After the dust has settled on all this, I will give you a watch list of films which may get those old grey cells of yours working." Second finger: "I'm happy to do this, and I will try to ensure that nobody will know about what is taking place." Third finger: "Copy, maybe, I will explain why in a minute. And yes, you will get the original USB back." Fourth finger: "Not insurmountable." He holds up his thumb in an okay sign, to make the fifth point. "Okay. Now can we proceed, as I am on a tight schedule and have the latest version of a video game that needs testing? I can tell you, there is more money in that than Government work."

Alpha surveys this man-child, who has the brain of a computer and an unwavering belief in his ability to unlock the information, hidden away in the small USB stick and random daubs on a wall.

"Right, as I can multitask, I will give you a crash course on encryption while getting access to the data."

Happy to let his nephew lecture away, Alpha sits back and drifts off like he often does in meetings, but with an ability to pick up on random words. In his nephew's talk, it's encrypted flash drives, different types of keys, physical security fobs, known passwords, physical locations, GPS, company address, IP address. He rambles on about the average person who will choose a simple password and then write it down on a Post-it pad and stick it to the PC. In Alpha's quickly filling head is the vibrating hum of geek speak, which he doesn't understand. Sighing deeply, he hopes that at some point today, the tech boy may get to the point, as it all just sounds like bollocks.

His nephew gives a shy laugh, as if he knows a secret, and then whispers to no one in particular, "Don't worry about all of this; I have it covered." And with that, his lecture stops, as though a thought has just popped into his head. Until he has assessed its importance and how to proceed, he picks up the chrome USB stick, rolling it round in his hand, before addressing it rather than his audience.

He murmurs, "On every computer there are logs which record everything that happens on the computer. If they have the wrong access rights then anyone can read them and change them. Access rights for a computer means what each user is allowed to see and do, on all computers. When you plug in a USB, then in the log it will show that the device has been plugged in. This is the first location that any security professional will check to see what information has been captured about the specific object/data/information that they are looking for."

Momentarily stopping, he scans the room, locating what his eyes are searching for, his drink. Grabbing the mug, he empties its contents in one large, audible gulp. Wiping a sleeve across his mouth, you can tell he is trying to find a convenient place to put the vessel. Not happy with any of the possibilities on offer, he throws it into the bin. "Don't worry; I will fish it out later. Where was I? Yes, boring the pants off of you both, sorry about that. You found the USB in the wall on which a number of swatch colours had been painted?"

The commander realises that it's time to wake up as he is being addressed; he can only nod.

Not waiting for a verbal response, K continues. "Pictures can contain hidden information, one being that the image contains certain arrays of colours which then can be transferred into binary. Each colour has a certain number, and that number can have multiple different meanings, one being to play music. Another way is that the image contains multiple little images of the same thing which, when mapped, create a QR code. QR code is a way of telling another computer to do something different by reading the QR code; simply having multiple objects in one picture can do this. The objects can

142

be any size and can all be in one location or overlapping each other. Another way of doing this is that the picture contains multiple letters and numbers which, when put in the correct order, create the code or password. This can be done by placing each letter in a random spot within the picture, without looking unnatural so everyone notices there is a code hidden in the picture."

Trish, drawing in a large gulp of air before making a comment, says, "You, young man, are like your cousin Ellie, too clever for your own good. Remember I used to wipe your snotty nose and your bottom. Where did that little boy, who struggled to do his English homework, go? It is bad enough that your uncle is drawing you into some clandestine operation, but it seems you already inhabit a world of spies. Who are you, George Smiley in the twenty-first century, or is it Joe 90?" Noticing his look of confusion at these references to popular culture, she frowns at him. "Don't look at me as though I have lost my marbles, young man, you know who they are."

Winking at his nephew, the commander turns his attention to his wife. "Calm down. Your geeky nephew knows exactly how the world works. Once the data has been accessed, we can be on our way, okay?"

With a wobbly voice, Trish replies, "Okay, but how long will it take?"

Both turn to the young man in charge. Looking up from his array of computer screens, he says, "Oh! The data from the colours is done. As I said previously, most people are stupid when it comes to keeping information secure. Here you go." He hands his uncle a piece of paper with a string of numbers on it. "I recognised what the number meant straight away and no doubt so do you?"

Scanning the paper, the commander laughs. "Thank you, my favourite nephew. What about the USB?"

"Uncle, I'm your only nephew. But when it comes to the USB, I would rather I didn't open it. It's not that I can't, but it is best that I don't." Seeing his uncle crestfallen, he continues, "Sorry, one of my other jobs may see me compromised if I do. You can have it back and, as promised, I haven't taken a copy. May I ask, what are you going to do with the other piece of information?"

The commander takes on the pose of *The Thinker* before speaking. "Right, I need a telephone number of a friend."

K is overjoyed by another task. "Name and address of your friend."

The commander writes down the details, shows Trish, who smiles before passing the paper to his nephew, who is shocked by what he sees. "Really?"

"Really."

"Bugger me, will have to start being nice to you. Ha, only in your dreams, big man."

From anyone else, Alpha would not have taken it, but he has a soft spot for his nephew, letting his disrespect slide. The young man's fingers dance across the keyboard and, within seconds, a telephone number is pulled up. "There you go, knock yourself out," he says as he indicates to the highlighted numbers on the screen.

Retrieving his mobile, the commander keys in the number. Placing the phone to his ear he waits, in the hope that his friend picks up and the call does not go to answer machine. A strong voice is heard. "Hello." That's it – no name, number or address, just a hello.

Taking this as his cue, the commander jumps in, "Can I speak to the duke please?"

"Sorry, sir, but His Grace is not taking calls today; the only exception is those that come from His Majesty."

Not one to take a negative as an answer, he continues,

"You owe me a bottle of Scotch you took from my rooms, you devious little turd."

A shocked voice answers, "How did you know it was me?"

"I remember your father, the late duke, used to get you to do the same trick for him. How are you, old friend?"

Now laughing, his friend replies, "Fine, but this is not social, or am I wrong? I hear things on the grapevine, you know."

"Bet you do. I also hear things, one of them being that you took over your father's job as well as his title."

"Yep, family business, don't you know, so what do you need?"

"Are you at home, because we need to meet, as soon as possible, like now?"

"Yes, I'm home. Do you need directions, and do I need anyone to be with me?"

"Very funny. I will have Trish with me, and two bodyguards, don't ask. Suggest that you call in your nearest and dearest."

"I take it you cannot tell me where you are or when to expect you?"

Looking at his watch to calculate the journey time, he replies, "No, but it will be within the hour. Watch out for the Jabberwock, my friend." And with that, the mobile is disconnected.

Trish breaks his reverence. "Can we go now?"

Still lost in his thoughts, the commander replies, "Yes, we can go." Moving towards her, he takes her in his arms for an unusual public display of affection. Releasing her from his grip, and now turning to his nephew, he says, "Thank you for all you have done for me today. Do you need anything?"

"Uncle, Aunty, I need nothing. Keep safe, the pair of you, and now get out of my domain, no pun intended."

The commander squeezes his arm in a sign of affection,

while Trish bundles him up in a warm embrace. Although he has had most of the air taken out of him, he manages to speak. "Will you two go and take Tweedledum and Tweedledee with you; I have a reputation to uphold." He points to a very impressive bank of CCTV monitors that are not only displaying the whole area surrounding the cathedral, including their car, but also the city centre and both the rail and bus stations. And with the order given, and his relatives back in the passage, he closes the dividing door between his world and theirs and is left with the only company he wants, the electric hum of machinery.

Retracing their footsteps through Coventry Cathedral and then onwards to where the car hopefully is, the commander stops and waits for the signal. Seeing the passenger lightly tapping the car roof, they move swiftly to the vehicle. Reaching the car, the pair take their seats once more.

The driver turns to Alpha and asks, "Where to, sir?"

"Not far, we need to get back onto the A5 and head south; I'll tell you when you need to turn off." Sitting back, he can't help thinking of Ellie and if she will ever forgive him for the danger he has put her in without reason. Half an hour into the journey, the directive is given. "At the sign coming up on our left, turn sharp right down the dirt track. Keep going and you will eventually come to the big house. Mind your manners, lads, don't want to upset the gentry; they usually have big guns and know how to use them. When we arrive, you two can stay with the car. Take in the fresh air, stretch your legs, but don't go too far; we're not staying long. The two of us will be joining His Grace for tea; I'll see if a cup can be sent out for you lads."

The driver eases the car into the lane and down to the house as instructed. On hearing the car draw up, the front door to the house opens and a man, similar in age and height to the commander but dressed in jeans and pullover, is standing waiting for his guests. Trish gets out of the now stationary car first, followed by her husband. She runs into the waiting outstretched arms.

With a great deal of relief, the welcome is mirrored.

"Hello, Pip." She uses the shortened version of the duke's given name of Philip.

"Hello, Trish, how do you put up with the big man?" Releasing his grip and then draping an arm across her shoulder, he continues, "Come in, have made us lunch. Are you having tea or a drink with it?"

"How about both?"

Now with an element of sarcasm in his voice, he turns to the commander. "How about you, old friend, do I get a hug as well?"

"Sod off, Pip. Can we get inside before we talk with too many ears around?" he suggests, nodding towards the car. "As you asked, a nice red would hit the spot, not that muck you gave me last time, nearly gave me gut rot. I was ill for days."

Not liking the reference to his poor hospitality, Pip replies mockingly with an upturned eyebrow. "So, it wasn't the amount you drank then. Had to ring up my suppliers the next day to restock. Asked if I had a party, replied yes, party of two," he says as he puts his other arm around the commander's shoulder and shows him and Trish into his ancestral home. "Come, we will sit in the kitchen; I always believe people are more open in that environment, don't you agree, Trish?"

"Best place in the house, and yours is like ours, homely."

With the three friends happy to be in each other's company, they move through the grand house and secrete themselves in an equally grand kitchen, which would not be out of place in a top hotel or in the pages of a glossy magazine.

The duke begins in hast, "As I said, I hear things, so what do you need me to do, Alpha?" At school, for that is where they met, the commander was always called Alpha. At the beginning, it was because he was much bigger, brighter and more athletic than the others in the year. Due to this, the older boys would attempt to bully him – his classmates would always say the same thing: 'how far' would he be pushed before he fights back? 'How far' became 'Alpha' as, one by one, he picked off the bullies, without becoming one himself. Neither age nor size of his opponents saw him back down from a confrontation. He would do this either in a fight, or on the playing field, in the gym or through debate. As his reputation and the respect he was shown intensified, he was bestowed the moniker of Alpha Dog by the whole school, pupils and tutors alike. Over time, people forgot what his given name was; only a few ever called him by it, well, only his wife, usually when she was mad with him, and then she used his full name – James Patrick Sutherland – followed by, 'you are in trouble now'.

"Thank you, Pip. My nephew the geek in Coventry has decoded the pictures I sent him. These were of colour swatches on the minister's study wall in the mansion which, you may have heard, is now rubble. It was there together with a USB, which we found hidden behind the same wall. *They* are meeting up with us at some point this week regarding the USB, but they do not know about the colours and their significance."

"Yes, I heard about Wales but, more to the point, do you know what's on the USB?"

"No, although with all that has come to my attention in recent times, I have a good idea what is and why *they* are very interested in getting hold of the data it contains. As to actually seeing the contents, as I said, no, as my nephew wouldn't open it, could but wouldn't. Gave us a very boring lecture. Didn't understand a word, glazed over after the intro, just nodded politely in the right places, was like being back at school. However, I do need to give you the numbers he gleaned from deciphering the colours. Your office will know what to do with them; see where it leads your team." Alpha extracts a till receipt from an inside pocket, for a lunch that his nephew had the day before, then passes it into a waiting hand.

Taken aback, Pip asks, "What's all this?"

"Geeky boy thought, and rightly so, that no one would be looking for information scribbled on the back of a receipt. You have got to hand it to the lad, anyone would think he has done this stuff before."

Surprised by what he is reading, Pip exclaims, "Oh! I know these numbers. Well, not these, but I know what the significance of them are. So, you would like the British Government, or should I say, my office, that has a very close business relationship with Interpol, to act on the information you have just handed to me but without any of it leading back to either you or your family, especially your nephew or friends?"

"Bedfellows with Interpol more like, and yes to no comebacks if you don't mind?"

"Do you want to know the outcome?"

"Of course, that would be very nice, as you know I am covered by the Official Secrets Act. So, posh restaurant just outside Oxford, a few old college friends and a number of bottles of wine, each, and a reminisce about how we became embroiled in this saga. Never know, may lay a few ghosts to rest. What do you say?"

"If all goes to plan, I think my office can pick up the bill, so champagne it is?"

"Agreed."

Not to be left out of a party, Trish butts in, "What about the wives? We were with you at Oxford too and have been dealing with the fallout of it all."

Pip chuckles. "Only right that they come as well; someone has to drive us home afterwards. Anyone else?"

The commander thinks for a brief second before putting forward additions. "Maybe a couple more, but they are family. If not by blood, by loyalty, and I think we will all stay over at a hotel, safer for all as I don't want to encounter a domestic." He says this with a knowing wink.

Finishing their most welcome refreshment, the gathering is at an end as they rise from their chairs.

Waving the till receipt in the air, Pip says, "So, Alpha, thank you for the information, and I will be in touch. Keep safe and kiss my goddaughter and army godson for me; tell them to visit soon."

"Ellie may have a boyfriend in tow, Tommy's boy. Tell you more when I see you next, and you keep safe as well."

Surprised by this snippet of gossip, Pip replies, "No, you can tell me now; my wife and my mother will kill me if I don't get more information."

"Trish doesn't even know the ins and outs of it, but the bare bones are that Ellie and I met with Tommy and Smithy. The two kids hit it off straight away – he asked her out on a date; she said yes; and what more can I say?"

"I'm so pleased, as I always hoped they would meet. Oh! Did I tell you that Tommy's boy is also our godson?"

"Yes, we were at the christening, remember?"

"No, you weren't, as memory serves, you were halfway round the world. My father had sent the pair of you on a much-needed holiday." This is said with a sly look that carries the shared knowledge that it was anything but a holiday.

"So we were, lovely holiday, all paid for by your father as he didn't want his office to know that he was a soft touch and had taken pity on an overworked civil servant. God rest his soul, the old bugger."

Laughing, while remembering his father, Pip says, "Thank you for that; I am sure to tell him you called him an old bugger in my prayers tonight. Are you off home now, may I ask?"

Happy to be reminded of the Bramptons, Alpha replies, "Gosh, home, yes, we are – bath, dinner and then bed with the love of my life. But if she is busy, then it will have to be the wife." With that, all three of them laugh out loud once more, before the commander finishes with a bow and, placing his hand on his heart, declares, "Your Grace, I am, and will always be, your obedient servant."

While reciprocating with a double-finger salute, Pip smiles and replies tenderly, "Up yours, Alpha." Moving to Trish, in order to give her the warmest of hugs, he whispers in her ear, "As always, it has been lovely to see you, and take care of Alpha. Sorry Brenda wasn't here, but she did say that she will catch up with you at yoga next week, and it's her turn to pay for lunch."

Slowly moving through the house, the three friends stop at the closed front door. The duke and the commander turn to face each other. Although not of the same flesh, like brothers, they warmly embrace, not scared to openly share their affection for each other with a kiss on the cheek.

"Love you, Pip, I'm always here for you; don't forget that, and good hunting."

"Love you too, my brother, you are always in my heart."

Trish knows that they need to get on, so it's down to her to break the tension. "Come on, darling, need to get home, and Pip has an important task to undertake for you. Today is nearly over, so let's see what tomorrow brings?"

Holding back a tear, both men move away from each other, not having to say the word 'goodbye' as it has already been said, just not out loud.

Taking his wife's hand, the commander looks from his friend to his soulmate and enquires, "Shall we go outside to our waiting taxi and home?"

"That would be lovely." Turning to their friend, she just gives him a knowing smile and mouths the words 'thank you', before blowing him a kiss, for she knows the strain her husband is under, and so does Pip.

Waving his visitors off his grounds, he knows he has work to do and has to be quick about it. Classified work, interesting work and, if successful, and he must be, it will bring his Government office and his family great kudos. But he has no need for financial rewards as he, like his best friend, believes in justice, regardless of the timescale to achieve it.

Once back in the car, the driver looking at the commander's reflection in the internal mirror asks, "Where to, sir?"

"Home for us, and no doubt your onwards journey is already mapped out?"

"Yes, sir, the major has planned it all, including contingences."

Placing a hand on the shoulders of each of their guardians, the commander speaks softly on behalf of him and Trish. "Thank you, lads, for your assistance over the last twenty-four hours, ensuring we stay safe. But I must ask that you forget you ever met us. Forget the conversations you have overheard and the places you have been with us. If we do happen to meet again, it will be for the first time, and let's all hope it is under better circumstances. Once again, much appreciation to you both, and good luck." With that last comment, he removes his hands, sits back and rests his weary head on his wife's shoulder, as though it is a place of safety.

He doesn't look at this watch but calculates that home is less than an hour away. *Oh! To close my eyes and sleep, but I am nearly at journey's end*, and with the talk of Tommy, Tennyson pops into his head again. He recites in a quiet voice 'The Eagle', which he feels is very apt, "'He clasps the crag with crooked hands; close to the sun in lonely lands, ringed with the azure world, he stands. The wrinkled sea beneath him crawls; he watches from his mountain walls, and like a thunderbolt he falls'."

He is the eagle, not falling into the void to his certain death but actually diving headlong to capture his prey, Cassandra Trevisa, in his mighty talons.

CHAPTER 14

THURSDAY

Tolly has refused to leave me at my parents' house in Northamptonshire, insisting that I should come home with him. I must confess, I don't relish the thought of being by myself, in our big house, with what has been happening. So, with just the two of us alone in his apartment, we hold each other, frightened to let go, lest we will collapse on the floor. The journey back from Salisbury had been arduous. Not because of traffic, although there had been plenty of it, but because Tolly had already driven from Oxfordshire to pick me up and drop *bitch face* back into the loving embrace of the army. He told me that he very rarely drove outside the city limits and therefore was not used to concentrating for so long on unfamiliar roads. While I had offered to do some of the driving, he wouldn't let me take over. For my part, I feel as though I haven't stopped and actually slept since Sunday night, having a very, very early start on Monday as I was undertaking a double shift at the hospital. I've had the odd catnap, but a deep and refreshing sleep, no. It has not been for the want of trying, as each time I have had a chance to snooze, something or other has interrupted my slumbers, usually a man shouting.

I'm getting a lovely feeling; his hug is so comfortable and warm I could stay in his arms forever. However, moving his head from our deep, welcoming embrace in order to speak, Tolly looks deep into my eyes before gently whispering, "What do you want to do?"

Without hesitation, I reply, "I want to go to bed." I can feel his body tense against mine, but not in a good way. I need to clarify my answer and quickly. "Oh! I don't mean sex; I'm whacked, and I need to get some sleep. I haven't slept for days, and my body is crying out for rest."

I note a sense of relief wash over him as his grip lightens.

I continue to speak. "Oh! Sex would be nice, yes, but I think it's a bit early in our relationship, if that's what we have, to… you know, to take it to that level of intimacy so soon?" I cannot believe I'm uncomfortable talking about sex when I have to approach the subject with complete strangers at work without flinching. Anyone who knows me well will observe that this man has definitely put my head in a spin. And of course, I will deny it vigorously as we have only just met.

He takes in my befuddled manner before making a heartfelt comment. "Sleep is good and at this moment very welcome. As for sex, yep, agree we may be best to take it one step at a time. We have only just met." Breaking his hold on me, he takes a single backwards stride. Running his hand through his hair, he comments in a tentative way, "Sorry, Ellie, the last few days have been all a bit of a whirlwind, and like you, I'm dog-tired. The journey to Wiltshire and back has, well, washed me out. Will it be okay if I join you on the bed? Yes, I said on and not in. We can keep our clothes on and just lay together like two peas in a pod, but no touching? What do you say? Please say yes as, like you, I want to lie down before I fall down. It is a very big bed and the only one in the flat; if you say no then I will sleep on the sofa."

Looking at his puppy-dog eyes and relieved at the growing ease between the two of us, I do not hesitate to reply. "Sounds good to me, but can I have a cuddle?" As I say this, I can feel tears of tiredness forming in the corners of my eyes. By Tolly's reaction, he has noted them too. The space between us vanishes, as he once again takes me in his arms but this time gives me a deep, passionate kiss. Breaking his hold once again, I murmur, trying to catch my breath, "On the bed and a cuddle, I would very much like that – is it okay with you?"

He reaches down and grabs my hand, while repeating my last utterance. "Yes, on the bed and a cuddle, and I would like it very much too. My bedroom is this way. Come on, you'll like the decor, if you can keep your eyes open long enough to see." With that, I'm ushered into a man's bedroom with the promise that he will be a gentleman. I have every confidence that is what he will be. *Please, just don't tell my dad, brother or Freddo what is taking place; they wouldn't believe it anyway. Mum's reaction, I know, would be, "How sweet, he must come round for dinner." Not on your life, as by the time the pudding comes out, she will know everything about him, his family and his prospects and have the church booked.* I can honestly say, I don't remember getting on the bed and Tolly joining me. What I do know is that it's dark outside when I wake on this Thursday morning. *Can't say I'm very refreshed. Guess it must be something o'clock. Do I care anyway, am I meant to be somewhere? Not that I can remember, past worrying if truth be known.* I'm pleased to report that my sleeping, more like snoring, companion Tolly is rolled up in a ball, with his back to me. As you might have speculated, yes, still in all his day clothes. Have to chuckle to myself and wonder if this is usual attire for solicitors when they go to bed. Shoeless in a very expensive suit, that now needs to go to the dry cleaners to have all the wrinkles ironed out, and still wearing a tie. *It's a wonder he didn't strangle himself in the night. Bet it has been a method of killing someone in* Midsummer Murders. *Will ask my aunty; she is an ardent fan of Mr Barnaby.* My need for the bathroom and then a cup of tea pushes this happy thought out my head, that's Tolly still in his suit, not killing him off.

Remaining where I am, I concentrate on getting my bearings before moving. The curtains are open so the light from the street lamp illuminates the room. It only takes me a minute to get focused. Swinging my legs off the bed and into a seated position, I note three doors. Eliminating the one to the sitting room, I surmise that one of the other doors leads to the en-suite and its partner to, no idea where, closet maybe? As my host is in the land of nod, the only option is for me to open each in turn. Left or right? Left, correct, *oh, this is good – the light comes on automatically and so does the ruddy extractor fan.*

Woken by the infernal hum, "Els, you okay?" says a sleepy voice from the only occupant of the bed.

Stopped in my tracks and now forced to do the dance routine of the full bladder, I answer quickly, "Yep, sorry to wake you, but I need the little girls' room – won't be long."

Talking in a puzzled way from a now seated position, but with his back to me, he asks, "Why am I still dressed in my suit? Oh! I remember now. Yes, sorry, would you like tea and toast, pretty sure I have bread in the freezer?"

Now on to my second dance, I reply, "Sounds wonderful," trying to appear enthusiastic, with my crossed legs shaking and a hand on the door jamb, hoping I do not wet myself.

Still I haven't moved, as he does a just-woken-up stretch and groans, "I could do with a shower and a change of clothes. How about you, can lend you a fresh jumper or shirt? Might have a pair of jeans; you will have to turn over the bottoms. You'll need a belt also, to stop them falling down, which can be supplied, free of charge. See, us solicitors don't charge for everything. Not sure how giving a damsel in distress my clothes would be shown on my tax returns?"

Ignoring his work reference and me being likened to a cartoon character, I do acknowledge his bathing and clothes offer. "Yes, shower and a fresh outfit would be heavenly, but are you saying I smell?" With that revelation, I stop dancing and now smell my armpits. *Ah yes, a bit whiffy.*

Now moving off the bed towards me, Tolly laughs and replies merrily, "I'm sure I heard it said somewhere that only true friends will tell their mates they smell."

"You just made that up, but thank you for thinking of me as your friend."

"Oh. I see you more as a sleeping partner," he says with an element of mischief in his voice, as he walks past me on his way back to the sitting room and hopefully to the kitchen. And with him out the way I move, crossed-legged, towards the bathroom and relief. After my much-needed ablutions, I follow the sound of cups rattling to the kitchen.

On my entry, I'm greeted with a pleasing smile. "There you are, better?" I nod, allowing him to continue the conversation. "If you wait two minutes, I'll make your tea, milk no sugar if I remember correctly, then get you fresh towels and some clean clothes. Sorry, don't have bras or knickers in the place but do have socks. Although these will be for someone with size ten feet."

His kitchen could be described as cosy if I was hoping to sell it. If, on the other hand, I was buying, it would be classed as small. So, whichever way you turn in the room, it is inevitable we are only an arm's length away from each other. I'm happy to report we are also only a kiss length away. While the kettle is boiling, I am given a very good morning kiss, just wish he had put more water in the kettle so it took longer to boil. Cannot help but think – when the kettle turns itself off and with it, he breaks the connection between our two bodies – *well, someone has woken up in a playful mood.* After the past few days, it is a welcome distraction, and one I am more than happy to go along with. "Tolly, do I get the first shower? Hope you have some nice smelly soap. What should I do with my dirty clothes?" It has to be said, sooner rather than later. "What will your girlfriend think about me staying the night? She might not believe you when you tell her that nothing happened, and you only kissed me... how many times? No, think it's better if you don't tell her we kissed, or shared a bed. Best not to say anything." I realise I said all this with a slight edge of panic in my voice – why should I care what his girlfriend thinks?

Sighing seriously, as though he is about to take a great weight off his shoulders, he answers, "Let's get a few things out into the open. Yes, you can go first with the shower, and there is plenty of shower gel and shampoo. There is a new toothbrush and toothpaste in the bathroom for you as well. Put your dirty togs in the laundry basket, and no, I don't have a girlfriend. The last one dumped me, saying I was a boring old fart. Actually, she told me to F off." Trying to lighten the mood and his tone, he continues, "My mother will like you very much; she will be over the moon to see female clothes in the house. By the way, my dad is bowled over by you and glad we are dating. Did you know our parents were at university together, all four of them went to the same college?"

Rising up to my full height, I reply, "May I remind you, Ptolemy, our first date is not until Saturday. Destination, unknown; what I need to wear, unknown, but hopefully it will be something that belongs to me and is not borrowed, ill-fitting, smelly and army." I cannot resist saying with a wicked smirk, "Not sure if we are dating, as I need to see how the first one goes. And as for our parents, like everything else that is happening around me, it comes as no surprise, and no doubt we will experience other bombshells along the way. Don't think bombshell is a good word for what has happened to me. May be best if we just wait and see what tomorrow brings and hope it's not more shit hitting the fan. Yep, shit and fan seem to sum up the week." And with that passing comment, I turn, teacup now in hand, and head for his en-suite, to be luxuriated by litres of cleansing hot water.

With a slightly raised voice, Tolly says to my retreating back, "Don't be too long or I will have to come in there and fish you out of the water. May have to give you the kiss of life; I know you like my kisses."

I happily think to myself, *said by a man who has to have the final word. He can have it this time, but we will wait and see about next time. And what is it about mums, because mine would like him too. I already know Dad does. On second thought, he doesn't deserve the last word.* "In your dreams, lover boy." No verbal reply is forthcoming, only a roar of laughter that lifts my spirits even higher.

Happily discarding the clothes I am wearing into the laundry basket, I step into a very swish shower cubical. The temperature of the water is to my liking, hot. With the intense water cascading over my body, I can feel muscle knots and arching joints easing. Applying a second dose of shower gel, I notice how silky smooth my skin is becoming, and the smell is very pleasant indeed. Ensuring every part of me has been washed, twice, with a foot, I swirl the falling water to push the suds towards the plughole. This done, I sigh and turn off the tap. My last job in the shower is to collect strands of my wet hair clinging to the drain. I wrap them in a piece of lavatory paper and put them in the small waste bin next to the sink, something else for his mum to consider.

I cannot resist taking a deep breath in when I pick up the warm bath towel from the en-suite's radiator. Like the aroma of the soap, I let the smell lovingly envelop me. Remembering the need to get on, I wrap a smaller one around my hair. The tea that came with me is now cold, but I still swallow it in one go. I am so grateful I can now clean my teeth. I wonder if Tolly will mind if I keep the toothbrush. I will ask. Feeling human again, I shout to the next bather while I wipe the steamed-up mirror with the edge of a towel to check my face is still as I remember it. "I'm out and halfway decent. Shower is free – see, us doctors, like solicitors, don't charge for everything either." With this last remark, I laugh to myself.

Feeling a change in the temperature in the room, I turn to see that the door is now open. Standing there, as though butter wouldn't melt in his mouth, is a suit-less, shirt-less, sock-less Smithy. In his hands are my clean clothes in a neat pile. I know it's going to happen, but I mustn't.

Angel on my shoulder: *Keep looking at his beautiful eyes, but don't look at his body. Resist, girl, you can do it; you have seen naked bodies before; his is the same as everyone else's.*

Devil on the other shoulder: *Go on, you know you want to give him the once-over, and you know – you've been to the gym – all men are different. I'm sure I've seen that body in a museum, standing there throwing a discus, naked as the day he was born, like some Greek god. Go on, just do it – look, nothing you haven't seen before. Maybe a quick look, just up and down, and up and down again. So, what do you think?*

Angel: *Don't look. Resist, young lady.*

Devil: *You looked, didn't you? Come on, tell; it will just be between you and me. I know you saw a gorgeous body, and I believe you thought,* yep, that will do nicely, my Greek god.

Angel: *Stop it. You didn't look, only at his eyes. His eyes, his big, beautiful eyes, one left and one right.*

Devil: *Can't fool me – you gave him the full once-over, or was it twice? Liar, liar pants on fire – is he wearing any pants, and what colour are they?*

With my head in a spin, I move to the door slowly; I make sure the towel wrapped round my body is secure and covering all parts that I don't want exposed. I gingerly take the clothes from the outstretched hands, trying not to touch any part of him, hoping that Tolly does not possess telepathic abilities. By the look he is giving me as I walk past, I think he does. Oh, shit, forgot he's in a profession where they are trained to read people. Barely out the room, I hear the door close between us. I cannot help but give out a sigh of relief.

I didn't realise my sigh was so audible, as he shouts from the bathroom in a concerned voice, "You okay?"

Gathering my thoughts quickly, I reply, "Yes, just a bit cold, that's all, coming from a hot shower to a cold bedroom."

"Oh! Okay, won't be long."

Not sure how long he bathes for, I make light work of putting on the fresh clothes, but not before smelling each item in turn. *What do they smell like? you may ask. And my reply to you is, mind your own business, but it is amazing.* As I do this, I hear the initial sound of running water quickly followed by an ear-piercing noise. By the song the tone-deaf solicitor is attempting to sing, I cannot help but think he is far too happy with himself. As for me, I'm now wearing a beautiful red V-neck cashmere jumper over a tailored white shirt. I haven't tucked the shirt tails into the borrowed jeans, held up with a belt, but let them hang below the sweater. The jeans are black and, yes, I have turned them over a few times so that I don't walk on the ends. I have foregone the need for socks, far too big.

As I look at my new outfit in a full-length mirror, my roomie emerges from his bathroom, and all he is wearing is a towel, and a very wicked grin. Time to make a hasty retreat to the kitchen for toast and more tea.

I must say that I am now past the stage of being embarrassed by my present situation, so I ask nonchalantly, "Shall I make some tea and toast for us both, while you dress?"

Picking up a pressed grey T-shirt from the bed, he says, without making eye contact, "That will be great, if you don't mind, Ellie? It's all in the kitchen, will be with you in two ticks as soon as I get some more clothes on."

Although used to seeing naked bodies as a doctor, I don't want to be around to see his, well, not yet, so I make a hasty retreat. *Eyes forward, girl; nothing to see here; move along.*

Trying to make myself at home in an unfamiliar kitchen, I hear footsteps moving my way. "Hope there is some bread left as I could also do with something to eat?" a jeaned, T-shirted and jacketed Tolly says from his position in the doorway.

Munching my way through a fourth piece of toast, I just motion towards the rack of toast sitting next to a pot of strawberry jam and carton of easily spreadable butter. I have put a mug, a plate and knife on the table for him to show that I can be domesticated when I want. However, the bubble bursts with the words I cannot stop myself from saying, "Tea's in the pot, just help yourself."

Answering jovially while taking a chair, he replies, "When I last looked, this was my place." We sit at the small kitchen table, happy to brush up against each other in the knowledge we survived the night together, and just as we agreed, sleeping in the same bed like two peas in a pod.

However, his mood changes when he tells me what is next for us. "Once we have eaten, I will drive you to the hospital."

With this disclosure, my anxiety level goes through the ceiling. "What? Why? Are you okay? Tell me – I am a doctor – I can help?"

"Me, yes of course, no I'm fine." Gaining his composure as he realises none of what he is saying is making sense, he explains, "No, sorry, I'm okay – it's Mac's son, Fred. He has had an accident, and he is in Northampton General. I believe, from the brief conversation I had with Mac earlier, that you two are close?"

"Yes, he's like another brother. What happened? And how do you know Mac? When did he tell you about Freddo?"

He knows at once that he has to be honest if this relationship is to get off the ground. "I don't know what happened." With this comment, he touches the back of my hand but not before catching some jam on the sleeve of his jacket. "Fuck, sorry, just get a cloth to wipe it off." A deeply apologetic look is now on his face, replacing a gentler one only a moment before. "I met up with Mac and the corporal when he came back to Northampton from Wales. Being available, I was tasked with taking the corporal back to your brother in Salisbury. Fred had to pass over his orders to me, hence the need for me to go to the hospital. I honestly don't know how he came by his injuries, but he was fully awake when I saw him. Well, his mouth was definitely working. You can imagine what he said to me; your brother's words were very similar."

"So, you know the major is my brother?"

"Oh, yes, didn't take much working out by the family resemblance and by the way he spoke to me when I told him who I was. He had been expecting Fred, but as I said, I stepped in at the last minute, due to the accident."

"You've known about Freddo since yesterday and you've said nothing?"

"Mac asked me not to tell you until the hospital had dealt with his injuries. Before you ask, Mac doesn't know how he got them either. However, he went on to say that you needed a good night's sleep as the past few days have been hectic for you. Sorry, but I could see how tired you were when I picked you up, and I needed your company; I know you needed mine. Gosh, I cannot tell you how pleased I was to see you in one piece. I know we have only just met, but I hope that you don't think ill of me or that I am being selfish. El, I'm deeply sorry for keeping this from you until now, but I would not change a thing. I enjoyed sharing my bed with you last night and sharing my bathroom and kitchen with you this morning. Please say something, even if it's to shout at me."

Analysing my overreaction to the situation, Tolly needs to know I am not mad with him. "I understand Mac's need for me to be kept away from the hospital until today. He knows, being a doctor, I would put my oar in regarding Fred's treatment. I hate it when it happens to me." Changing tack to sound grateful for his hospitality, I continue, "I did have a good sleep – your bed is very comfortable – and the company both in the car and last night were very comforting; the kisses and the cuddles were the best parts. I don't think what you did was done out of malice, and I will only shout at you if you really piss me off, so you have been warned." Noticing he is still to finish eating, I add, "You are hungry, so I will wait patiently while you eat and drink; it is only fair," but my agitation is plain to see. When Tolly takes his last sip of tea and munches the last piece of toast, I jump up from the kitchen table, declaring, "I'm ready, Tolly, can we go?"

Brushing the crumbs from the front of his clothes, he breezily answers, "Sure, let me get my shoes and yours, need the car keys and we can be on our way. Sorry, but do need to get gas on the way. You may want to grab a couple of bottles of water from out of the fridge when you put the butter and jam away? Leave everything else; I will deal with it later." Before he heads for the bedroom, he catches my hand and pulls me towards him, giving me a reassuring kiss.

When I am able to speak, I say, "Thank you for taking care of me, and I do like your taste in clothes. However, I will have to come here again, as I didn't notice the decor in the bedroom you promised I would adore." It is now my turn to instigate a kiss of forgiveness for all that has passed between us since we woke up.

The look of surprise at my action quickly turns to one of joy as he goes to fetch the bits needed for our journey to Northampton. While he does this, I do as I'm told: put the breakfast things in the fridge and take two bottles of water. And although not asked, I put the dirty cups, knives, spoons and plates in the dishwasher before proclaiming, "That's better."

Out the corner of my eye, I see I'm being watched.

Trying to sound annoyed but without much success, Tolly comments on what has just happened. "Sorry, but didn't I say I would sort the mess out later? You are hopeless – what am I going to do with you?"

"Take me to see Freddo, and we can discuss what you are going to do with me on the way. Will you be taking me home after?"

"No. I am due to meet up with my father and you with yours. Give him a ring to tell him you're safe, and you will need to be picked up at the General later this morning. In the meantime, put on your shoes, and we can go, 'Miss Eager'."

Speed dialling, then waiting for the phone to be answered, I smile at Tolly. The call is picked up. "Oh! Dad, yeah, I'm fine with Smithy – we are going to the General to see Freddo. Have you heard how he is?" A short pause while he speaks, then "Oh! How's Mrs Mac? Is she with him?" Another pause as I listen to my father's response. "Okay, so she is at our house with Mum; that's a good sign. Dad, can you pick me up from the hospital in a couple of hours? And yes, I'm fine, Dad, as I've already said, no need for you and Mum to worry." Yet another pause while I receive a fatherly missive. "Okay, okay I will tell him to drive carefully, and I love you both. Bye, Dad, see you at the hospital, and you will be in the car park at the back, okay."

Pressing the red button and then looking up at Tolly with a pleading expression, I ask, "Can we please go?"

Casually leaning against the connecting door, he replies, "Been ready for the last five minutes, just hanging around." And with that, he moves to the front door, which he opens, allowing me to go first. He then gives the room a quick glance – checking lights are off – follows – closing and locking the door behind him – grabs my hand, then leads me down the stairs to his car, hurriedly speaking, "Gas then hospital, and we need to discuss what I am going to do with you."

I cannot resist replying in a coy way, "My mother always warned me about men like you. But I never thought it would be my father who would introduce me to one, and with his father's approval." With that revelation, we both laugh out loud, not worrying who can hear us.

Gaining his composure, and speaking with a twinkle in his eye, while fingering an imaginary moustache like an Edwardian rake, Tolly speaks with a sly edge to his voice, "I will try not to disappoint our fathers. Or you."

Still trying to act demure, with my hand acting like a pretend fan, covering the lower half of my face, I reply, "Oh! Sir, I will not be able to show myself in polite society ever again." This time we both blush at the realisation that the Rubicon has just been crossed. Neither of us dare to speak as we get in the car, but it doesn't stop me thinking, *what just happened?*

CHAPTER 15

THURSDAY

Freddo refuses, point blank, to tell me how he came by his injuries. While desperate to know, I don't press him for an answer in his present state; it can wait, but not for too long. The reluctant patient wants to discharge himself. I can see by his medical chart this is not an option open to him. Although he is sitting up in a hospital bed in his private room, with a broken leg and ankle and various cuts and bruises over his body, I doubt if he could make it to the bathroom, let alone the car. With a great deal of coercion on my part, he is not going anywhere.

When I tell him I am to attend a meeting today and Tolly will be there, and also that he has asked me out, Freddo grumpily moans, "I'm coming with you as I want to know he is acceptable. I've come across his type. Everything is given to them on a silver platter working for Daddy's company. Bet he drives a posh car, wears nice clothes and splashes the cash. They're all arseholes."

His comments raise my hackles, not least because I'm wearing Tolly's 'nice clothes'. "Firstly, you drive a Porsche and a Range Rover, wear posh suits and stomp around town in Church's and Jeffery West shoes; you have plenty of cash to splash, so are you an arsehole too? Well, at this moment you are. Secondly, how do you know he is?"

Like a rally at Wimbledon, he serves first. "I just do."

"Bullshit. You are jealous."

"No, I'm not. As the major is not here to protect you, it's down to me."

"You may not have noticed, but I'm a big girl; I can look after myself."

"I may be gay, but I do have eyes, and I don't like the way men look you up and down."

"Stop it, enough. Smithy is a gentleman."

"They are the worst."

"Are you going to throw any more outdated clichés into the mix?"

"No. All I'm saying is, if you have to go out with this guy, just take care; I don't want him breaking your heart."

"You great big softy. I will, and he won't. Now, your job is to get better." And with no reply forthcoming, it's 'New balls please and first set to Sutherland'.

He mutters under his breath, as though not sure whether to ask, "I need you to do something for me."

Not fully hearing what he said, I ask, "What did you say?"

"Need you to do something for me, please," he says with the look of a little boy lost.

I reply without hesitation, as the conversation has turned serious, "Of course, name it."

"Before you all went to Wales, the commander asked that I kept my ear to the ground and let my dad know if something out the norm turned up. As I was covering a couple of shifts in the office, I could root around. I remembered Dad saying Michael would often talk about a series of flights abroad which followed the same pattern. For some unfathomable reason, I couldn't shake the feeling that my brother had been a pawn in all of this..." he waves a bandaged hand in the air before he speaks again, "...you know, this 'shitstorm'. So, I decided to visit the duty security manager, who was there on the day of his accident. She has since retired due to ill health, mainly due to a large element of guilt she is carrying for that day, which is illogical. Well, unbeknown to her colleagues, she kept copies of every cargo manifest that left and entered Cranfield. She had already figured out something was amiss with some of his flights, but it was not until the crash and the subsequent inquiry that feeling grew. So much so, she had compiled a dossier on his journeys, and others that didn't add up, which she was happy to give to me. I could tell that by doing this one thing, a great weight had been taken off her shoulders."

Before continuing, he motions towards a glass of water on his bedside cabinet; I help him take a few welcome sips. Continuing refreshed, "When you leave here, can you go to the Spencer Arms and ask Jack for the box file I left behind the bar? Then get the information to the people who matter. Please, for my mum's sake, also for Michael, Chris and Steve. Before you ask, I have briefly scanned through the contents, and it doesn't make for a happy read. The minister's name, Trevisa, was all over them."

He knows I would do anything for him and his family. "Of course, but can I tell our dads, or is this only between the two of us?"

"Tell them, as they will help you get the documents to the right people."

"No doubt you want to know what takes place at today's meeting?"

"If you don't mind, especially if it involves Smithy. Not even a proper name, so what is the dickhead's real name? Oh!

And take the Porsche keys from my jacket pocket. Motor is still in the pub car park, if you could move it back home, parents' not mine." When he motions his head to his coat, he moans as he is still battered and bruised.

There is no way I am going to rise to the bait about Tolly, and he knows it. And there is no way I'm going to enquire if he is okay after that moan. So, I saunter across to his jacket, it's torn and bloody, but only pause to retrieve the car keys. I leave him without so much as a backwards glance or a kiss goodbye, just a, "See you later, Fredrick." I can feel his eyes boring into my back, fully aware he knows he has overstepped the mark with me. Leaving my injured old best friend in the hospital to wallow in his own self-pity, I quickly march through the multitude of corridors, avoiding patients in wheelchairs or on crutches. Swinging open the doors at the bottom of a sloping passageway, I am now standing by the largest of the car parks at the back of the hospital. After fishing my phone out of my bag, I give Dad a call.

Picking up on the second ring, he answers, "Hi, sweet pea, we can see you; I'll get Mac to flash his lights."

With a relieved voice, I reply, "I see you – don't move – I will come to you." Negotiating hospital traffic, I reach them in Freddo's Range Rover with its engine running.

Jumping in the back of the car, déjà vu, I can tell Dad is shocked by how I look. "What are you wearing?"

"Tolly's clothes as mine were a bit smelly," I say while I pull at the very expensive jumper I'm wearing.

"Who the hell is Tolly?" both men say in unison.

"Smithy's given name is Ptolemy – don't laugh. So, like you call Mr Smyth-Tompkins Tommy, Smithy is called Tolly by friends and family."

"So, which one are you, young lady?"

"Dad, really."

Mac butts in, "Okay, you two, but how is the patient in your medical opinion, Doctor?"

As we slowly leave the General, I relay Fred's prognosis, which reassures Mac, and subsequently will take some of the stress off his wife. Then I get to the story about the dossier and how it came into Freddo's possession. I conclude with my need to change, which Dad and Mac both whole-heartedly agree with, but only after we first visit the Spencer Arms.

On entering the pub, situated in our village, a grinning landlord asks, "What's your poison?" Remembering Dad's a serving police officer, he changes tack quickly. "Not open yet, gents and Eleanor, but can do you all a proper coffee or English breakfast tea? Just about to make one for the team, help yourselves to a biscuit."

Leaning over the bar, I speak to Jack as coolly as possible, "Freddo is fine, you will be glad to hear, and he asked me if I would pick up the little something he left with you on Tuesday for safe keeping?"

Sheepishly, he answers, "Team will be glad he is okay, gave us all a bit of a shock. Pass on our best when you see him next." Bending down behind the bar, he retrieves a box file, relieved to pass it over, as though it is burning his hands. "So, he told you how he ended up in hospital then?"

Keen to know, I reply honestly but somewhat sarcastically. "No. I take it you know, or you wouldn't be making a song and dance about it."

"Let me tell you then." As we all draw close, Jack happily avails us of his tale. "Fred was in a terrible mood when he came in. Asked me to keep the box safe while he had a drink, refused the offer of food. By the end of the evening, he was drunk as the proverbial lord; the team refused to serve him anymore, so he went on his way, staggering home, leaving the Porsche in the car park. But *bang*, literally, outside the restaurant as he fell off the kerb into the road, straight into the path of a delivery van. The driver of the van went into shock and had a heart attack. No doubt so did the household who didn't receive their shopping."

And there is me thinking that an assassin was after him, idiot, him not me. When I see him again, the strongest drink he is having is squash.

Mindful of the time, Dad hurries us along; he has already finished his much-needed cup of coffee, not concerned Mac and I are only at the sipping stage as our drinks are far too hot for our palate.

Leaving the barely drunk tea and waving the Porsche keys in my hand, I say, "I'll meet you back at the house, Dad, as need to drive Freddo's car to the Macs first." I notice Mac is still drinking his coffee, and has taken another couple of biscuits, before he leaves.

Back home, my loving father waits impatiently while I rush in. Charging, two steps at a time, upstairs, I change out of Tolly's sweet-smelling clothes. Dad has already made it clear in the hospital car park that he is not prepared for me to go to our next destination in clothes that look like I'm going to a scarecrow convention. Well, it would be a very fashionable scarecrow who has expensive taste, judging by the makers' names in each item. I know Tolly and his father are going to be there, so I make sure I'm wearing a different outfit from the one I wore at our breakfast meeting. This includes a change of handbag and shoes, also a slightly different hairstyle, just to enhance the ensemble.

Three beaming faces look up at me when I come down into the hall: Mum, Mac and Mrs Mac.

Dad's comment bursts my bubble. "Move it and get your arse in the car; Mac's driving."

It is just the two men and I going to the meeting. Mum

173

and Mrs Mac are left at home and are no doubt going to drink copious amounts of coffee while waiting for our return. With the steady hum of the engine, I'm happy to just sit back and let my mind drift, looking aimlessly out the window at the passing countryside. From what little information I can glean from Dad, it would appear we are meeting those who sanctioned, underpinned, orchestrated this little operation that started all those years ago. Oh! And then disposed of the bodies in Wales, literally. How they managed this in today's age of twenty-four-seven media feed, I don't wish to know. However, the big question that needs answering is waiting on my lips. *Just go for it*, I tell myself.

"Dad, what did Mum say when you told her about the Mini? You did tell her?"

"Of course, I told her, and now I'm going to be dragged round every dealership from here to Timbuktu."

"Dad, what do you always say? 'What Mum wants, Mum gets.'."

"Correct, but I didn't blow her car up, yet I got the blame. Thinking of a new model Countryman, maybe personalised number plates."

"What, something that has the numbers 007?" Only two of us laugh in the car; you can guess which one doesn't. Talking of spies, I realise I have yet to fulfil a task I was given back at the army base. "Dad?"

"Yes," he says as though wanting to concentrate on what lies ahead than general chit-chat.

"In Wales, my brother had been instructed to take me to an army base to meet someone. This turned out to be a very scary city gent, a man who is so non-descript that I wonder if he was real. Armed bodyguards in civvies surrounded him. The meeting lasted ten minutes tops; its sole propose was to give me an envelope for you. Smiled when your name was raised. Do you know who he is?" I ask, reaching into my bag to extract the envelope, with my name emblazed across it, and pass it over.

"Oh! Yes, I know laddie. Now let's see what he has given me." He takes great pains to open the stuck-down flap gently so as not to tear any part of it. He then takes out a piece of high-end quality paper that has been folded in half. It contains an equally high-spec, elegant but oversized business card. Reading the note, he nods agreeably.

Thankfully, we are going to hear what is written.

"Well, well, the family, and I include yours, Mac, regardless of outcome, are not to be sent to jail, arrested, investigated or even looked at in the wrong way. No mention of collecting any money when we pass Go."

Still curious, I enquire, "So, Dad, who is he? And what is he to our family?"

"No one to worry yourself about, sweet pea. Just be thankful your old man resisted the temptation to knock a very irritating prefect's teeth down the back of his throat many moons ago. Don't you just love it when these little acts of kindness are remembered?" And with that, he laughs at a happy memory while looking longingly at the business card.

Looking over his shoulder, all I can make out is the embossed mark of a portcullis; if I look hard enough, will I see his school coat of arms and motto? Is there anyone left in the world who doesn't owe him a favour or two for services rendered?

Over the canal at Whilton Locks, quickly followed by under the railway bridge, we have right of way. In two hundred metres, up to the junction with the A5, we indicate left and onwards towards Towcester, but for only two minutes. Towcester is not our objective today but the Heart of the Shires emporium. The slow *click, click* of the car's indicator, the dropping down through the gears and then the turn of the wheel off the road onto the tarmac drive, which announces our arrival. I'm surprised the satnav does not spring into action with, 'you have reached your destination. Thank you for travelling with Range Rover. Please remember to take 'all your belongings and mind the gap'.

Two apparent workmen are waiting by the shut metal five-bar gate. Momentarily stopped, Mac rests his arm on the now windowless door and speaks to one of the men. After a brief exchange, the gate swings open, allowing us to carry on our journey up the tarmac drive. The gate is swiftly closed behind us, just in case someone has the audacity to follow us in. Mac is not stopping in the very generous emporium car parking area but continues to the staff parking at the back of the complex. Four top-of-the-range motor vehicles are already there – an Audi, two Jaguars and a soft-top Morgan – together with a beaten-up old Polo. I could hazard a guess who the owner of the Morgan is, as it screams 'solicitor', senior not junior. Tolly, as I already know, drives a Range Rover, like Freddo. Oh dear, just had a thought, *Freddo and Tolly are starting to look like two peas in a pod. On balance, is it that bad, having two eye-catching people in your life?*

Parked, Mac turns in his seat to look over his left shoulder to speak to me. "A few ground rules. The people we are going to meet are the goodies, but don't for one minute think they can be trusted. Speak only when you are spoken to and give the briefest of answers. Alpha will take the lead; please resist the temptation to butt in. Other than the Smyth-Tompkins, you recognise no one. I repeat, you recognise no one, understood?"

I didn't understand the need for the last point but agreed anyway. "Yes."

"Good. You can now jump out, and you look very nice."

Dad has already alighted and is adjusting the jacket part of his suit in order for it to sit comfortably on his back. Next, he pulls at the cuffs of his new white shirt and then fiddles with his tie, ensuring it is still correctly knotted. Glancing up from his deliberations, he notices I'm watching. Speaking quietly, his tone is one of seeking a positive endorsement on his appearance. "Do I look okay?"

I chuckle at my father's need for approval. "Dad, you look wonderful – you always do – don't worry." I take his hand in mine and give it a gentle, reassuring squeeze. It is so unlike him to be nervous. Letting go of each other's hands, I ask, "Shall we?"

Before we move, my father looks at me hesitantly. "Before we go any further, Eleanor, I must ask for your forgiveness. Please do not interrupt, as my heart is already about to break. I should never have put my job before my family's well-being. I let my obsession blind me, as you were the bait on the hook that I hoped would catch what ministerial officials and I were fishing for. I am no better than Trevisa and his daughter when it comes to using people."

Not knowing how to respond to such a bombshell, I can only kiss him on the cheek as a sign of my exoneration.

Shaken by this loving sign, he gives me an answer to a question I asked him what seems like a lifetime ago. "Fred found out your house was raided by mistake. It should have been three cottages down, 16 not 10. An idiot officer wrote on the back of his hand the correct number, but he rubbed it and 16 became 10. Save us from the company of fools." And with that, he leads us to the French doors of the Tea Rooms.

Two burly bodyguards stop our entry, briefly, and then move to one side to allow us to move forward. One of the men goes to the where the cars are parked, while the other moves inside with us, then closes the door. He takes up the position of sentry in front of it, baring the way for all, in or out.

The area we are in is comforting, calming. The space

consists of eight square tables, with four seats at each. Each table is adorned with condiments, menus on dark green tablecloths that sport an abundance of small white stars. Coffee, tea, water, croissants and cake have been laid out in one corner of the room for us all to help ourselves. While the area is warm, none of us take off our coats or jackets, as though waiting for a quick getaway.

Dad and I take our seats; Mac refuses to sit, instead taking up the position as our bodyguard, like a falcon protecting his prey. Noticing Mr Smyth-Tompkins senior, we trade nods; in contrast, furtive smiles are exchanged with Tolly, whose eyes light up before disappearing under downturned eyelids. Hopefully there will a moment when we can talk. Not sure if this is going to be possible as Mac's hands are on my shoulder, keeping me put. Tolly remains seated by his father. Nearly missed, in a dark corner sits a young man with a laptop and a small assortment of electronic equipment. A black hooded sweatshirt is flung over the back of the chair, daring to drop to the floor, only saved by part of it being sat on. He is so engrossed with what he is doing, he ignores our entry. Not sure he could tell, if asked, how many people are in the room. Doubt if he cares. I take it the two gentlemen seated at another table, with teacups and now empty cake plates, are here to meet us. Dressed in expensive city garb, they rise and walk towards the three of us. While doing so, they both extend their right hands in order to give a welcoming handshake. Looking at our hosts, you can tell they're used to dining at the Connaught or the Langham, not some country eatery.

Now Dad and I are standing *they* acknowledge our presence.

First official: "Commander, Doctor, Mac."

Then the second official repeats the same, "Commander, Doctor, Mac."

Father, being the leader of our pack, shakes each hand in seniority, while extending spoken politeness to each in turn, "Sir, sir."

These men must be well up the food chain if Dad is calling them both 'sir'.

When their attention turns to me, I'm mute, as it would appear we're doing no names, so it is just handshakes and a nod to each in turn.

Mac is equally polite and follows Dad's lead by treating the men with great respect and in order of rank. "Sir, sir."

Formalities finished, it would appear that the conversation is going to be conducted between the officials and my father only. Mac and I are unnecessary. With a raised eyebrow, the lead man enquires, "Any problems, Commander?" *They* know exactly what problems we have come up against and what mayhem we created.

My father, in a measured way, with no irony implied, answers, "No, sir. All went well, as you forecasted, and you, sir, any problems?"

The senior government official coughs as though the question has stuck in his throat. Composing himself, he lifts the back of his right hand to his lips. Behind the knuckle of his first finger, he asks in a whisper, while looking into my dad's eyes, "Do you have a little something for us?"

Reaching into the breast pocket of his suit, Dad retrieves a folded white handkerchief. He takes great pains not to put his fingers on the surface of the object it contains as he unwraps it. He lays the, now open, handkerchief and its contents on the table for all to see: an old, oversized USB, not like the slick USB sticks you buy today. "I believe this is what you may be looking for, sir?"

Witnessing a scene from *Lord of the Rings*, I expect 'Precious, my Precious' to come out of the mouth of the bureaucrat, but all he says is, "Have you opened it?"

"No."

Scanning the room, I have to do a double take at the techie in the corner – yep, my cousin. I knew he was good at his job but never realised he was so talented that the Government went to him so much for security and in-depth checking on family relationships. The USB is passed to him; now I know why he is here.

The second official enquires of me, "Doctor, I would be grateful if you would consent to sign a few legal documents?" He motions to Smyth-Tompkins senior, who steps forward.

Hesitantly, but in a gentle way, I ask of Tolly's father, "What do you require me to do?"

Laying out paperwork in front of me, he speaks in a businesslike fashion. "The Government," nodding to both men in turn, "would like you to turn over ownership of your property in Mayfair to them. There is no content in said dwelling as this has been removed, but not before an unsuccessful burglary had been attempted. Also, the incumbent of said property has been detained, at His Majesty's pleasure pending further investigation. The house has been under surveillance for some time."

Well, it's news to me that I own another high-end property. Gosh, what colour is it on the Monopoly board? Think it may be purple. Likewise, I'm sure there is more to the story regarding the burglary; one day I might get told.

Continuing as solicitor to client, Tolly's father says, "As you have been well rewarded on the sale of your other property, it is felt that no money will change hands on this occasion. I doubt this is a problem for you." He's now speaking in a reassuring manner, a paternal way. "Ellie, as your solicitor, and hopefully as a trusted friend to your family, I can assure you the paperwork is in order. You just need to sign," adding in a whisper, "like you did before." Talking normally again, he continues, "And you will be back to owning no properties. However, you will have a nice bit of money under trust for you to enjoy as you like."

He gives me a warm smile as though I know the amount in question, but I still don't, so frustrating. If it means I get my life back by signing the paperwork, then I am happy. Not sure there is sufficient soap in the world to wash away how dirty I feel at this moment in time. And believe me when I say that I have been very dirty this week, smelly as well.

We are interrupted by a squeak coming from the dark corner, followed by a call to his masters, "In accessing data, how do you want to proceed?" *They* move to see more closely what information has been found. Whatever is flashing across the screen, *they* are mesmerised, as though unable to believe their eyes.

I'm not so far away from my cousin to realise he is scrolling down line upon line of bank account details – they say 'follow the money', and the minister appears to have followed the money, put plenty of it away, and none of it his. No wonder his daughter wanted it and was happy to kill us to get it.

As my geeky cousin's fingers race across the keyboard again, *they* bring their attention back to us.

Dad motions to Mac and I. "Think it's our cue to go."

Curiosity gets the better of me as I whisper, "So it's account details on the stick?"

With a note of caution in his voice, Dad warns, "Leave it, Eleanor, will tell you later, promise; we just need to go before the proverbial hits the fan and we all get covered."

With my given name ringing in my ears, we move to depart; however, *they* now saunter across to join us, with broad grins and the smugness of men who have won the lottery.

Addressing my father, one official says, "Alpha, on behalf of the Government, we thank you, your family and your colleagues. You will be rewarded, whether you like it or not."

Giving me his unwavering attention, he holds out his hand. "Thank you, Doctor."

While our hosts appear to be in a generous mood, I dive in with Freddo's request. "May I ask a favour on behalf of Mac and his family, as I know he would not ask himself?" I can feel daggers from Dad, but I don't care – a promise is a promise.

"Please."

"Mac's son Michael and two of his colleagues were killed, as you know, in a plane crash. I would be most grateful if you could look through these documents pertaining to the transportation of cargo that certain parties believe can be laid at the door of the minister. It is also believed that people under the pay of the minister murdered Michael along with his two colleagues and has left two women with unremitting guilt. Although any findings will not bring those killed back, it may in some small way bring peace of mind to Mrs Mac and the, now retired, duty security manager of Cranfield, as well as Chris and Steve's families. Hopefully, through your contacts, you may be able to pin something on those involved." I hear Mac give a sigh of approval at my request.

Looking away from me, *they* wave forward Mr Smyth-Tompkins. "Ah! Tommy."

Oh! Yes, another school friend, that small world just got smaller.

"Please would you tell the doctor, as her solicitor, that she has signed the Official Secrets Act, and we will be forced to take legal steps if its terms and conditions are broken."

Mr Smyth-Tompkins looks directly at me. "Ellie, do you understand the ramifications if you go against the Act?"

I answer assuredly, "Yes I do," but am unsure of the reason for the question.

Nodding his thanks to both of us, the senior government official begins his story. "Your father has already passed over certain information regarding the whereabouts of items that the minister had taken from various foreign governments around the world, as well as their secrets, when he held the position of Minister for Cultural Affairs. While his properties in London and Wales contained many of the purloined treasures, the 'mother lode' was hidden from our sight, but not anymore, as a mutual friend is now working closely with Interpol, analysing some colourful data." He smirks as though he has just made a clever pun, about the data K had unlocked, regarding the colours on the wall of the mansion.

I get it, we all get it; now move on, don't have all day.

He resumes. "The documents you have given me I will pass over, as I believe our friends will be happy to have the additional pieces to the jigsaw."

If you are interested, the jigsaw's picture is 'shit hitting the fan'.

The official continues, unaware of my thoughts. "We had two people on the inside helping us – one of them was killed and the other now needs our protection, which she will get as she has accumulated an invaluable amount of information and documentation. Hopefully this will open up other avenues of investigation for a fair few Government offices, not all of them ours."

Mac's face and mine must have shown shock at this disclosure. *Michael was working for them.*

"Doctor, I will leave no stone unturned regarding a relationship between the minister and Cranfield, as well as his dealings with other small aerodromes here and on the Continent. I will get my best people on the case and please be assured this will be given top priority. Similarly, who orchestrated, and undertook, the attack on you in Wales will also be part of the investigation. I will take it on myself to be in touch to let you, Alpha and Mac know of the outcome of each inquiry. Thank you, Eleanor." And with that, he doesn't shake my hand but kisses it. "Until we have an occasion to meet again." Then he calls to my cousin, "Come on, K, say goodbye to your uncle and cousin and get your gear into that heap outside." With that, security close ranks on our hosts and my cousin.

Tossing his car keys to his son – yep, the Morgan – Senior tells Junior what is going to happen next – "Don't worry, I'll pop into the office on Monday, keep Henry on his toes. Enjoy yourselves." It would appear that Mac and Dad have already arranged to take Mr Smyth-Tompkins back to Oxford or wherever he lives.

At long last I'm able to give my full attention to Tolly. "So, where are you taking me?"

Moving close, he asks, "How does London sound?" It's said with a twinkle in his eyes.

Shocked by the announcement, I check, "Don't tell me, my dad's flat?" I turn round in order to look at my father, who just winks in a sly way.

Tucking my arm into his as though it is the most natural thing to do, Tolly purrs, "Shall we? How does dinner, wine and a film sound? We don't have to go out, can stay in and chill?"

"It sounds good to me. Will you be staying 'on' the bed? Oh! I will need to go home and get some things first."

"No, you won't, all sorted, and as for sleeping arrangements, we will see." And like me, he now looks at my father, who nods in an approving way.

Nothing or nobody is going to sully this moment for me as I ask, "Does this count as our first date?" And with that, we both laugh, happy and comfortable to be in each other's company, oblivious to what is happening around us, as he leads the way to the Morgan.

If we had stayed a moment longer, we would have heard the conversation between our respective fathers. With a hand round Tommy's shoulder, after serious consideration, Alpha bestows his verdict, "I give it four months," as he watches the couple pull away in the Morgan.

Likewise, his friend weighs up the situation, before answering solemnly, "No, three months tops."

With that, the commander's pronouncement is, "So, engagement party at yours or ours?"

Thinking quickly on his feet and anticipating the number of school and college friends that will want to attend, Tommy imparts a bold suggestion, "I think it's only right that Pip and Brenda have the pleasure, being their godparents? Their house also has a ballroom and an overflowing wine cellar. Might wear a cloak for the occasion; I will leave the dagger at home." Both men laugh in the sure and certain knowledge three wives will be overjoyed. Tomorrow will bring not only family and friends together but the reminder that, as Alpha's Lord Tennyson said, 'love is the only gold'.

CHAPTER 16

SUNDAY A FEW WEEKS LATER

The last couple of weeks have flown by. I have moved in with Tolly and, in order to keep our respective parents reassured all is well in our world, we often dine with them.

Now standing on my parents' drive in the Bramptons on a chilly Sunday afternoon, I look at them both, commenting light-heartedly, "Dinner was wonderful, but we have to go as I have an interview tomorrow and Tolly is back at work."

Gripping my hand while replying in a manner that shows she is sorry to see us go, Mum asks, "Are you sure you don't want to stay and leave first thing?"

Adamant that we must be on our way, but without wanting to causing offence, I reply, "No, it's okay, Mum, but thanks for the offer." After exchanging kisses, I join Tolly in his Range Rover for our journey to our apartment in Oxfordshire.

Alone in the car, Tolly speaks first. "Thank you."

Touching his arm in a possessive manner, while smiling, I reply, "I picked up on the vibe that you didn't want to stay. Our lovemaking can be a bit noisy, and it would be embarrassing for us both, especially when we face them in the morning."

With the remark barely out of my mouth, he laughs before answering, "Oh, Ellie, you make me so happy. I think we should look for a place with thicker walls, maybe detached. And what's all this about an interview tomorrow? You've been quiet on the subject."

"Well, it's a half truth. Sir George Khan wants to talk about my future. Thought my life was all mapped out for me as a doctor and then a surgeon, but after what has happened in the last couple of weeks, it's all up in the air. Not sure which way to turn, cannot see a way through the fog."

Our banter just took a serious turn. "Oh, Ellie, I didn't realise; I'm so sorry."

Surprised by his comment, I ask, "What are you sorry about?"

"Don't know, just seemed like the right thing to say."

I move my hand down to touch his leg.

He moves his left hand off the steering wheel to place it on top of mine. Then brings my hand up to his lips and kisses my fingers in a sensuous way. Speaking softly, trying not to break our emotional connection, he asks, "Do you want to talk it through? Might help to simplify the predicament you find yourself in."

I muster a fuzzy response to go with my fuzzy head. "Oh! Yes, good idea, well, here goes. I must warn you that my thoughts are going to be a bit all over the place." I don't have time to say anything else as two large black BMWs, with pulsating blue lights, force us to stop. Hemming us in, barring our way.

*

Back at the Bramptons, Alpha looks up from his reading and is momentarily taken by surprise by his wife Trish walking into the room with Fred. "What are you doing here? Did a taxi drop you off?"

"No, able to drive Mum's automatic until my leg and ankle are mended. Came to check up on Ellie as Smithy's car is parked along the Holdenby Road and thought it might have broken down?"

Trish cannot keep the shock out of her voice. "What are you talking about? They left here just after lunch. Had a text saying they're home."

The commander, realising something is not right and needing to seek further clarification from Fred, asks, "You did say you saw Tolly's car down the road just now?"

"Yes, it is definitely his car, been trying to pin a motoring offence on the bastard, so yes I do know it's his."

The commander looks from Fred to his wife with her mobile to an ear. She shakes her head worriedly. "It keeps going to voicemail."

Turning back to Fred, he barks, "Show me," as he flings his paper on the floor.

Kissing Trish before leaving the room, he tries to keep his voice calm, more for her sake. "I'll be quick, just need to check. See if you can contact Mac? I know he is away, but I like to keep him in the loop." She knows what he truly means: *tell Mac to get back here — I need him.*

Departing the house, he runs to his car parked on the drive. While trying to keep his mind open to all possibilities, the text message is filling him with the greatest concern.

After a very brief journey, they are now parked in the road where Fred saw Tolly's car.

Swiftly alighting the car, even with a plastered leg and a booted foot, Fred points to a muddy area of the country lane.

"It was here; I swear on all that is holy it was here and neither Ellie nor Smithy were with it. I came from my place in Long Buckby, through East Haddon and then onto the Holdenby Road. I stopped but didn't get out the car, came straight to your place." Inspecting the road surface, both men notice that freshly made tyre marks are visible. Fred is the first to break the silence. "Three large cars, by the marks." He doesn't have to say any more, as he knows the commander has already come to the same conclusion by the look on his face. Fred instinctively knows what to do and reaches into his jeans pocket for his mobile.

Alpha is doing likewise. Once the call connects, he says, "Pip, don't fart arse about – the kids have been hijacked, kidnapped, taken."

Stunned by the quickness of the message spoken, the duke, somewhat perplexed, asks, "Alpha, what are you on about?"

Still talking at a pace, Alpha continues, "Ellie and Tolly, I'm standing where the lad's car was last seen, and there is no sign of either of them. Trish received a message to say they were home, but she cannot reach them. Pip, where are they?"

The duke had never known his friend to sound so panicky, fearful. "Alpha, I need to put you on hold but just for couple of minutes while I make a call. Stay calm, my friend, stay calm." Picking up the landline telephone on his study desk, Pip shakes his head at his wife Brenda. She automatically knows the call he is about to make is grave. Instead of leaving, she goes to him as he is holding out his free hand for her to take. His need for her reassurance will no doubt become clear by his phone call.

With the call connected, the duke dives straight in. "Sophie is that you?" This is followed by a barely audible sound on the other end that Brenda cannot make out. He continues, as it's his turn to speak. "Good, top priority – I want everyone working on this, now. It would appear that the commander's daughter Eleanor and her boyfriend Tolly Smyth-Tompkins, my godchildren, have been kidnapped from the road going past Holdenby House, close to the family home in the Bramptons. You have two minutes to find out by whom. Get our forensics to the location now and report back to me. I will be on my mobile heading for the commander's place. Tell Lewis and Harvey to meet me there, fully armed. Warn them to hope for the best but prepare for the worst." With that, he puts down the phone.

Brenda looks at him, horrified, but knows what she must do. "I'll get our things as Trish will need me. No doubt you and Alpha will be doing what you both do best?"

As she leaves the room, Pip realises that his friend is still hanging on. Taking the mobile off hold, he resumes the call. "Alpha, I'm on my way; two of my lads will join me at your place. Bringing Bren with me to help Trish. My forensic team is on the way – is someone with you, big man?"

In a state of shock, a condition that is a stranger to him, the commander replies half-heartedly, "Yes, Mac's boy Fred, the local police officer."

"Good, get him to block off the area as best he can. I will speak to the chief constable of Northamptonshire immediately and send officers to help with the blockade. What's that noise?"

"Fred has already rung it in and is getting the Holdenby Road closed at both ends as we speak. He's as concerned as I am, Pip – what is going on? I will swing for them if they harm my girl, I will."

Sensing his friend's growing anxiety but knowing the need for both of them to stay focused, he relays comprehensively what needs to happen next. "Okay, Alpha, we will be at your place in less than an hour. Your immediate task is to go home to Trish, leaving Fred and forensics to do their jobs."

Holding a mobile with a now black screen, Alpha speaks to

himself, not in any rush to move. *Where are you both? Must ring Tommy; Tolly's father needs to know. What do I say?* Speed dialling Smyth-Tompkins senior, the phone is picked up by Katie, his wife. *I can do without this.* Trying to be upbeat, Alpha says, "Hi, Katie, is Tommy there?"

"Hello, Alpha, yes he is – I will pass you over. How were the kids at lunch, and did they get off home okay? I haven't seen them since they had film night with us last Tuesday. Of course, Tommy sees Tolly in the office."

Lying through his teeth, Alpha replies, "Fine, we enjoyed lunch very much, then they went on their way. See you both soon," not wanting to prolong the dialogue any longer than necessary.

Tommy comes to the phone and takes up the conversation. "Good afternoon, Alpha, this is nice of you to ring. Is there something you would like me to do for you?"

"Tommy, take a walk out of earshot of Katie please?" The commander can hear his friend saying something to his wife, followed by the sound of footsteps and a closing door.

Now another bewildered friend asks, "Alpha are you there, what's the problem?"

"Ellie and Tolly have been kidnapped. I don't know any more than that. Rang Pip – he has taken charge; he is on his way to my house." No response is received; Alpha starts to panic, as indicated by his tone. "Tommy, Tommy say something please?"

A solemn voice is heard. "How long ago? Who has taken our children, Alpha, and why?"

"The kids left us just after lunch at about 2:30pm. Fred, Mac's boy, spotted their car at about 3pm, abandoned close by our village. When we went to look, the car had gone. Before you say anything, I must tell you that Trish received a message saying they were home. Tommy, it isn't possible. Fred is waiting for Pip's forensic team. I'm going home to wait. As for why, I have no idea, but once I find out who it is, I will kill them and nothing or nobody will be able to stop me. They will find out that they don't want me as an enemy."

"Get in line, Alpha, as I will tear them limb from limb if they touch one hair on their heads."

The commander doesn't reply straight away but can hear the low sound of his friend crying. Sensing the right moment to butt in on his friend's grief, he says, "I will keep you and Katie in the loop at all times, and if you want to come to our house, then just turn up. I must go now, but I will be in touch. If I'm not able to, I will get Trish to ring you both on the hour until they are back with us. Will ring at 5pm."

All that Tommy can muster is a downcast, "Okay." Then silence as the connection goes dead.

*

Earlier – looking through the windscreen and then at the internal driver's mirror at the scene playing out in front and behind them – a dazed Tolly enquires of me, "What's going on? Do you know these people? Are they police?"

All I can muster is, "No, and they are not police for all their blue lights."

Two men appear on either side of the car and attempt to open the locked doors of the Range Rover. Pulling out guns, they forcefully give orders, "You two out – I want your mobiles and the keys to the car." Tolly deactivates the locks. Opening the door with purpose on the driver's side, the man grabs Tolly's mobile from his hand.

Rummaging through my bag, I find my mobile and hand it over to the brute on my side.

He then barks at me, "Stand there as I need to verify you haven't sent any messages." Tolly's mobile is thrown over the car to also be checked. As one of the carjackers examines our phones and his partner, still on Tolly's side of the car, looks out for traffic, it gives us the briefest opportunity to run.

Being manhandled, all I can muster is a whimpering, "Hey, you are hurting me," for all the good it does me. *Surely what they want is the car, not us. Nope, we don't get any further than arm's length as it would appear that we are the targets.*

"Be thankful I don't hit women," the carjacker says while looking Tolly's way, who is equally restrained by a thug.

Inwardly, I think, *Tolly, he has no qualms about hitting men; it's no time to be macho – wait and see what they want and don't panic.* Dragged to different cars, it would appear they don't want us to travel together or in the same direction. Thrown roughly onto the back seat of one of the BMWs, I'm unable to see what is happening to Tolly as he is driven away.

I have to say to my captives, "When my dad finds me, because he will, he is going to stand back while I pulverise your bodies into the ground. Then we are going to have a barbeque to feast on your corpses." Both the driver and the thug laugh. Passing through East Haddon and then dropping down onto the road which leads to Long Buckby, I'm surprised I'm not on my way to a derelict barn or a dilapidated old farmhouse. Both of which would see me hidden away from prying eyes. I calculate my journey has lasted less than ten minutes. It may be an unknown place to my kidnappers, but I know exactly where I am, Long Buckby wharf, less than two miles from a cottage I own in the village.

Saying calm, at least on the outside, I'm manhandled out the car, this time by a man who had been standing on the bridge over the canal. *Why is there no traffic when you want some?*

The driver turns the car round in the narrow road and heads back the way he came. A hand grips my arm more firmly, and its owner drags me down the stone steps leading to the water below. Waiting at the water's edge is a boat, just one of many that travel up and down these arteries of the United Kingdom. I notice the name on the side: *The Corvid Family*. A striking piece of artwork shows a group of flying, predominately black, birds that I can only think are crows, get them mixed up with ravens, together with magpies and jays. Now the holiday season is well and truly over, the boating traffic has slowed to a trickle. So much so that this part of the waterway is empty of moving boats. Those moored are empty as, on a cold day like today, smoke would be emanating from their chimneystacks. Unceremoniously, I'm pulled on board by my hair and then pushed down through a small wooden hatch into the space below. Gaining my balance and trying to take in my predicament, I cannot fail to see how nice the cabin area is, clean and tidy.

My jailer says in a sarcastic way, "Hope you like your living quarters; you're not staying long." He enquires, as though I've just popped in for afternoon tea, "Would you like a drink, water, tea or coffee?"

I shake my head. *May be drugged; I would rather become dehydrated.*

"Oh dear, too bad." And with that, I'm Tasered. The last words I hear as I slump down on the sofa are, "Sweet dreams."

Waking in a funk, I have no idea how long I've been out, but it is dark outside. Lying on the sofa with a blanket over me, I can hear the lapping of water hitting the side of the narrowboat but no engine noise. It would appear that we are moored, as we are not permitted to navigate the canal in the dark. Hearing me stir, my jailer glances up from his reading. *Well, as I've been spotted, no point in pretending.*

Attempting to sound menacing, the jailer says, "Welcome back – did you have a nice sleep? Be good and I will not have to send you into dreamland again."

Sorry, it just doesn't work on me; I've met men that are truly bloodcurdling, who would have you shitting your pants. Right, I need to get a grip of the situation, come on, I need to ask; it would be rude not to. "So, who are you, and why am I here?"

Quick as a flash, the answer comes back, "I'm nobody, and I am not interested in you. I'm here to make sure you don't come to any harm."

Whose dirty work are you doing? Swinging my feet round in order to sit up, I ask, "So, who is interested in me? As, like you, I'm a nobody." I can sense he has been travelling on his own for some time by his nervous demeanour and no doubt been told not to talk to anyone. *Did you think I would be crying by now, wanting my mummy and daddy? Let's see how a little bit of chit-chat goes while I take the measure of you.* Trying to be unashamedly friendly, I continue, "Northamptonshire must be strange to you as I can tell you're not from these parts; I would say London?"

No reply is forthcoming, so I soldier on. "Hear they have a lot of top-class football teams in London? I remember my sister, who is a doctor in London, telling me." With that lie about having a sister, his face freezes for a brief moment. Blink and I would have missed it.

Astonished by this revelation, he speaks, unsure of what he just heard. "You have a sister?"

"Yep, she is a year older than me, but people think we are twins. She is really clever. I work in a shop, just come back from Ibiza. Popped in to see my parents to say I'm back, a friend gave me a lift. Had a great time, sleeping all day, partying at a different club every night. Have you ever been there? Can tell you all the best places to go, where the cheap booze is and the best music."

Again, all he can say is, "You have a sister that looks like you?"

"Yep, same size, same colour hair and eyes. Do you like what I'm wearing? These are hers. Raided her wardrobe while I was at home. Couldn't afford these on my wages. Don't even get the living wage, stingy bastards." *Oh! I am so good at lying; do I see a fragment of doubt worming its way into your brain? Good, now let's throw out the line and see what I can catch.* "Do you have my bag?"

Confused, he replies, "No. Why?"

"Ladies problem, must go to the lav. You do have one on this boat, or is it a bucket? I don't mean the boat is a bucket," faking a laugh before getting back to the task in hand, "you know, or do I have to spell it out? I'm on my monthly." *Did I just see you squirm? Good, will keep you away from me, and now I need to find out if we have moved away from the wharf and how I'm going to get out of this hole.* "Have you got anything I can use before I bleed all over this lovely seat?" I am happy to be as graphic as I need to make him drop his guard and let me move about this area freely.

Clearly knocked for six, he replies, "I'll find you some cloths – will that be okay?"

Is that empathy I'm witnessing? "As long as they are clean. Do you have a pair of scissors if I need to cut them up?"

"Yes, then I must make a call," he says, slightly distracted by events.

When I was last on the canal, I remember that the signal was very hit and miss, hope it's miss or I'm in the mire. He passes over a couple of new tea towels and a pair of scissors, and I go about cutting the material up, with one eye shut. He goes outside to hopefully not make or receive any calls. When done with my handy craft, I shout to him that, "I'm going to use the lavatory." Once in this tiniest of tiny rooms, I grab some water in cupped hands, doubt he has drugged his water tank. I open the closed eye, which is already adjusted to the darkness.

Peering out of a porthole window, the size of a tea plate, into the night, I cannot tell if I'm still at the wharf. The view out the window is taken up with greenery, trees and bushes. *So, you canny bastard, you have moved the boat to the opposite side of the towpath while I was asleep. No way am I going into freezing, muck-infested water. Remember, I am now my drippy sister, and I must get out before you get a mobile signal.*

Coming back into the cabin, my captive closes the hatch behind him, swearing like a trooper.

I gather no signal, so it's Plan A, entry level one – let's party. Swaying slowly on the spot to the beat of unheard music and singing a song that I am making up the words to, I say, "Hey, if you are not going to give me your name, I'm going to call you Dave. I'm Sue. Do you have anything to drink in this place, not tea or coffee? How about some music? I want to dance." I fling up my arms. Love the look on his face, one of pure horror. "Can hear the music from Ibiza if I close my eyes. Wow, I'm back there on the dance floor."

He passes me a mug with some unknown spirit in it, which I have no intention of drinking, but he does not know that as long as he keeps drinking his fill.

"Come on, Dave, get down with the beat."

Getting agitated, he says, "Sit down. I know what your game is."

"Games, Dave, don't play games. Leave that to my sister." *Let's have a go at a crash course on Stockholm syndrome – I will play Beauty and you will be the Beast.* Still carrying on with the dancing, I say, "Did I tell you she is my parents' favourite? They don't care about me. She went to medical school; I failed my A levels. Been in trouble with the police, bastards, it wasn't even my stuff; it was my boyfriend's. They didn't believe me, pigs. Sun shine's out Little Miss Wonderful's backside; she may have her boring career, but I know how to party."

Level one of Plan A can be ticked off, need to move to level two. "Come on, Dave, put the music on, and what do you have to eat? Can't boogie on an empty stomach – haven't eaten since lunch." I can sense it – *you don't know how to deal with the situation – good.*

Sounding befuddled, he says, "Sit down please, and I will get you some toast."

Making full eye contact, and talking in a subservient way, with a drooping lower lip, I ask, "Toast with what, Dave?"

Moving to one side, he opens up one of the small cupboards in the equally little galley kitchen. As he does that, I dance swiftly around the cabin, checking the place out. *Where is that Taser? Scissors are still on the side; if needs must, I will stab you. Hopefully, this will be in a place that will just maim you, who knows, who cares? But I am a doctor? Yes, but that is not going to save me from being killed.*

He calls out over his shoulder, "Have beans or jam?"

"Beans sound great, if that's okay with you? Thanks, Dave, you're the best." Dishing up the makeshift meal, he hands over the plate with only a fork to eat it with. With pouting lips, I ask like a child, "No knife, Dave, can you cut up my toast for me, please?"

He takes back my plate and proceeds to do my bidding. Placing my soldiers and beans in front of me, he sits down, his mug refreshed with another slug of spirit, and watches me eat, as though it's a spectator sport.

Finishing off the last bean, putting down the fork, I give him one of my very best smiles, trying not to reach across the table and strangle him. I deliberately burp, laughing while saying behind a raised hand, "That hit the spot."

With this, he smiles. *Level three coming up.*

I nod approvingly at my surroundings. "Nice boat." This allows me to glance round even more without too many questions being asked. "And so neat and tidy. You look like a man that likes things orderly, Dave. I do like a man who looks after himself." A small clock on the side shows 7:35pm. *Is it right? Well, it's dark. but it gets dark early this time of year – not sure how long Tasering knocks you out for. This, being blatantly nice to my captive, is hard work; I need a break. I think it's time to tell you I need to pay another visit to the lav.* Smiling flirtatiously, wondering how I'm doing this while keeping a straight face, I say, "Sorry, ladies' problem, don't touch my drink." Once more into the littlest room, *think, girl, think.* Cupping my hands again, I drink some more water from the cold tap, in order to keep my fluid intake up. Coming out into the warm cabin, I notice that he has adjusted the hatch door so it is now slightly open to the elements.

Pleased that I like my prison by the compliment I just made, he acknowledges this with a, "Thanks, like to keep the place neat and tidy." As though to demonstrate this, he sets about puffing up the cushions, then moves to the minuscule sink to wash my meal things up. I can tell this is more out of habit than the fact I am present.

Right, so the question that I need to ask, or should I say be expected to ask, as I still don't have an escape route, is, "What is going to happen to me, Dave? You said that you are here to make sure I don't come to any harm." He does not answer, as I suspected. *So, you are merely a cog in a much bigger wheel, and you need to be given directions; let's hope you don't get a signal, as I could find myself on very dangerous ground playing my not-needed sister.* Faking a yawn, I say, "Sorry, Dave, would like to have a nap, if that's okay with you? All that dancing has made me tired. Need all my strength to party tomorrow," once again giving him a girlish smile. *Yuck, I'm starting to hate Belle, or should I say Sue, with this playing up to the Beast.*

Throwing another blanket at me, while trying to sound

macho, he says, "You can sleep where you are sitting. Don't do anything stupid, or I will have to Taser you again. I'm going out."

Yawning again for show, I reply, "Goodnight, Dave, thanks for the beans on toast and for looking over me, keeping me safe. Can't be easy?"

I can tell he is taken aback by my acquiescence by how he replies, "Yeah, goodnight, Sue, glad the food was okay." With this, he strides up the couple of wooden steps to the deck above, no doubt to try and make that call again.

I deliberately don't sleep but lie still, listening. I can feel the narrowboat move slightly down as though another person has stepped on board. I pull the blanket under my chin in a protective way, for all the good it will do me, moving my head slowly and silently towards the back of the craft. The hatch door opens to its full capacity and my jailer falls head first down into the cabin. His mobile hits the ground and slides along the wooden floor until it comes to a halt against the table leg. The boat then moves slightly upwards and, after the briefest of moments, travels sideways. The ropes must have been untied by someone, no time to contemplate by whom. Throwing off the blanket, I rush to check on the man; I have seen enough dead bodies in my short medical career to know that Dave is now another one to be added to that list. *Right, move, Ellie, move, girl, this may be your only chance.* I grab whatever I think I may need: one of Dave's jackets – not worried that it swamps me – scissors, his unbroken mobile. *Check his pockets* – keys, wallet – *take them.* I keep the mobile in my hand but the other things I shove into the deep pockets. Glancing around, I still cannot see the Taser, so it's quickly up and through the open hatch, without any regard for who might be on board.

Relieved I'm alone; I can only surmise whoever threw Dave through the hatch is gone, otherwise they would have come for me. As the craft is touching the towpath, I swiftly jump off the boat. Wanting to kiss the ground, I resist; however, I do push the boat off the bank so it floats in the middle of the canal. Momentarily, I start working out in my head which way I need to run. Standing looking at the canal, Long Buckby wharf is to the left. Looking up at the night sky, a large yellow and orange cloud hangs omnipresent, not too far in the distance. I speculate its light pollution is coming from Daventry. *Doubt if we have travelled as far as Buckby Top Lock. So, my best bet is back towards the wharf and then on to Whilton Locks. I can do this on the same towpath. Easier to hide in an area that I'm more familiar with. So, start running down the path towards home and keep those eyes and ears open.* I run along a flat, fairly dry and well-maintained towpath. The phone in Dave's coat pocket starts pinging. *Don't have time to stop to look, keep going, girl.* I ignore the green direction signs as I'm unsure of my ability to traverse fields without any light. *Who to ring? Mac, ring Mac – he will know what to do, always does.*

Not recognising the unfamiliar caller ID, a cautious voice answers, "Yes?"

Speaking quickly and hoping he recognises my voice, I say, "Mac, it's me, Ellie, I've lost my bottle."

Relieved at what the hidden message means, he answers carefully. "How long?"

I calculate and respond, "Two hours, maybe less. Come alone – don't tell anyone please?"

"Okay." He presses the red button to disconnect the call.

Mac notices that Alpha is still in deep conversation with Pip who, along with Brenda, Lewis and Harvey, is now based in his neighbour's house. Keen to get going, Mac catches the eye of the lady of the house. "Trish, that was the wife; she has just made me something to eat. Will you tell Alpha I'm going next door to check up on her and maybe catch up on a couple of hours' sleep, if I can. Will be back, but if you need me sooner, just call." With that, he heads next door to grab his gear with a few extras, telling Mrs Mac his plan and then trekking across the back fields, keeping clear of people and cars. He knows the house must have been being watched all these weeks, waiting for the right moment to occur. That moment was this Sunday afternoon.

Getting back to the task in hand, the proverbial, *can do this journey with my eyes closed*, is very close to the truth when it comes to Mac's trek from his home in the Bramptons to the old, disused shooting range outside the hamlet of Nobottle, the 'lost my bottle' of the message. In his mind, he can create a well-constructed argument as to the direction Ellie is coming from, based on their brief conversation, but not her precise route. One thing he is sure of is that his journey will be the quickest and safest. Leaving from the back of his garden has allowed him the ability to cut across the far-reaching fields and golf course to his destination, Nobottle. Taking a chance, he moves onto country lanes, this being a quicker route. With their twists and turns, he can easily dart into the adjoining woods to take cover. Although in a game bird shooting county, he doesn't want to be questioned as to why he is carrying a high-velocity weapon, with silencer and night sight, hence one of the reasons for stealth.

Moving closer to the village, he is ever vigilant for the dog walkers. He glances at his watch, noting both the actual time and the time taken so far. He does a speedy calculation: *estimated distance still to travel, two and a half miles; ETA twenty minutes but looking for eighteen, then you better get going.* Finally coming into the blink-and-you-miss-it hamlet of Nobottle, he moves assuredly along its main road, hoping he doesn't meet any traffic. Relieved, he darts down the lane to the old gun range. Reaching the abandoned buildings of the range, fully aware of its layout, he sets up camp in the most advantageous position at the site. Having already calculated the direction Ellie will be coming from, he waits, silently and without moving any more than necessary. He has his rifle, with night sight and silencer attached, and is happy to wait as long as it takes.

It is her movement that tells him that it is Eleanor, regardless of what she is wearing. Diligently, he continues to monitor the landscape. *Good girl, come to your uncle Mac. No need to rush, gently, calmly, I have you in my sights.* Although straining his ears in order to pick up every sound, he doesn't lose sight of his target. Coming into range, he points his night sight to the ground in front of her and then moves the red dot in the direction he wants her to take. He is thankful that she obeys his signal and moves quietly to stand, as though glued to the wall of the bedraggled, disused building. Mac moves cat-like towards her, so as not to startle her. He cannot help himself, grabbing her and kissing the top of her head.

*

Drawing me no more than an arm's length away, he quickly pats me down, checking I am whole.

Cupping his hands on my face, Mac enquires in a controlled but protective manner, "Okay, sweet pea? Come on, I'll take you home."

I cannot help but fall against him; however, I hesitate at his suggestion. "Mac, I'm not sure that is a good idea – can we talk this through before we, I, do anything hasty that may put others in danger? It's bad enough that Tolly and I are in this predicament." Realising what I have just said, I cannot stop panic worming its way into my voice. "Mac, tell me he's safe, tell me?"

Before I can say any more, Mac stops me and agrees to my

request, ever watchful of our surroundings. "Okay, start at the beginning, and don't forget to eat and drink." He gets a snack and a bottle of water out of his rucksack and hands them over to me.

Sliding down the wall into a sitting heap on the ground, I thirstily drink between bites of a healthy bar, while putting another one in my pocket. "So, Tolly and I left Mum and Dad's after Sunday lunch. Is it still Sunday?"

"Yes, it is still Sunday, just. Go on with your report."

"We took the Holdenby Road for a change as we were in no rush to get home. Before the entrance to Holdenby House, and therefore out of range of their CCTV, we were pinned in by two large black BMW cars. They took our mobiles, and I had to go in one car and Tolly in the other." I close my eyes to replay the nightmare in my head so that I get everything right. "I was taken to Long Buckby wharf and put on a narrowboat named *The Corvid Family*, as in crows and ravens. There is a beautifully painted picture of crows, jays and magpies on its side. One man held me captive. He didn't touch me; I think he was as frightened as me – he is dead."

With this revelation, Mac grabs my arm tightly. "What? You killed him?"

Ignoring him, I continue telling my tale. "He went on deck to make a call; he had already said that the signal was bad. He zapped me with a Taser when I was first taken prisoner, and while I was out of it, he moved the boat to the opposite side of the towpath and further down the canal towards Daventry." I pause to take another drink. Mac fishes in his bag for another bottle as I have nearly finished the first. "Alone in the cabin, I felt the boat drop down as though someone stepped onto the deck. Next thing I know, my jailer comes head first though the hatch, landing on the ground dead. The boat then floated towards the towpath. I grabbed his mobile and legged it. I came along the towpath to Whilton Locks up the hill, working my way here. Rang you rather than Dad. Not sure if I was followed but kept to the shadows as best I could, although I did have to go on the road for much of my journey."

"Well, you were right to call me. I will take the mobile and give it to K, your geeky cousin, to analyse; he has set up shop at my house – yours is getting a tad crowded. What else did you take?"

Reaching into Dave's coat pockets, I bring out his wallet, a set of keys and the scissors. Looking at the unimpressive bounty, Mac murmurs, "Is this it?"

"Yes." I think for one brief moment he doesn't believe me.

"Right, I'll take the mobile, the keys and the wallet; you can keep the scissors." He puts them all into a side pocket of his bag and then, reaching back into the main part, pulls out another mobile. "Take this – it has been programmed with a few numbers. Press any speed dial number from one to five; tell whoever answers your name and that you need help immediately. Help will come running. Now, what to do with you."

Rising from his squatting position, he then lifts me up off the floor. Making sure his rifle and his rucksack, which now contain two empty water bottles and a couple of snack wrappers, are safely on his back, he enlightens me on what is to happen next. "Right, I need to arrange for the boat to be secured and get you somewhere safe. Then we have a one-mile run eyes and ears open, mouth closed. Keep on my shoulder – if I tell you to drop, you drop. Let's get going back to Great Brington." With the calls made, we move quickly and with purpose.

I find the ground under my feet well known to me, having jogged these paths and lanes many times, often with Mac. Not having to concentrate on the placing of my feet too much, my mind starts to drift, worrying about what is happening to Tolly. *Once my family knows I'm safe then they can pool all their effort into finding Tolly. Okay, now keep up with Mac.* Adrenaline is gushing through my body, giving me a high that makes me believe I can run to the moon and back without getting out of breath, even though I only need to make it to somewhere in Great Brington.

Stopping a little way from the back entrance to Althorp House, the home of the Spencer family, Mac takes out his phone and makes another call. Once finished, he turns his attention to me. "Right, keep in the shadows and wait, not long, trust me." A proper Land Rover, not a Chelsea tractor, appears on the other side of the foreboding gates.

A man's voice quietly calls out, "Mac, Mac."

"Our ride is here – come with me." While the vehicle slowly ticks over, its driver barely opens the gates to allow us access. Quickly moving into the grounds of this fine house, I shift once again into the shadows. I hear the heavy click of the lock and then watch as the driver retakes his seat. With passenger door open, Mac motions for me to join the two of them in the car. "This is Addy – you are going to stay with him and his wife Jo until I can get you safely relocated sometime tomorrow." As we unhurriedly move within the walled grounds, Mac and Addy talk in an easy-going manner. "When I've settled Ellie with you and Jo, any chance of letting me out?"

Addy speaks with a very pleasant and reassuring voice, "Of course, Mac, can get you high up near to the main road; I take it that an old man like you can still climb our outer stone wall without doing it any damage? Once on the other side, then it's not too far for you to run home."

CHAPTER 17

MONDAY

I slept restlessly, even though Jo has made me feel most welcome. I can only pick at my breakfast, just eating a slice of toast and downing a large mug of tea. I ask if it is okay for me to sit in their back garden. She is happy for me to take a breath of fresh air. Addy, who it appears has finished his morning chores, comes out to cut the lawn, but I can tell it is to keep an eye on me. Within the vast grounds, a rather grand car stops a little way off. Noticing the vehicle, Addy seems to be happy to leave me on my own. For my part, I find myself grazing into the distance.

Without looking round, I hear a man quoting Mearns, a poem I instantly recognise.

Yesterday, upon the stair,
I met a man who wasn't there
He wasn't there again today
I wish, I wish he'd go away...

Craning my neck, a man in a very expensive overcoat covering an equally pricey three-piece suit is looking down at me. With a hint of mischief in his voice, he asks, "Is that what you thought of me? Your father told me you believe me a scary man, whom you were not sure you had met. Thank you, as I do like to keep up a modicum of mystery, threat, intrigue." Sensing I'm downcast, he changes tack to a tone that is more genial. "Tell me, why so glum, have you lost something you treasure above anything else?"

With that I can only nod while tears start to form in the corners of my eyes.

"And would you like me to help you find this missing something?"

Once again, I nod, trying to hold back the tears without much success.

Reaching into his coat pocket, my mystery man brings out a pure white, neatly pressed and folded handkerchief. Passing it over, he speaks in a concerned way as he sits beside me. "Go on, have a good blow, always makes me feel better when life drags me down. Did your father say how we met and became friends?"

This time I shake my head, still unable to speak, while having a good blow. Once finished, he puts his arm round me and brings me close. I'm surprised I let him do it, but it seems right.

Talking into space with my head resting on his soft wool coat, he begins his tale. "We went to the same boarding school, cast adrift by absent parents. We weren't in the same house as I'm four years older than Alpha. I was jealous of your father, from day one. Even at a young age he had this aura. He wasn't one of the biggest of lads then, but you could tell he could take care of himself. Like now, he was able to get people to hang on his every word, do his bidding if he asked. I gave him and his pals hell; being bigger, older and a prefect, it was easy. Even if it was somebody else who did the deed, his gang were the ones that were dragged to the headmaster's office. I didn't realise, what I thought was a bad boy act came at a cost to me. I lost friends as your dad gained them. I came to understand that his role at school, as in life, was to protect those who were unable to protect themselves.

"I went into town one night, against school rules; it was to meet a friend, a male friend. Your dad got wind somehow that I had been set up. He followed, just him. He waited and watched until it all kicked off. I didn't realise how vile people could be to the likes of me. It was one against six rugby-playing lads from the local comprehensive. Thankfully, it became two against six, with Alpha taking out most of the lads on his own. We legged it back to school, bloodied but alive. Your dad said we had a fight in the dorm; we were pretty roughed up from our town encounter. Understandable he was fed-up with me picking on him and threatened to knock my teeth down my throat. That was when the two of us, allegedly, squared up to each other and had a bloody fight. We both got detention and told that we had to spend the rest of the term together. I never forgot this one act of kindness by your father and his unstinting friendship ever since. Our paths crossed on numerous occasions, at various official functions, and I'm pleased to report he remains the same loyal school friend to me as I am to him. Well, enough of that story for today as we need to get you cleaned up; I need you to meet someone and then dazzle my guests."

Stunned by his last comment, I reply, "Sorry, what? Where are you taking me? And if you haven't noticed, I'm wearing jeans and jumper. Unless you are taking me to a fast-food outlet, I'm not dressed to dazzle anyone?"

Touching his nose while smiling, he remarks, "I knew the first time we met I would like you, even in that ill-fitting borrowed uniform. May I call you Ellie? Please say yes, and you may call me Ted, short for teddy bear." With that he laughs as he sees himself as a large soft fluffy toy.

However, by the size of him, his white hair and the very short meeting that my brother and I had at the army base a couple of weeks ago, he is more of a polar bear, with teeth and claws to match. Taken aback by the softness in his manner, I reply calmly, "Yes, you may call me Ellie, but as for calling you Ted, we will see." With that, he smiles a nice friendly smile that lifts some of the gloom surrounding me. "May I keep your handkerchief, just in case I need it again?" I'm holding it tightly in my hands.

Standing up and then tapping his coat breast pocket, he replies, "Please feel free to keep it, as I have another two in my pocket if needed by a damsel in distress." Grabbing my hand, without letting go, he pulls me up so I now face him. "Carl, my driver, will take us to a little dress shop; I know where we can pick out something that will make you feel like a million dollars. Then I will take you to dinner with my visitors, who will help me find what you have lost."

First, I thank my new friends, Addy and Jo, for welcoming me into their home. They hope we will meet again, but under better circumstances. With goodbyes complete, I am slowly ushered towards Ted's car. He is true to his word as we pull up outside a very select fashion house, hidden away from the main street. The door to the property opens at the same time Ted's 'special forces bodyguard' Carl opens the passenger door, first for me and then for my benefactor to alight the vehicle. A casually dressed and tanned middle-aged man shepherds us into the establishment. Once the front door is closed behind us, the two men embrace tenderly. Pleased to be in each other's company, they smile lovingly before their attention turns to me.

Ted gestures from me to the proprietor and then back

again. "Where are my manners? Simon, this is Eleanor whom I am taking to dinner tonight, where I will try not to throw her to the lions. Therefore, I want you to dress her so that she radiates sophistication, style and intelligence. She already processes these virtues, like her mother Patricia, but no one can see them while she is dressed in jeans. Is Susie here to do her hair?"

Well, I don't expect Simon to reply with an Australian accent, "Sure thing, Teddy. Have just the thing for you, Eleanor, it will make you look like the princess you truly are. I will dress you as though you are going off to a red-carpet event. Susie will style your hair to match the cut and design of your dress." Looking me up and down, in a nice way, he continues, "Eleanor, I would say dress size six and shoe size six. Colour of outfit, I would say hints of blue, to match those glorious azure eyes and that mane of beach blonde hair. Whoever did your fake tan did a good job. May I ask, is it all over? And do I have to worry about strap lines?"

Taken aback that I have been summed up in so few words, I answer assuredly, "Yes, six and six; I do like blue in all its tones; and my tan is all over with no lines."

Giving me a reassuring nod, he talks like a man whom you would be happy to take charge of your wardrobe, maybe your life. "Let's get to work. If you will come with me, I will introduce you to Susie and we can weave our magic. I have a couple of dresses put to one side you will like, together with very flattering lingerie, and of course heels. Teddy will be the judge. But might I suggest a very quick shower?"

Why is everyone concerned about my personal hygiene and not afraid to tell me so?

Wow, within the hour I am washed, dressed and my hair coiffured. 'Ted', or should I say Teddy, loves the first dress I put on and the way my hair is styled to complement it.

Giving a small clap of appreciation, he cannot contain his joy. "Wonderful, Ellie, Alpha would be so proud of you. May I add that I can see you on the front cover of *Vogue*? Don't you agree, Simon?"

Studying me for a few moments, a positively beaming Simon remarks, "Off to the ball, my princess?"

Having been gifted the make-up used and a clutch bag to match my ensemble, Teddy gently takes my other hand as he steers me towards the front door.

Simon touches Ted on the arm. "Take care, Teddy, and dinner tomorrow?" Turning to me, he blubbers, "And, Ellie, you look magnificent; if the doctor thing doesn't work out, you can always do some modelling for me?"

Sitting in the back of Ted's car, I notice that he cannot stop smiling. "Thank you for allowing me to be Professor Henry Higgins to your Miss Doolittle; it was great fun and a small debt repaid. I hope you are hungry; I know I am. But now we need to meet my first guest."

He has given no indication of where we are going that needs me to be dressed up so glamorously. As we seem to be on friendly terms, I jump straight in. "Ted, I like Simon and absolutely love his fashion house. Oh! Now I'm ready for my photo shoot. Where are you taking me?"

I'm expecting to be told a swanky restaurant, but this is not the case. Rather guiltily, he answers, "Mine and Simon's weekend place in the country."

Eventually, we come to a halt outside a property hidden away from prying eyes. All I can muster is a, "Bloody hell, Ted, it's awesome."

Seeking my approval, he sheepishly enquires, "You like?"

I'm still not able to take in the enormity of the property before me, but I know he wants a positive answer. "What's not to like? But it's colossal, in a good way, I might add."

"Come, you will meet my guest, and then I will wine and dine you."

Ted darts round to my side in order to be gentlemanly and lead me into his mansion and onwards, hopefully to dine or have nibbles. I am getting more curious by the minute – who is his visitor? I'm ushered into a small, cosy room sporting a dining table that seats only four people and two large sofas, positioned round a large coffee table close to a blazing open fire. Seated on one of the sofas, with a whisky tumbler in hand, is a man I recognise and am very pleased to see.

Rising, he affectionately utters, "Hello, my little Ellie-phant." I rush into his arms and cry uncontrollable tears. Ted steps forward and offers me another one of his beautiful handkerchiefs. Too late, for my tears and my runny nose are being mopped up by my brother's jacket. However, I still take the offering anyway.

Ted, seeing my predicament, tells me in a fatherly way, "Blow, girl, blow."

Letting go of my brother, I cannot help but give Ted a lopsided grin before blowing. My once scary man is actually a big teddy bear, regardless of what his external façade is saying. Taking control of myself, I stare at my brother, demanding, "What are you doing here?"

Surprised at my question, he replies, "Trying to locate your boyfriend before he gets himself killed." Seeing my shocked expression, he says, "Come here and give me a hug. I'm glad you are safe, but it's Tolly who needs our help now." My tone-deaf brother sings tenderly in my ear the same song he sang weeks ago. 'Get me to the Church on Time'

Interrupting a warm family moment, Ted butts in, "Major, we all still have a job to do. Carl," who has been waiting patiently, "will show you to the powder room so you can freshen up."

Before leaving the room, confused, I ask, "I thought we were dinning here?"

Ted takes my hand, remarking, "Hopefully one day, with your fiancé, but not today." Then, addressing his bodyguard, "Carl, if you wouldn't mind?"

Returning with make-up reapplied and now composed, my host once again gives the orders without question. "Please, your audience awaits."

Moving to the front of the mansion, the Rolls Royce has its doors open waiting for our arrival. The journey is taken in relative silence, only interrupted by the lightest of dialogue.

On arriving at our destination, I cannot help but feel that I have stepped into another world: a bygone era of old Hollywood meeting *Bridgerton*. While a uniformed attendant moves towards my brother's side of the car, Carl has already alighted in order to open our host's door. Standing at the main entrance, Ted takes my arm, tucking it into his. The three of us proceed into a very grand entrance hall. As we pass staff, each give a slight bow as though in the presence of royalty. In this dress, it's just how I feel; I'm so pleased my make-up is perfect. Entering the gentleman's club-type restaurant, with its wood panelling and richly decorated ceiling and walls, the feeling of time warping has increased.

My escort pulls my arm even closer to his body and whispers in my ear, "The men are looking at you with desire and the women enviously."

I am unable to give a private response as a pleasant waiter guides us seamlessly to a corner table, out the way of the other early diners, laid for a party of four. It is covered with a thick, pristine, white linen tablecloth, a small pile of gold-rimmed plates ascending in order of size, a whole canteen of cutlery, glasses that you cannot fail to notice reflect the light from the chandeliers, and equally pristine white napkins held in gold rings. The waiter proceeds to seat us but is stopped by our host who pulls out my chair. I am positioned so my back is to the room. My brother waits while I'm seated before he and Ted sit.

The hovering waiter is now allowed to place the napkins on our laps before bowing and departing, making way for the sommelier. "Good afternoon, sir, may I be so bold as to ask if it is to be your usual?"

In a tone of familiarity, Ted answers, "You may, William, the young lady will have a glass of wine, will leave it to you on that front, and my young friend here will have a pint of Guinness." Before I can say anything, a rather pompous man comes across to our table and, without introducing himself, directs his remarks to our benefactor.

"Who are these people, Edward?" He flaps his hands and arms animatedly in the air as though trying to fly. "Don't tell me they're yours?" Horror crosses the man's face before he continues, "But they can't be, because…"

I touch Teddy's arm as I can sense his blood starting to boil; his utterance reflects his rising fury. "Spit it out, man." He is not concerned with the fact all in the room are now looking over at our table. "Are you saying that because I'm a homosexual that I am incapable of fathering children? I will have you know that I have all the equipment and it is still in good working order." With that very heartfelt reply, this insignificant man scurries away, not back to his table but out the room. With the little show over, the rest of the restaurant's clientele return to their conversations as though nothing has happened.

Pleased with how he conducted himself, I ask, "May I call you Teddy? It suits you better than Ted." He nods, grabbing my hand and giving it a squeeze.

Turning to my brother, he enquires, "And you, my boy, would you like to call me Teddy also?"

Keeping a passive face and his voice low, my brother

responds, "If you don't mind, as you are my superior officer, I believe that, even in private, I should continue to call you sir."

"Very wise – don't want unrest in the ranks due to overfamiliarity." With the waiter standing discretely to one side, Teddy remarks enthusiastically, "Oh! Yes, the food to go with our drinks. May I choose for all of us? Doing my Professor Henry Higgins again – I observe from your very poor singing, my boy, that *My Fair Lady* is something of a favourite of all of ours." Looking over at the waiter, who comes to our table immediately, Teddy cheerfully proceeds to give our order – without need to consult a menu – as though his outburst didn't happen.

In an establishment like this, I surmise, *no doubt they have seen much worse... I wonder if they have a medical team on standby,* giving an inwards chuckle at the very thought.

While I cannot see what is taking place over by the maître-d's station, both my brother and Teddy can. Placing their napkins on the table, the two men rise, as inborn manners dictate, to meet another guest. Still seated, as a lady's privilege, the first glimpse I get of our other diner is what she is wearing. The sheer luxuriousness of a most exquisite silk dress interwoven with gold and vivid coloured silk threads makes me feel like I'm wearing rags. I don't have to look up far to view its Japanese wearer, as she is petite. No one could fail to notice her rich, sleek, black hair that reaches down to her hips. It has been styled to show off her delicate, flawless features most pleasingly. A glorious jade pin has been inserted into her locks to add balance. She offers a small, gloved hand to Teddy, who kisses it chastely on the knuckles.

She speaks first while placing a single pointed finger on his chest. "You look well, Edward, too much time on your hands had made you soft. Recent events have invigorated you, most agreeable, most agreeable."

Now clutching her hand close to his chest, he softly speaks in reply, "Gracious of you to say so; your opinion is always welcome. May I introduce you to my other lunch guests? Elizabeth, please meet Eleanor and her brother. Before you ask, you may call him 'Major'."

Waving the ever-dutiful waiter away, he seats Elizabeth himself. I have come to realise Teddy likes to be a most conscientious host.

Her lyrical voice is most pleasing to listen to; however, it's a voice that draws you in before she strikes like a cobra. "It is an honour to meet you both, especially you, Eleanor."

I can only nod, as I believe our paths have never crossed.

Directing his enquiry at Elizabeth, Teddy asks, "May I tempt you with wine and a morsel of the finest food that you will ever taste in England?"

Purring, she replies, "You are so sweet, Edward, but I must decline. Water will be sufficient as I must leave you once my task is fulfilled."

Motioning once again at a waiter, he asks for, "Water, still not fizzy."

You can tell she is fully aware of her surroundings and is forever on her guard by the way she holds herself. However, she directs the conversation at me as though we are the only ones in the room. "Eleanor, let me start by saying that I admire your bravery, but dark times are with us, and what you must do goes beyond being brave for yourself. You will find that you may have to shoulder the burden of others, like your father." Without being given a chance to answer, she continues, "I was placed into the service of Madam Trevisa, the minister's daughter. My position in the Mayfair property was as general dogsbody in the guise of PA." She nods at Teddy, before continuing her tale, "This was in order to monitor her and the coming and goings of visitors and possessions. With the recent events in Wales, you now know how dangerous this person is. With heartfelt regret, the authorities let her go and then lost track of her."

With this pronouncement, I know my face mirrors the astonishment shown on my brother's and Teddy's.

"She is on the loose once more and seeking revenge – against you, your family, everyone she blames for her predicament – and will stop at nothing to achieve that end. Hence the kidnapping of you and young Mr Smyth-Tompkins; I surmise she hoped to use your both as bait to trap all the players in her evil web. Our one saving grace is that she does not know you have escaped, bravo." Taking an envelope from a secret pocket in her dress, she presents it to Teddy.

He touches it to his head in thanks; she silences him with just one look. He once more takes her tiny hand and, not worried who sees, gently folds down the glove to expose her hand so that he can kiss the back of it. I'm starting to wonder if Teddy isn't a closeted heterosexual. Elizabeth blushes as she lowers her delicate eyelids over her striking olive brown eyes that contain the minute traces of emerald green.

As though not wanting her to go, I hear an element of earnestness in his tone, "When we meet again, you must allow me to wine and dine you?" Now placing his hand on his heart and giving a most beautiful bow of his head to a woman whom you can tell he has a high regard for, he slightly stutters, "Your most humble servant."

Only as early as this morning, I would have found that creepy, but not now, as I'm starting to fall a little bit in love with Teddy – *what is it with Dad and his school friends with their manners from a long-gone age? I adore them, and yet I'm still a feminist.* I crane my neck to witness Teddy walking Elizabeth towards the exit of the restaurant. On his return, retaking his seat, I note a light has gone out in him.

Trying to be upbeat, although I have nothing to be upbeat about, I ask, "Okay, Teddy?"

Shaking the malaise from his head, he composes himself before answering, "Yes, thank you for asking. Let's get on, as we need to reunite you with Tolly. May I say, although I don't know the man, I hope that he is more chilled than his father. Tommy is so... like a solicitor?" With that, a boyish giggle emanates from our host.

In all this, my brother has sat passively, like our father, just listening, analysing to then regurgitate it at a later date.

After such a glorious meal, we forego the delights of the sweet trolley being wheeled across to our table, much to the horror of Teddy, who looks like a man raised on school puddings with heaps of custard. Coffee is served, with cheese and biscuits as a compromise.

Putting down his knife, Ted answers the question playing out on my face. "Eleanor, Elizabeth has provided me with five places in the immediate area that need to be searched. All of these locations are where Madam Trevisa has boltholes, which fall within the GPS signals." Seeing my confusion, he explains, "The mobile you took from your guard on the canal has been very useful – it has allowed K to access their communications by voice and text, sent and received. This has been translated into the GPS co-ordinates. As the major is aware, you may not be, all mobiles, provided they are switched on or do not have a blocking device activated, will show where the phone is, phone not person. GPS triangulation will put the phone into an area of the country. The locale may be a house, a street, a block of flats, or it could be an area the size of a town centre."

Trying to control my tears and my voice, I ask, "So what do you want me to do so that we can get Tolly home and that woman off our backs once and for all?"

"Thank you, but patience, my little sweet pea. I know

Alpha calls you that; I will too as your brother has already claimed Ellie-phant." All three of us smile, but it is not a smile of true happiness.

Looking over my shoulder, I can see that the head waiter is working the room; I can tell we are his final destination. He bends his torso just enough to talk intimately to Teddy, displaying a mask of serenity the entire time. With message delivered, he stands upright, lingering for a response. Teddy informs us that, "William has given you both the greatest of honours by requesting our presence to view his cellar, where the finest of his wines are stored. Shall we go? Let me lead the way." With that, we are escorted, with Teddy acting as though he owns the place, to this most hallow enclave below the restaurant.

William, the sommelier, is waiting for us in front of an ancient-looking door that a company of soldiers would have a job to smash. He swings open the door to allow us entry into a rather chilly room. His last task is to turn the lock shut.

Not liking being confined, I enquire in a somewhat aggressive way, "What is going on Teddy? I've already been kidnapped. If this is some twisted joke, I'm going to start smashing every one of these bottles until you start treating me as an adult." Teddy reaches out to grab my arm, but I step back from him and take the first bottle by its neck, raising it above my head. I notice that William is starting to sweat, even in this 'fridge'.

Just short of crying, he pleads, "Please, madam, sirs, that's an 1870 Chateau Lafite Rothschild."

Oh, I do like this game. "How much? Don't bother as it's bombs away." Dropping it on the cellar floor, a smash and splash follows. William wobbles, and at one point I am sure he is going to join the smashed bottle on the floor.

I pick up another dusty and web-covered bottle. "Please,

madam, that's a 1921 Chateau Yquem; if you are going to smash something, can you start on the bottled water? Please, sirs, tell her why you are here before I have a heart attack."

Teddy raises his voice in the manner of a pissed-off teacher. "Give William the bottle, Eleanor, as I don't have the time or the money to allow you to create havoc. We need to walk quickly to the far end of this cellar, and I mean now. Move, girl, or you will get my royal boot up your petite arse."

Wow, where did that come from? True colours coming to the fore, Edward? Always wanting a victory, no matter how small, I toss the wine bottle at William, who catches it and then holds it lovingly before returning it to the stack. *Yep, that's not going to be drinkable for a little while.*

Teddy speaks with authority, "Major, next room, if you would?"

I cannot see what my brother does, but the racks move just enough for three of us to slide between them into a room beyond. A large pot of coffee and five espresso cups sit on a cheap, circular pine table with five, not very special, chairs around it. Two men emerge from the shadows, Dad and Mac. I cannot hide my joy at seeing them. Mac moves to my brother and gives him a hug; Teddy gets similar treatment.

Dad wraps me in his arms as though never to let go. "Mac told me what happened; sorry, sweet pea, should have realised our family was being watched. Can you ever forgive me for putting you in danger? I heard the bitch is on the run. Rest assured we are working behind the scenes to locate and get Tolly back."

As if on cue, Teddy hands over the envelope Elizabeth gave him.

Knowing its content, Dad responds, "Thank you, Edward, for this and for guarding our girl. Did you put her in these glad rags? Of course you did; I am forever in your debt." Nodding his head in appreciation to Teddy for his kindness, Dad turns his attention back to me. "Tommy and Katie are at our place, surrounded by Pip's team, so you don't have to worry on that score." Motioning for us to sit, he delicately opens the envelope and spreads the contents in front of him. After studying what he sees, he focuses on my brother. "One of these boltholes is where Tolly may be. With K's GPS data, we should be able to narrow down the search area. My worry now is with so few of us, how are we going to hit the closest five all at the same time? Any chance of calling in the two guys from Wales?"

"Take it as done. Just need to decide where you want them to go and with whom."

"So, five areas needing five teams of two. With your guys, Mac and I, that's only two places covered. We are three teams short as Pip and his men must stay at the house, just in case there is trouble."

"I can cover one, leaving two, any suggestions, anyone?"

Raising a hand, I interject. "As I'm bait and she doesn't know I've escaped, put me back on the narrowboat and see what happens? Chances are Tolly is close by to also be used as a lure."

Mac acknowledges my request. "Makes sense to attack the closest three targets. If no joy and the enemy has been neutralised, we can swiftly move on to the other two."

Giving consideration to what I just said, my brother sighs and then talks to us all. "I'm not happy with Ellie going back on the boat. However, describe the fellow on the boat for me, Els?"

Closing my eyes I begin, "White, male, short dark hair, Londoner, mid-twenties, about five foot ten, slim, no outstanding facial features. Does that help?"

After a moment of thinking, Dad says, "I think one of Pip's boys will fit the bill. Looks like he is still in his teens but, with a bit of luck, may work. Right, I need to make some calls. By the way, where is the narrowboat now, not floating still in the middle of the canal, I hope?"

Mac replies, "At the rifle range. Rang Ted and asked him to deal with the situation. Too soon for the boys in blue to find a dead body."

It is now Ted's turn to interject ."The craft is moored securely, in a mobile dead zone, with an armed guard nearby. Eleanor's dead jailer has been taken away."

The major outlines the plan. "So, Ellie will be put back on the boat with one of Pip's men disguised as her jailer. All the bits and bobs she took will go with her. Mac and one of my men will go to the first address; Dad and my other man will proceed to the second set of co-ordinates. I will go, alone, to the third location. We will hit the three targets all at the same time. Pip's team will monitor our communication. If we have no joy, then we move onto the other two, Dad with his man, and I will join Mac."

Giving Ted his attention, he continues, "Sir, can you liaise with Pip to clean up any mess we cause, and can you return Ellie and her protector to the boat but not in the Rolls?" Seeing his father's face, he says, "I know, but as you said, Dad, we are light on the ground. If all goes well, Tolly will be at one of the first two; if nothing else, we are reducing her gang numbers and closing the net. K has given us the ability to block mobile signals. Similarly, he can block CCTV and cut the electricity on our command. Sorry, sis, but you must change back into your jeans; before you do that, can I say that you look lovely?"

Not waiting for a reply, he looks at Mac, who nods, and continues, "Mac has all we need in his car, including new mobiles. Dad, your vehicle and buddy are not far from here. Similarly, Mac, your man is close by – Dad will introduce him." Turning to Ted, he says, "Sir, please take care of my sister; she is very precious to our family."

With genuine feeling, Ted replies, looking at our small band, "She has become very precious to me too."

I give Teddy a tender smile just for him.

With coffee finished, we all stand. Dad's old mobile phone pings with an incoming message; looking down, he opens it and reads the contents. "We are standing by outside, happy to meet for the first time."

CHAPTER 18

TUESDAY

Mac's target is just outside Stoke Bruerne. He reads the sign, not believing what he sees: 'Sinister House and Farm'. He doesn't say it out loud, but the coincidence is too much. *Canal access up to Long Buckby and beyond where a boat called* The Corvid Family *is moored and I'm looking at a farm with a strong reference to rooks, jays and crows?* Parking their vehicle in this busy, vibrant neighbourhood, no one will give them a second look with their rucksacks and gun cases held like cricket bags. Although cricket is not a winter sport and it is pitch black. Running hard across open countryside with all equipment necessary, Mac and his 'buddy' reach the outer limits of the farm buildings within fifteen minutes of leaving the car. Dropping down to a stop, both scan the landscape with night sights.

Mac whispers, "I count five, wait one is sitting. Make that six."

His companion concurs, "Six. Two on patrol, one seated, three in the house."

"This looks promising, but we are on a farm, so we will not count our chickens just yet. Right, need to get closer as all teams are striking the first three targets at the same time." Checking his watch, he says, "Four minutes, move forward, low, and check for bloody dogs." The moon is hiding behind clouds, so the sky is beautifully dark; a wind is whipping up, coming from the direction of the house, so the thugs' conversations are being picked up while their presence goes unnoticed. Much to the relief of Mac, no dogs are heard. Reaching into his jacket, he sets about disabling all mobile signals. There is no apparent panic within the house. "Attack in four, three, two, one." Mac heads for the seated man first; his buddy is scanning with a rifle. By how he is sitting, Mac is momentarily halted from landing a killer strike. He whispers, "Tolly, it's Mac, don't move – we have come to save you."

A forlorn, drugged voice answers, "Is Ellie okay?"

"Yes, she is worried about you."

"Must stay, Mac, please keep close. Must flush the wicked witch out."

Mac touches the young man's back and quietly says, "You don't have to do it."

"Must."

"I'll stay close by, son, be brave."

Moving into the shadows, Mac watches as the drugged Tolly is manhandled back into the building. He shudders at the fact that this young solicitor is now willing to play a dangerous game with his own life, a situation that he is not trained for. Moving to find an area where he can transmit a message from, Mac rings Harvey. Connecting, he says, "Mac here – I've located package, cannot secure, staying close. Package wants to remain a hostage to flush out witch. Ring when on move."

"Thank you, Mac. Will wait for your next report."

Pip ran into the room when the phone rang and now waits impatiently for Harvey to finish the call. "Well?"

Harvey plays a recording of the conversation.

"Have you heard from either Alpha or the major?"

"No, sir."

"When they call, get them back here."

"Yes, sir."

A somewhat perplexed man walks round the room. He should feel relief, but all he is feeling is dread. Unlike those who can wait, the duke is a man of action, happiest when he is fully occupied, but at the moment his hands are tied.

*

Neither the commander or his 'buddy' talk during the journey; orders were relayed when they met forty minutes ago. Checking his watch, the only words muttered by Alpha, when the long-awaited time is only moments away, are, "Off we go."

Leaving the car, they weave their way through a housing estate to the property pinpointed by intelligence. Alpha walks purposely, but before taking a small electronic device from his combat trouser pocket, a dog walker appears in front of them, with a yappy mutt. Acting calmly, slowing his step, the commander acknowledges the dog walker with a friendly, "Good evening," before starting up an inane conversation with his buddy. "Said to the wife, we are not going to Spain again – the beaches are full of tourists, and you don't like the sun." Once the man and the dog have rounded the corner, his conversation becomes monosyllabic. "There," he says, nodding to a non-descript property on the corner. With device in hand, he presses a button and counts to ten. Placing the device back in his trouser pocket, his hand dives into his puffer jacket pocket to retrieve a pistol and an oversized key. "Now." Walking rapidly to the front door, the commander jams the smart key in the lock. His buddy jumps over the back fence, also with gun in hand, to get into the house via the kitchen door. A quick search of all the rooms draws a blank. As all communications surrounding the building have been blocked, they move back towards their car, once the property has been secured. On the road travelling further east towards the fourth target, the commander rings the pre-programmed number to make their report. "Alpha team here, negative, empty, property secure."

The voice not giving away anything, "Thank you, sir please return to base.". The connection is terminated.

Harvey looks up at Pip. "Do you think that the commander believes that Mr Smyth-Tompkins is safe, Your Grace?"

Pip snaps, "Leave it, Harvey." Realising how harsh that sounded, he places his hand on the young man's shoulder before saying in a controlled manner, "They are safe." With that, he slumps in a chair, while the young man waits for the major to report in.

Unsure of what to make of his orders, Alpha tells the driver, in a very even voice, to, "Turn the car round; we have been called home. It may be best if you park in the golf club, I have the code for the barrier, and then we will sneak into my house."

At the same time that Mac is running across the fields to his target, the major spots the isolated farm building he is looking for. Only one light is on; its beam cuts across the front porch, illuminating a small section of the front of the house. Tolly's Range Rover is parked to one side of the building. There is enough cover from the still-foliage-rich hedges lining the property's driveway to hide his visit. Swinging his rifle off his shoulder, he holds it ever ready in one hand. His motorbike is in a ditch, away from prying eyes. Scanning the area intensely, he has counted two men only. After activating the blocking device given to him by K, he decides it may be best if he confronts them without his weapon. Placing it lovingly close by, he moves forward but now into the open, noting that, other than the car, there are no signs that Tolly is being held here. One man stands in the now open front door, shedding more light on the area, while the second appears from the side of the building. The major has no qualms about his abilities in a fistfight. Two against one is standard training, and he has fought bigger men than those standing before him. He has already planned his first opening salvo and, depending on their reaction, it could well come down to a bloody and no-holds-barred contest. *What do they say in all those old films – do you want to dance, or do you want to fight? Let's see if dancing is to their liking before we do the fighting.*

In a calm way, the major asks, "Hi, lads, car has broken down and I have no signal – can I use your landline?" All he receives is a grunt in reply.

The major carries on in the same manner, "Come on, let me in to use the phone." Another grunt.

Looks like I'm going to fight a couple of farm animals. But not one to give up so easily, he continues, "What do you say, fellows, a two-minute phone call to the garage, shake hands and say our farewells?" Once again, the response is a grunt. *Is that all you can do – grunt?* "So that's it then? Nice meeting you, boys; I'll be on my way."

The two heavies look at each other and take a huge step forward, closing the gap between them and him. In all the time that this one-sided conversation has been taking place, the major's hands have been resting inert by his side, but with them taking up an aggressive posture, his body awakens to the possibility of carnage. He's surprised not by their desire to fight but that it's one at a time. *Strange, I would do a joint attack and kick my head in.* Allowing 'contestant number one' to make the first move, he avoids the strike easily and then whacks an elbow into his nose, causing it to erupt. He had noticed in the run-up to the battle that the man's nose is very wonky and swollen, a sign it has been broken a few times, maybe in the boxing ring. While blood spatters in all directions, including into the thug's eyes, he takes the opportunity to add to his woes. This time it's a straight leg into the groin and then a grab and pull, and as the saying goes, 'head and brain will follow', in this case onto a volley of powerful strikes. The second guy, 'contestant number two', wades into the fray. *This one is going to fight dirty, maybe with a weapon.* The weapon of choice is a long, thin pole. *Not a good option; let me show you why.* As the man starts to wield the pole, the major sidesteps its downwards trajectory. With his opponent's upper body open to him, Mac performs a straight hand chop into the throat. Coughing, the man drops the pole in order to hold the area that has just been attacked. *Have I got your attention? Now take this: a knuckle sandwich in your face, a knee in the back, followed by a boot down your calf.*

As his second opponent takes an enforced break, the major leaves him and goes back to 'contestant number one'. These men have been trained but not very well. Regardless of the punishment he is dishing out, he is not surprised the boxer is still standing. Enjoying not having to pull his punches, he smashes his fist once more into that bloody and well-broken nose. Sucking in great breaths of air, he moves swiftly, jabbing his opponent in the eyes, the throat and the groin, with fingers, elbow and knee. His last act is to slap the whole of his body weight into him, causing them both to crash to the ground. The major ensures he lands on top of the toppled man. No time to take stock he jumps up, looking for the second guy. With him firmly in his sights, he goes to move towards him, but the man on the floor grabs his ankle. *Okay, laddie, for you it's a boot sandwich.* Raising his free foot, he rams it, unceremoniously, into the throat of the man on the ground, and on doing so, hears a satisfying crunch. *Now back to the task in hand.* Moving forward, the major raises both his hands in a boxing stance. His right hand is concealing a small knife that he has secretly taken out of a pocket. To use it, he has to get in close, and the man in front of him has a longer arm span. *So, it's going to be under and up.*

Before he can execute his next move, the heavy speaks breathlessly, "You shouldn't have come here, but now you're here, I cannot let you go. *Now.*"

The major hasn't realised there is a third opponent waiting in the wings. *Idiot.* He tries to swing round, while still trying to parry a strike from the one standing giant. He does not feel the knife go immediately into his leg. It is only when the second strike with the blade, by the third man, is buried into his torso that he knows it's going to be bad. Furious with himself, pain shoots along every nerve in his body. Staggering and stumbling, no matter how hard he tries, he cannot stop himself crumbling to the ground, but with the one saving grace, the blade is still in him.

Barely conscious, he can hear the panic in the third man's voice. "Sorry, mate, so sorry."

The third man is grabbed by his colleague and told, "Leave him – he'll bleed out so we will not have to worry about being recognised. Come on, grab an arm, need to leg it before all roads are closed." Together they lift their comatose colleague off the ground and hobble away, leaving the major to his fate. The next sound is a revved-up motor, with wheels spinning on the gravel lane as it rushes away.

In his head, all the major can think of is his sister. *I'm so sorry, Ellie, I promised to save Tolly, but I've failed. Forgive me, my little Ellie-phant.* He knows he must lie still, not moving so the blade stays in place, plugging the hole. *Breathe slowly, try and keep your stress levels low, control the pain. Keep awake; don't drift – help will come.* Quoting poetry like his father, today it's Thomas, not Dad's favourite poet Tennyson. "'Do not go gentle into that good night, old age should burn and rave at close of day; rage, rage against the dying of the light'."

A low, comforting voice breaks the building sorrow. "Hang in there, handsome, look at me; open those big blue eyes of yours and keep them focused on me and only me." His eyes find it impossible to focus, but he can feel well-practised hands touching the areas around the entry wounds, first on his leg but more probing on his side.

The more he is touched, the intensity of the pain increases. Close to passing out, he cries out, "Stop, stop, for goodness' sake." He knows that tears are running down his face; he can neither wipe them away nor halt them.

The comforting voice returns, not giving any hint of the damage to his body. "Stay with me; you are doing fine, but don't move – let me do my job and yours is to remain still."

Trying hard to focus on anything other than his pain, his ears pick up a distant noise. He would recognise that distinctive sound anywhere, the low rhythmic beat of helicopter rotors, slowly getting louder as they get nearer. He knows the air ambulance is on its way; a feeling of relief sweeps through him. He slowly closes his eyelids; his body relaxes and a prolonged release of air escapes his lungs.

The comforting voice whispers close to the major's ear, "Don't worry about your rifle; I'll take care of her. Tolly wasn't here, only his car. Can you hear that? Medics will soon have you carried airborne and then into the operating room to be patched up good as new." This is said more in hope, as the injuries inflicted are life-threatening. Moving back into the shadows in order to leave the major to the paramedics, his guardian's mobile vibrates.

Message received: 'Located package. Wait for orders'.
Reply: 'Major down, but not out, check A & E'.

CHAPTER 19

TUESDAY

True to his word, Teddy arranged for me and Lewis, as my protector, to be taken to the narrowboat, now moored on the towpath side. He assured me an armed guard would be hiding out in the woods opposite, within calling distance. It is now a waiting game. Having taken to patrolling up and down the towpath, Lewis hears the *ping* of 'Dave's' mobile. The message reads: 'Standby to bring the girl to the Whilton Lock bridge over the M1'. He forwards the text to his brother, as instructed to do by Mac. Rushing back to the boat, I am hastily informed of our next move.

Passing a flak jacket, Lewis answers the question playing out in my eyes. "You are to wear it, as my life will not be worth living if you refuse."

While I put on the jacket, my protector starts the process of 'tooling up'.

Once finished, he speaks slowly and evenly, "Once at Whilton Locks, I will stay as close as possible, reducing the angles of attack; keep in the shadows if you can, but don't make it too obvious. Keep calm, breathe and prepare to run and hide;

you know the area, chances are, they don't. Quickly go to the toilet, then we will have to run along the towpath."

Meanwhile, Mac can see that Tolly's jailers are getting ready to move. His 'buddy' has already moved their car nearby in anticipation of what is just about to go down. Now on the move and keeping a safe distance behind the thug's car, Mac rings base. Harvey picks up, noting the caller.

"Mac here. On the move, following one saloon car, four people in it. On the A508 heading towards the A5. Do you want me to remain on the phone?"

Pip takes over, "Mac, yes. Is Tolly in the car?"

"Yes, but this isn't right – we are missing something."

The duke knows what he means. "Yep, seems too by the book."

On cue, Alpha, with his buddy, run into the room. "What's up, Pip? Tell me we have Tolly."

Still pondering on what Mac said, Pip doesn't give Alpha his complete attention. "Mac found the lad but he stayed to be bait to fish out the bitch. The gang holding him are on the move towards the A5 along the A508."

Scanning the area, the commander asks, "Is my son back yet?"

Pip's face drops. Placing his hand on his best friend's shoulder, he looks into his eyes before he speaks. "Alpha, the major is in surgery with a couple of very deep stab wounds. Air ambulance lifted him just in time. As you know, we are all taking risks."

Shocked by this statement, he doesn't ask but demands, "I want to speak to Mac."

"Big man, I'm here. Have this feeling that something is not right, too easy."

Pip's mobile pings; putting it on speaker, he sighs. "Must take this – it's Brenda. Yes, Bren?"

"Darling, I'm upstairs in the dark. Glancing out of one of the back bedroom windows, I can see movement over on the golf course. I don't mean the odd late night dog walker. The movement is too... I don't know how to describe it. There is no wind, but it is odd, spooky, like waves rolling on the sea but not breaking. Sorry, that's all I want to say, except, miss you." Waiting for a response, wishing she hadn't put another problem her husband's way, she is surprised when Alpha starts to talk to her.

"Brenda, tell Fred that I want everyone, including him, into the safe room off the cellar. Do it now – take the phone with you. I will call Fred when it is safe for you all to come out." He presses the red button before an argument ensues.

Pip, taking his phone back, presses a speed dial number. The connection is instantaneous. "Sophie, I want eyes in the sky pronto, and I don't mean just police. Do it now. You are looking for bandits on the golf course at the back of our HQ in Golf Lane. I do believe we are the wicked witch's next targets any time now. Swarm the area with our men, no kills unless necessary. Numbers unknown, but they will be heavily armed. Complete media blackout, will deal with the fallout later. If you come up against insurmountable problems, refer them to Sir Edward. Thank you. I will be in touch."

Keen to know where Mac is, Alpha enquires, "Where are you now?"

"Travelling down the bloody A5 in the direction of Whilton bloody Locks."

"Take it you heard everything going on here – do you have anything to add?"

"Yes, what is the situation with Ellie? Is she still on the boat, or is she also on the move?"

Looking at Harvey, a brooding Alpha asks, "Have you heard from your brother?"

A worried Harvey can only give a firm negative shake of his head.

From Mac's open mobile comes, "Shit," followed by the sound of a car braking, then a series of bangs and then, "Shit, shit, shit."

A somewhat surprised Alpha asks, "Mac, what is going on?"

"A roe deer has just come out of nowhere and has taken our car out. No way can we follow – can you get someone to intercept?"

"Sorry, Mac, we have our own problems; it looks like it's the kids and then us. If the emergency services are on their way, use your initiative – nick a police car."

"Did I hear a senior police officer say, 'nick a police car'?" Not waiting for a reply, a very calm Mac continues, "Alpha, we are both okay; it's the kids you should worry about. We will get back on the road ASAP."

"Okay, Mac."

With the sound of a police car in the distance a joyful Mac exclaims, "Think our ride has just turned up."

Pip jumps in, shouting, "Harvey, Lewis?"

"On it." Trying several times to reach his brother without any luck, he gives 'Dave's' mobile a shot, a signal but line engaged. "Sir, it would appear that Lewis is being given instructions as 'Dave's' mobile is telling me that he is already on the line. Have sent a text message to Lewis's mobile." A message pings back: 'Whilton Locks, M1 bridge showdown fifteen mins, on the move'.

Alpha and Pip lock eyes. Pip knows what the commander's look means. Speed dialling, he says, "Sophie, we are to be hit in fifteen minutes. Tell me."

"Media blackout in place, sir. Special forces in position awaiting your command to begin attack, patching you through to Taskforce leader."

"Good, thank you, Sophie."

"Sir, Taskforce leader here, waiting permission to execute order to attack."

Very much in charge, Pip relays the orders, "Taskforce leader, we will block all electronic signals in zone before your attack and you will go in immediately. Blocking in," looking at his watch and quickly calculating, "twelve minutes from now."

"Thank you, sir, minimum force will be used if possible." The connection is terminated and then Sophie comes back on the line. "Sir, emergency services on standby, eyes in the sky deployed; K should have pictures. Good luck, Your Grace."

While Pip is nervous Harvey anxious, Alpha is composed. Meanwhile, K is in Mac's house relaying the video and audio feed of the golf course behind his uncle's house and is waiting to block all the enemy's mobile signals.

Pip gives a relieved sigh, then says, "Time coming up, Alpha?"

Looking nonchalantly at his timepiece, Alpha answers coolly, "Yes, it is, my friend. Ten, nine, eight, seven, six, five, four, three, two, one. K?"

His nephew calls out, "Blocking."

There is silence inside and, surprisingly, nothing to alert the neighbours that a synchronised and possibly bloody attack is taking place on the golf course behind their million-pound-plus houses. Star shells are fired into the night sky illuminating the scene, this is quickly followed by green and then red lights. Dogs can be heard barking, and no doubt their owners muttering, "Bloody kids letting off fireworks, waste of money if you ask me."

On the video link, it's like an old film. A number of shadowy silhouettes in black uniforms and helmets, in a pincer movement, advance in a hunched manner. A couple of them roll into sand bunkers to use them as makeshift foxholes. The 'eye in the sky' also has audio, which picks up the popping of gunfire. No loud, rapid fire, just a barely heard sound that stops as abruptly as it started. Whoever had been employed to take out Alpha's house with those inside were amateurs in comparison to Pip's task force. From start to finish, by Pip's calculation, the whole debacle lasts three minutes.

Harvey calls out, "Sirs, Taskforce leader the line." A more upbeat Pip and Alpha take their eyes off the monitor and join him.

An apprehensive Pip asks, " casualties?"

"Area secure and all weapons retrieved. Casualties, none for us, and just walking wounded for them; no kills I'm pleased to report. Golf course may need a bit of work though."

"Thank you, Taskforce leader, and congratulations on a successful outcome. We will put the damage to the greens down to the high jinks of youths. Once again, thank you."

While Pip is on the telephone, Alpha picks up the noise of a speeding car pulling up outside the front of the house. After what has just taken place at the rear of the house, he is now on edge that something may go down at the front.

CHAPTER 20

TUESDAY

After running down the towpath, Lewis and I move towards the motorway bridge at Whilton Locks. Two men appear from Spotted Cow Lane. They give no indication of noticing 'Dave' has been substituted.

Directing their utterance to Lewis, while looking at me, they say, "Take her to the far side of the bridge and wait. Once there, Madam Trevisa will come out." True to their word, the wicked witch appears on cue, wrapped in a blood-red coat with a turned-up black collar, which blends in with her shining raven-black hair. Her macabre, white face with its blob of red lipstick does nothing to take away the feeling that she is unhinged. Very high-heeled red shoes *clip-clop* on the concrete road, as she drags a drugged man like an appendage. Once she has slithered into position, her appearance is made more startling by headlights from the cars below, hitting her white face like flashbulbs going off.

Her two guards disappear back into Spotted Cow Lane. Standing on the bridge, it's just me against her. She has a rag doll Tolly by the arm. Lewis is still by my side, slightly in the shadows as my protector; she seems unperturbed by his presence. For someone so thin and waif-like, she is as strong as an ox to be able to hold Tolly up and point a steady-handed gun at me.

No way am I going to be intimidated by her. Without flinching, I ask, "What do you want, bitch?"

"Oh! You know what I want. Everything you and your friends stole from me. Maybe I will throw you over the bridge with this one. Oh! It will be like *Romeo and Juliet*, doomed lovers going to their death on the motorway below. Don't cry – I'll make sure it will be quick, and then I'm going to enjoy picking off everyone that got in my way. What do I care? My daddy will look after me; he is such a generous papa."

When is she going to get it? Her papa is dead and buried, may his corpse rest in hell. Gosh, this person is as mad as a bag of frogs, and if she thinks I'm going to cry in front of her, she is mistaken. Still looking directly at her with unblinking eyes, I say, "Talking about stealing things, you have someone who belongs to me, bitch."

Turning away from me, with her long tongue she licks the side of Tolly's face.

He is going to have to have a good wash before I will kiss him on that side again.

Looking back, her face, still catching the headlights from the cars travelling below, takes on a grotesque appearance. A red spot of a night sight appears where her heart should be if she had one. A cry of, "Drop," echoes around me. I do what I'm told; Lewis also obeys the order. No shots ring out, but looking up from ground level, my foe is falling backwards, hopefully dead. A moan comes from a drugged Tolly as he slowly drifts down, oblivious to what is going on around him.

Footsteps approach; shiny army boots position themselves under my nose. "Get up, bitch face." Looking up, I see a familiar person, my brother's corporal. She is holding a rifle in one hand and sporting a single raised finger on the other. I cannot help but smile with relief. "The major told me you are his sister. Still don't like you, but you do have a cute boyfriend. I prefer my men army and officers." She says this with a knowing grin.

Not able to move immediately to Tolly in order to gather him in my arms, I remain on the ground, waiting for my jelly legs to go. I enquire pensively, "Where is my brother? And congratulations on your promotion – you deserve it. Truly, you do."

Taken by surprise by my sincerity, she replies, "Oh! Thank you. Mac asked that I keep on eye on you without anyone knowing. Tracked you to the barge when you were kidnapped, sorry about the dead guy. As for the major, stupid idiot got himself stabbed. The air ambulance lifted your brother before he drowned in his own blood, on the mend now. I came back here to hide in the woods when you and the other guy – Lewis – were put on the boat to wait for the call from the creepy lady. I must say I do like your family and friends, never a dull moment."

Now able, I gather Tolly in my arms and cover him in kisses. Looking over towards where the sergeant was, she has gone and so has my other protector, Lewis. The rifle used, minus night sight and silencer, is on the ground. I can see blues and hear twos coming my way.

A sleepy man utters a few welcome words, "Did we win? Is the bad witch dead?"

Relieved, I reply, "Yep, we did, and yes, she is. Do you want to chill, get a takeaway and watch a film on the TV?"

Slowly coming round, but slurring his words, Tolly says, "Sounds good," snuggling closer. As he buries himself in my breasts, he murmurs, "At this moment, a woman who gives great cuddles is all I want."

Still sitting on the bridge surrounded by police cars and officers, two casually dressed men come rushing towards us, our fathers. Looking up, I catch Dad's eye. He speaks gently, "Okay, sweet pea? How about we get you two off the ground and checked over?"

Tolly's father squats down with his knees next to his semi-conscious son and then grabs him tightly. With Tolly secure in his father's arms, Dad reaches down and draws me up into an equally tight embrace.

Realising the mess we are in, I ask, "Dad, will I have to speak to the authorities?" whilst looking over at the discarded rifle and then at the dead body.

Letting go, he touches his breast pocket, smiles and then asks, "Do you remember the man you met on the stairs?"

"Yes, Dad. Why?"

"Remember Ted gave us an immunity card, which means no one will talk to us, investigate us, arrest us or look at us in the wrong way."

"Oh! Dad, I love you, Mum, my brother and all your strange and spooky friends."

"And Tolly?"

"I love him best of all." Between tears of joy and relief, we both laugh. Looking down at the two people still on the ground, Tommy joins us in our happiness, displaying a broad smile. While the medics hover to treat Tolly, his father kisses his head gently before handing him over reluctantly.

A firearms officer comes over and speaks to his senior Officer, Dad. Whatever is said, the officer shakes my father's hand and then leaves, taking his men with him.

"Sorry, Ellie, I need to retrieve a family heirloom." He walks purposely over to the rifle and carefully picks it up, checking it's safe.

I desperately want to depart, but my gaze rests on medics

carrying stretchers Three bodies, under sheets, are being taken to a waiting van with blacked-out windows, the bitch and two of her thugs.

Tolly is sitting in the back of an ambulance and, on seeing me, asks, "Can we all go home and sleep?"

"Definitely."

"Can we go to your parents' house as it's closer than Oxford? I don't think we are going to have trouble facing them across the breakfast table in the morning."

"How about going home in Mac's nicked police car? Much quicker. It was him who brought our dads here."

"Lovely, but no blues and twos – my head won't take it."

EPILOGUE

In frustration, a clenched fist slams down on the nearest surface. A protracted howl echoes in the cavernous space like it emanates from a wounded animal. There is no one to hear the sound or see the rage painted on the person's face. Picking up a loaded handgun with silencer from a nearby chair, shots are fired in all directions rather than at a selected target, done more to release the all-encompassing anger, which it doesn't. In one area of the dimly lit space, a number of A4 pictures of the same man's head are attached to one wall. His features are now obliterated by a cluster of bullet holes that have taken out the centre of his forehead and his eyes. Putting down the empty gun and picking up a marker that contains ink that is blood red, the person strides over to the pictures and writes on each 'BASTARD'.

On another wall are similar bullet-riddled pictures, but this time it's of a woman. The mutilation is the same, but her sweet, cheeky smile is set in a rebellious manner. Although just a picture, the owner of the image is setting a challenge that sends a shudder down the pen holder's spine. They hesitate to deface the offending mouth, as though the woman is all knowing and has some secret power over them, which the individual does. They want to write 'BITCH' but know it is not true, so they don't; instead, they allow the marker to drop to the floor. For one brief moment, they bow their head as though seeking forgiveness for even thinking of doing this act of disrespect. They already carry the guilt of despoiling the face of a most beautiful woman. Turning back to the now red-ink-spattered man, with real venom they spit out, sounding out the single word for as long as their breath allows, "Bastard." Standing up straight while gaining their composure, they pat down their clothes before moving towards the exit, up a small flight of stairs. With lights off and coat in hand, the last task is to make sure the street door is securely locked. As they step back into the world, the mask of respectability is now on show.